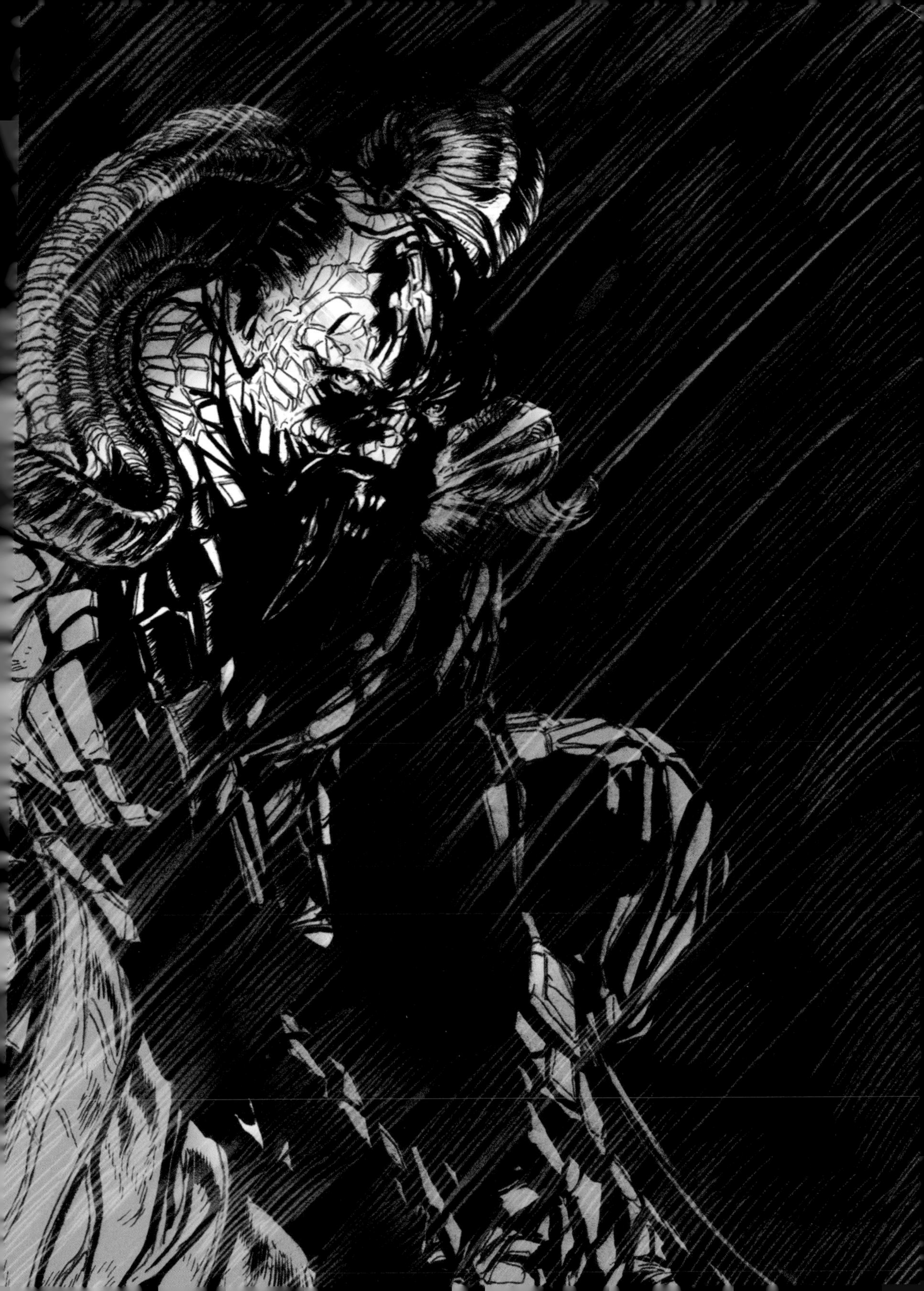

To my grandson, David Stemple, who knows Edinburgh well and loves graphic novels —JY

For Karrin and Big John, who loved the Auld Toun almost as much as we did —AS

This book is dedicated to the greatest parents in the world, Mark and Lisa Zangara, who are loving and always supportive of my drawing habits. Thank you for everything. —OZ

Story by Jane Yolen and Adam Stemple
Illustrations by Orion Zangara
Lettering by Bill Hauser

Text copyright © 2016 by Jane Yolen and Adam Stemple
Illustrations copyright © 2016 by Orion Zangara

Graphic Universe™ is a trademark of Lerner Publishing Group, Inc.

Graphic Universe™
A division of Lerner Publishing Group, Inc.
241 First Avenue North
Minneapolis, MN 55401 USA

For reading levels and more information, look up this title at www.lernerbooks.com.

Main body text set in CCWildWords 7/8. Typeface provided by Comicraft.

Library of Congress Cataloging-in-Publication Data

Names: Yolen, Jane. | Stemple, Adam. | Zangara, Orion, illustrator.
Title: Stone cold / by Jane Yolen and Adam Stemple ; Illustrated by Orion Zangara.
Description: Minneapolis : Graphic Universe, [2015] | Series: The Stone Man mysteries ; #1 |
    Summary: Silex is a talking gargoyle on a cathedral in Scotland who moonlights as a
    detective, assisted by a team of Scottish street urchins who do the grunt work.
Identifiers: LCCN 2014009423 | ISBN 9781467741965 (lib. bdg. : alk. paper) | ISBN 9781512411553
    (pbk.) | ISBN 9781512409031 (eb pdf)
Subjects: LCSH: Graphic novels. | CYAC: Graphic novels. | Gargoyles—Fiction. | Supernatural—
    Fiction. | Mystery and detective stories. | Scotland—Fiction.
Classification: LCC PZ7.7.Y65 St 2015 | DDC 741.5/973—dc23

LC record available at http://lccn.loc.gov/2014009423

Manufactured in the United States of America
1-36193-16977-3/2/2016

THE STONE MAN MYSTERIES
BOOK ONE

Stone Cold

JANE YOLEN AND ADAM STEMPLE

ILLUSTRATED BY ORION ZANGARA

GRAPHIC UNIVERSE™ • MINNEAPOLIS

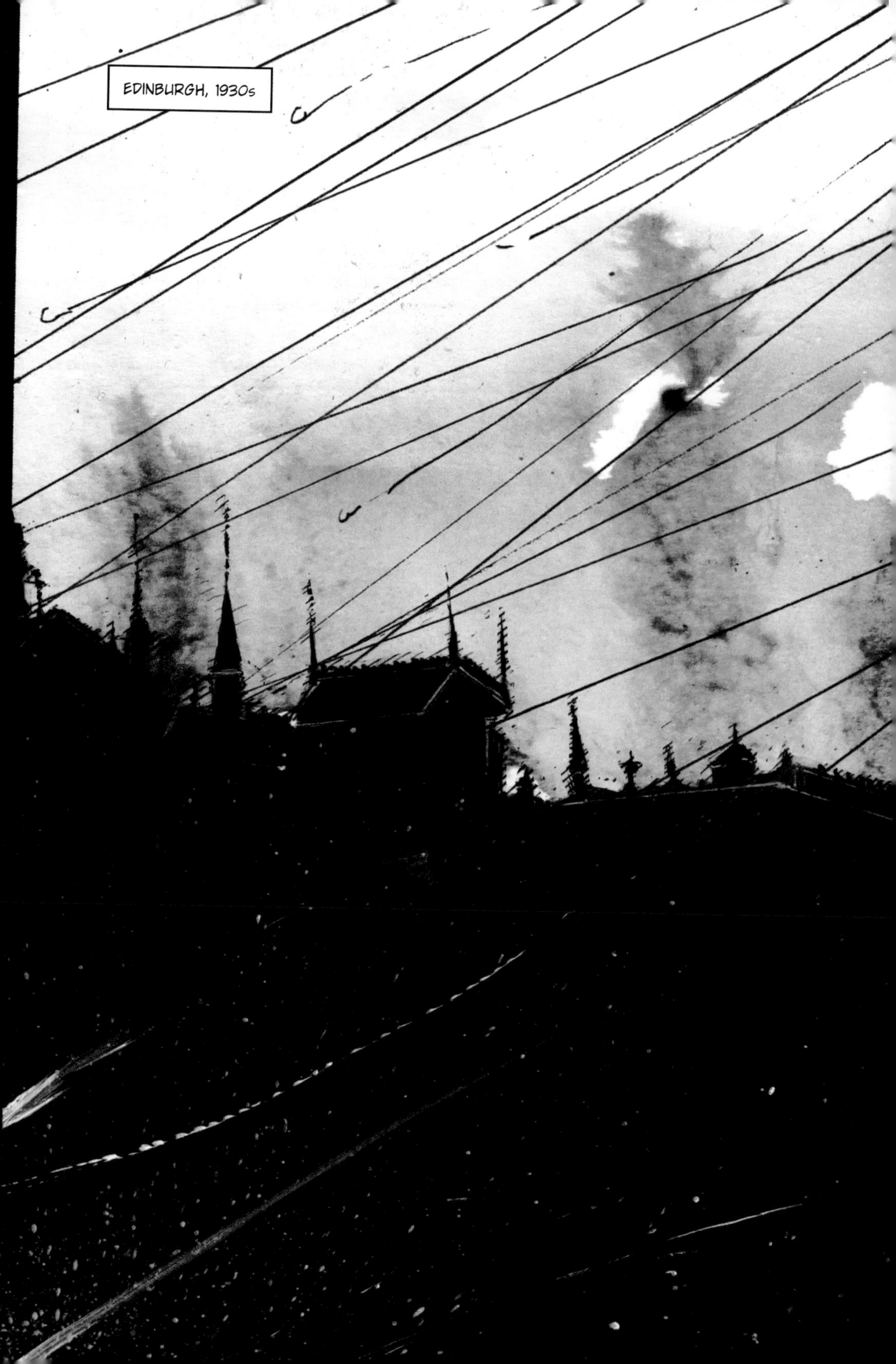
EDINBURGH, 1930s

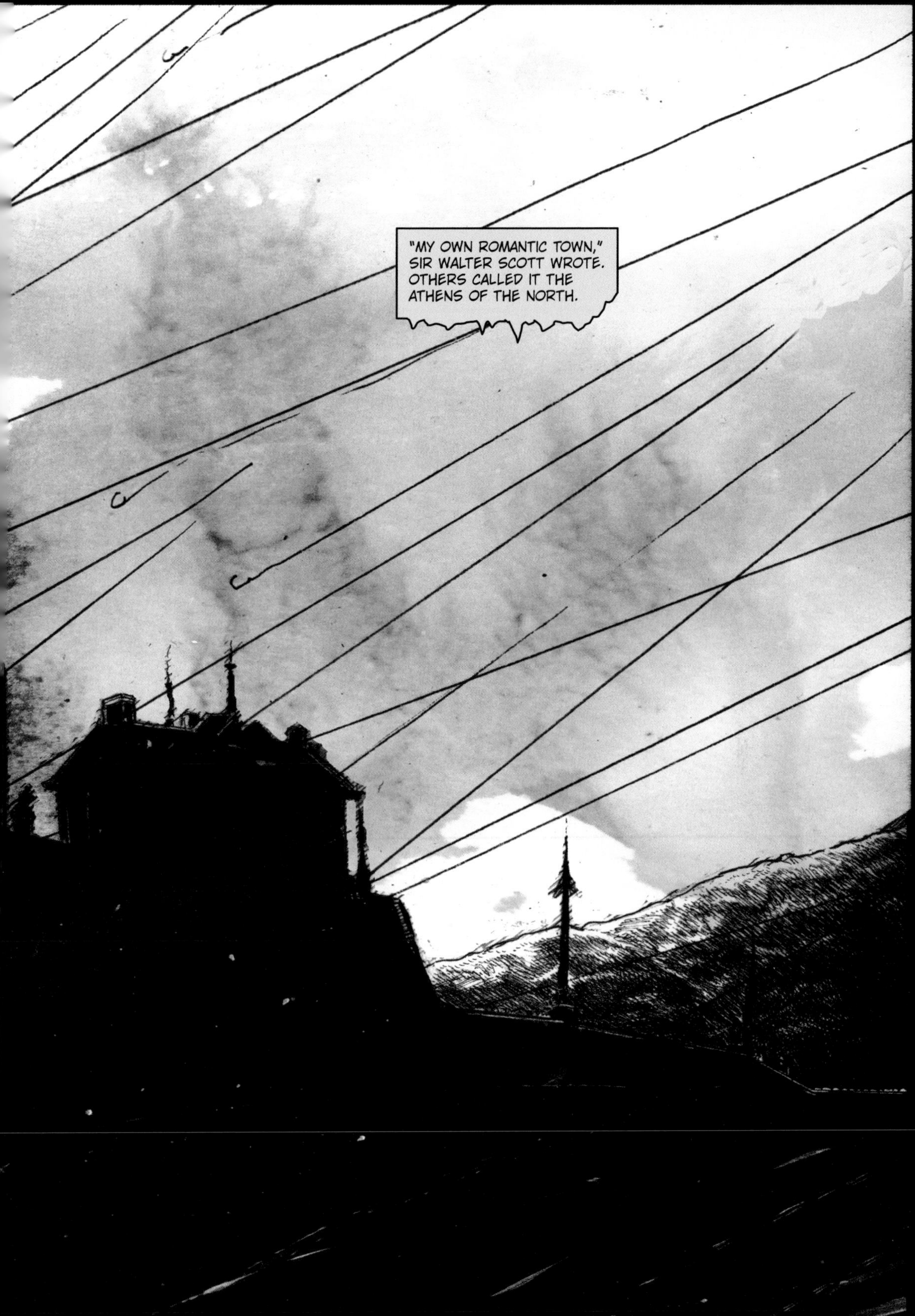
"MY OWN ROMANTIC TOWN," SIR WALTER SCOTT WROTE. OTHERS CALLED IT THE ATHENS OF THE NORTH.

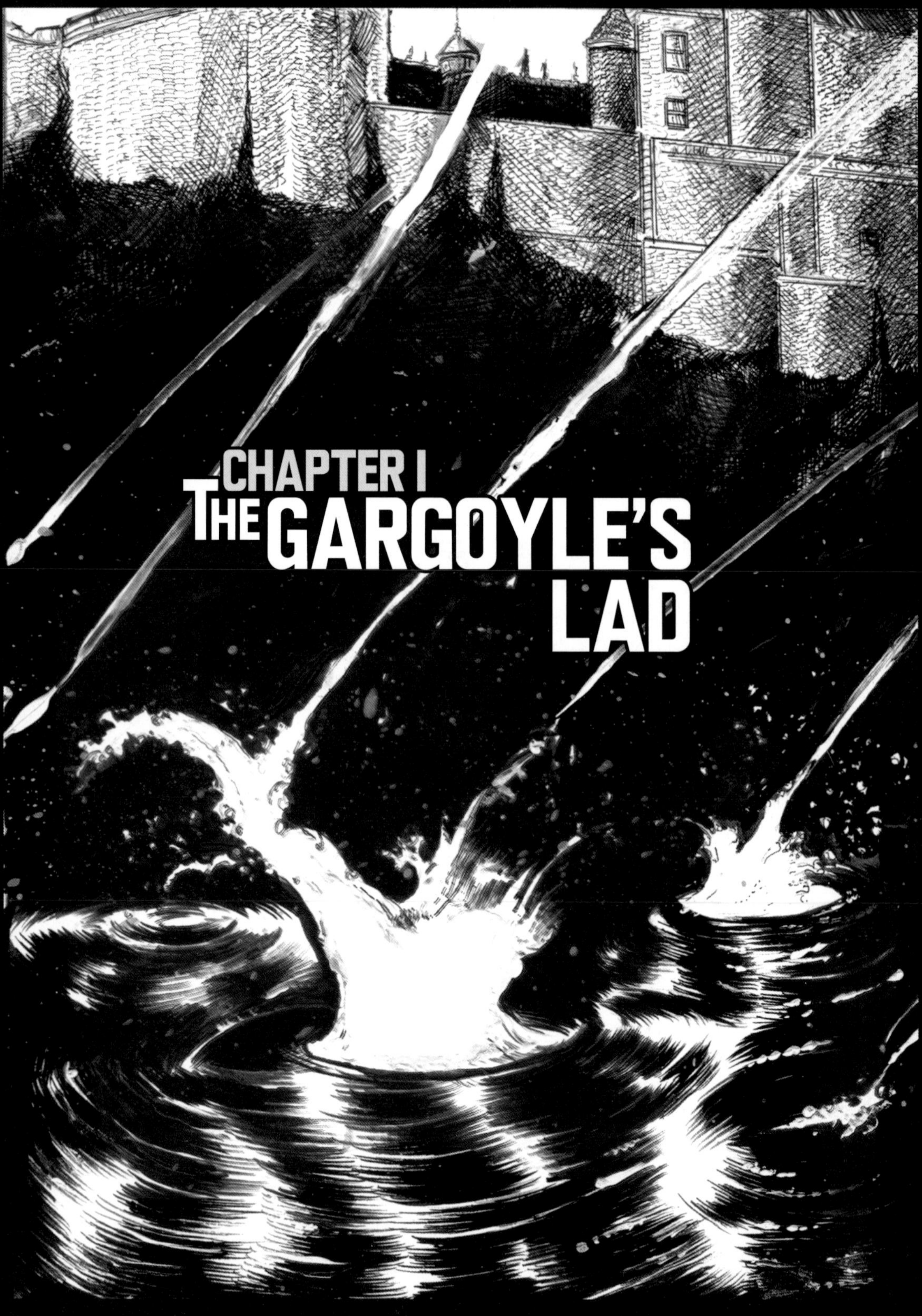
CHAPTER I
THE GARGOYLE'S LAD

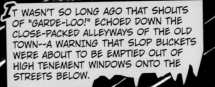

IT WASN'T SO LONG AGO THAT SHOUTS OF "GARDE-LOO!" ECHOED DOWN THE CLOSE-PACKED ALLEYWAYS OF THE OLD TOWN--A WARNING THAT SLOP BUCKETS WERE ABOUT TO BE EMPTIED OUT OF HIGH TENEMENT WINDOWS ONTO THE STREETS BELOW.

RAIN WOULD SLUICE THE COBBLESTONES CLEAN, BUT THE MUCK JUST WASHED DOWNHILL. IT GATHERED IN A RANCID LAKE WHERE WAVERLY TRAIN STATION NOW STANDS. AND THE LAKE SENT THE STENCH RIGHT BACK UP HIGH STREET, UNTIL EDINBURGH CASTLE ITSELF STANK OF SEWAGE, SMOG, AND SECRETS THROWN OUT WITH THE TRASH.

AULD REEKIE, WE CALLED EDINBURGH THEN. I DON'T CARE WHAT THEY CALL THE TOWN NOW...

IT STILL STINKS.

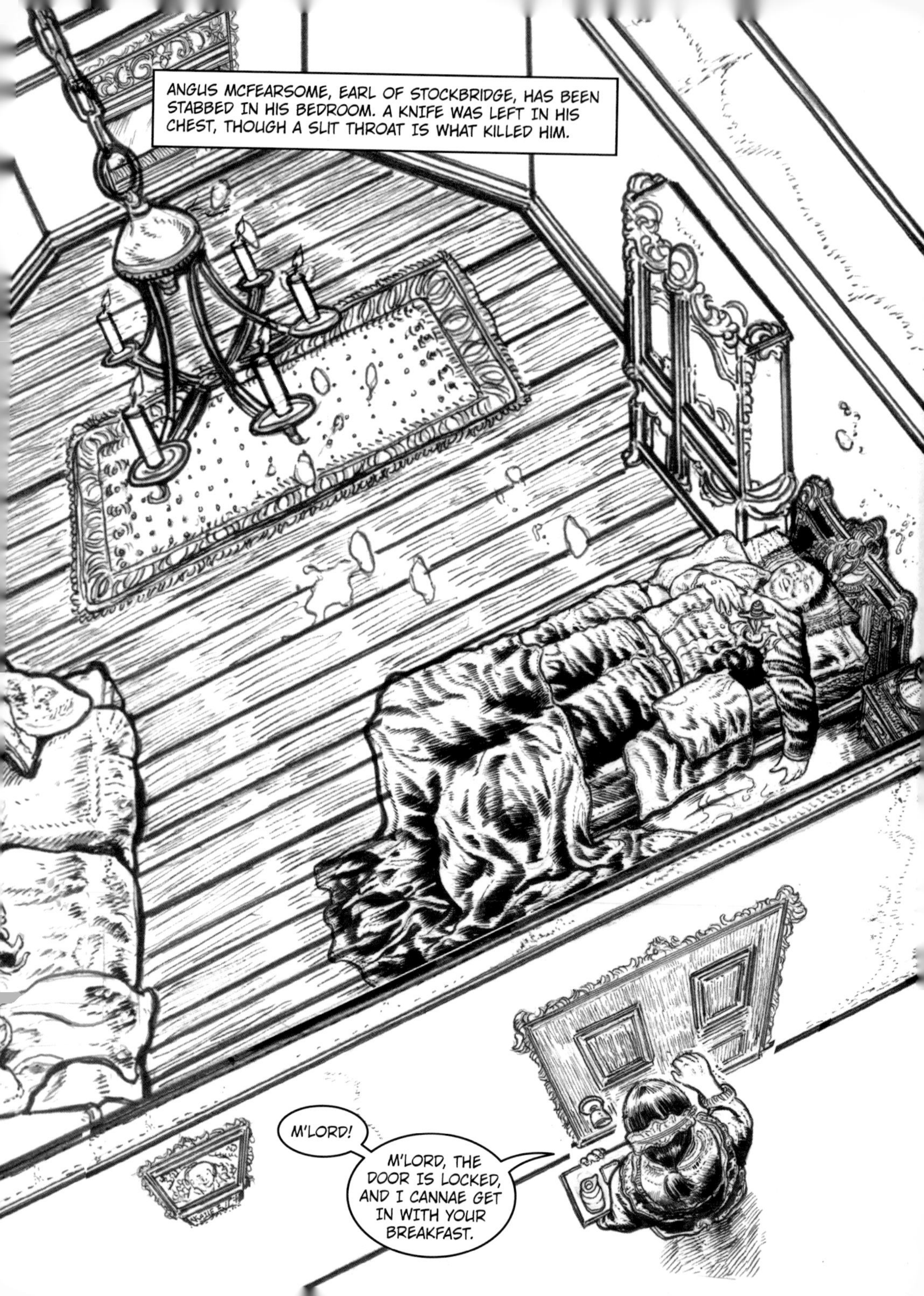
ANGUS MCFEARSOME, EARL OF STOCKBRIDGE, HAS BEEN STABBED IN HIS BEDROOM. A KNIFE WAS LEFT IN HIS CHEST, THOUGH A SLIT THROAT IS WHAT KILLED HIM.
M'LORD!
M'LORD, THE DOOR IS LOCKED, AND I CANNAE GET IN WITH YOUR BREAKFAST.

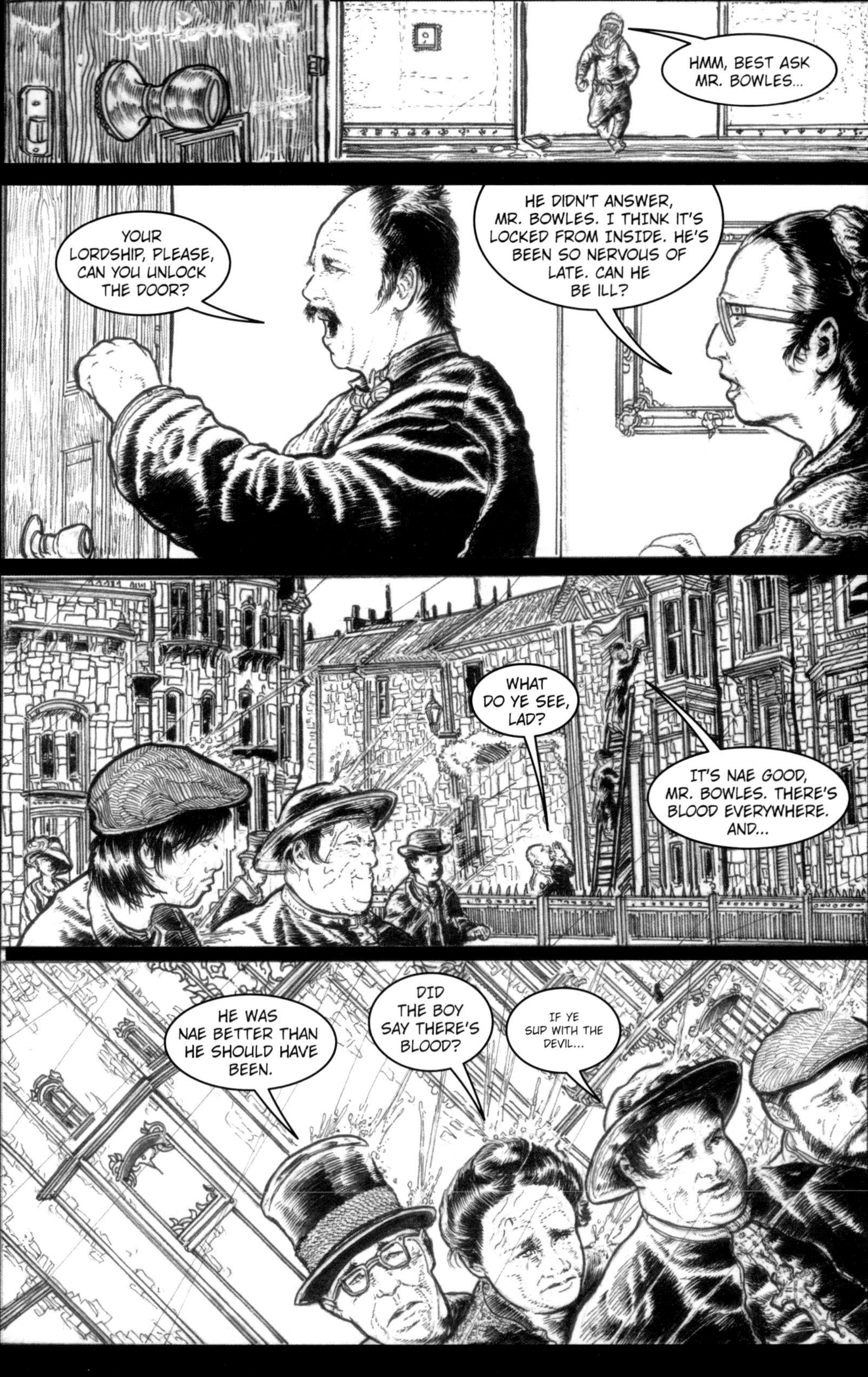
HMM, BEST ASK MR. BOWLES...
YOUR LORDSHIP, PLEASE, CAN YOU UNLOCK THE DOOR?
HE DIDN'T ANSWER, MR. BOWLES. I THINK IT'S LOCKED FROM INSIDE. HE'S BEEN SO NERVOUS OF LATE. CAN HE BE ILL?
WHAT DO YE SEE, LAD?
IT'S NAE GOOD, MR. BOWLES. THERE'S BLOOD EVERYWHERE. AND...
HE WAS NAE BETTER THAN HE SHOULD HAVE BEEN.
DID THE BOY SAY THERE'S BLOOD?
IF YE SUP WITH THE DEVIL...

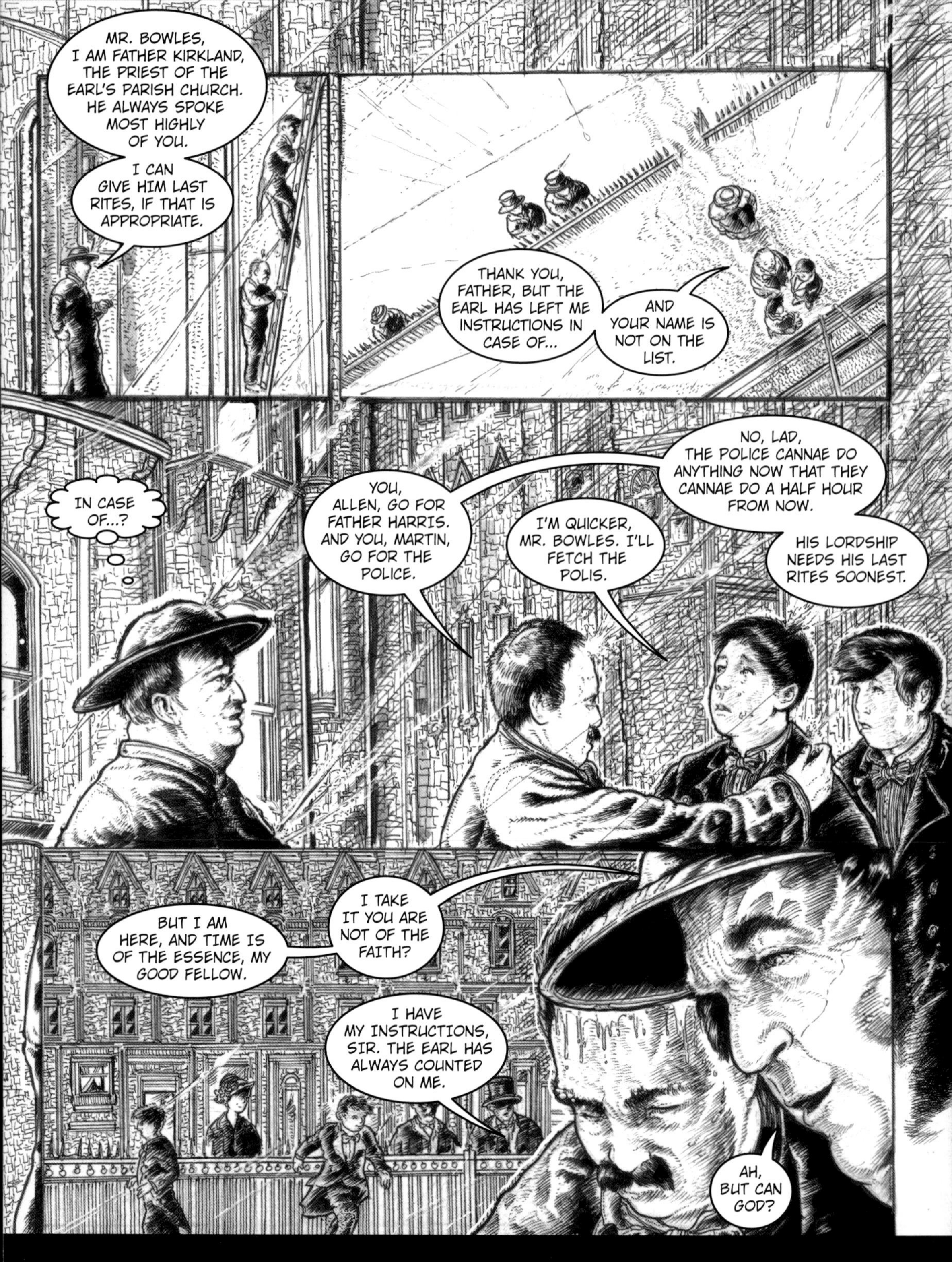
MR. BOWLES, I AM FATHER KIRKLAND, THE PRIEST OF THE EARL'S PARISH CHURCH. HE ALWAYS SPOKE MOST HIGHLY OF YOU.
I CAN GIVE HIM LAST RITES, IF THAT IS APPROPRIATE.
THANK YOU, FATHER, BUT THE EARL HAS LEFT ME INSTRUCTIONS IN CASE OF...
AND YOUR NAME IS NOT ON THE LIST.
IN CASE OF...?
YOU, ALLEN, GO FOR FATHER HARRIS. AND YOU, MARTIN, GO FOR THE POLICE.
I'M QUICKER, MR. BOWLES. I'LL FETCH THE POLIS.
NO, LAD, THE POLICE CANNAE DO ANYTHING NOW THAT THEY CANNAE DO A HALF HOUR FROM NOW.
HIS LORDSHIP NEEDS HIS LAST RITES SOONEST.
I TAKE IT YOU ARE NOT OF THE FAITH?
BUT I AM HERE, AND TIME IS OF THE ESSENCE, MY GOOD FELLOW.
I HAVE MY INSTRUCTIONS, SIR. THE EARL HAS ALWAYS COUNTED ON ME.
AH, BUT CAN GOD?

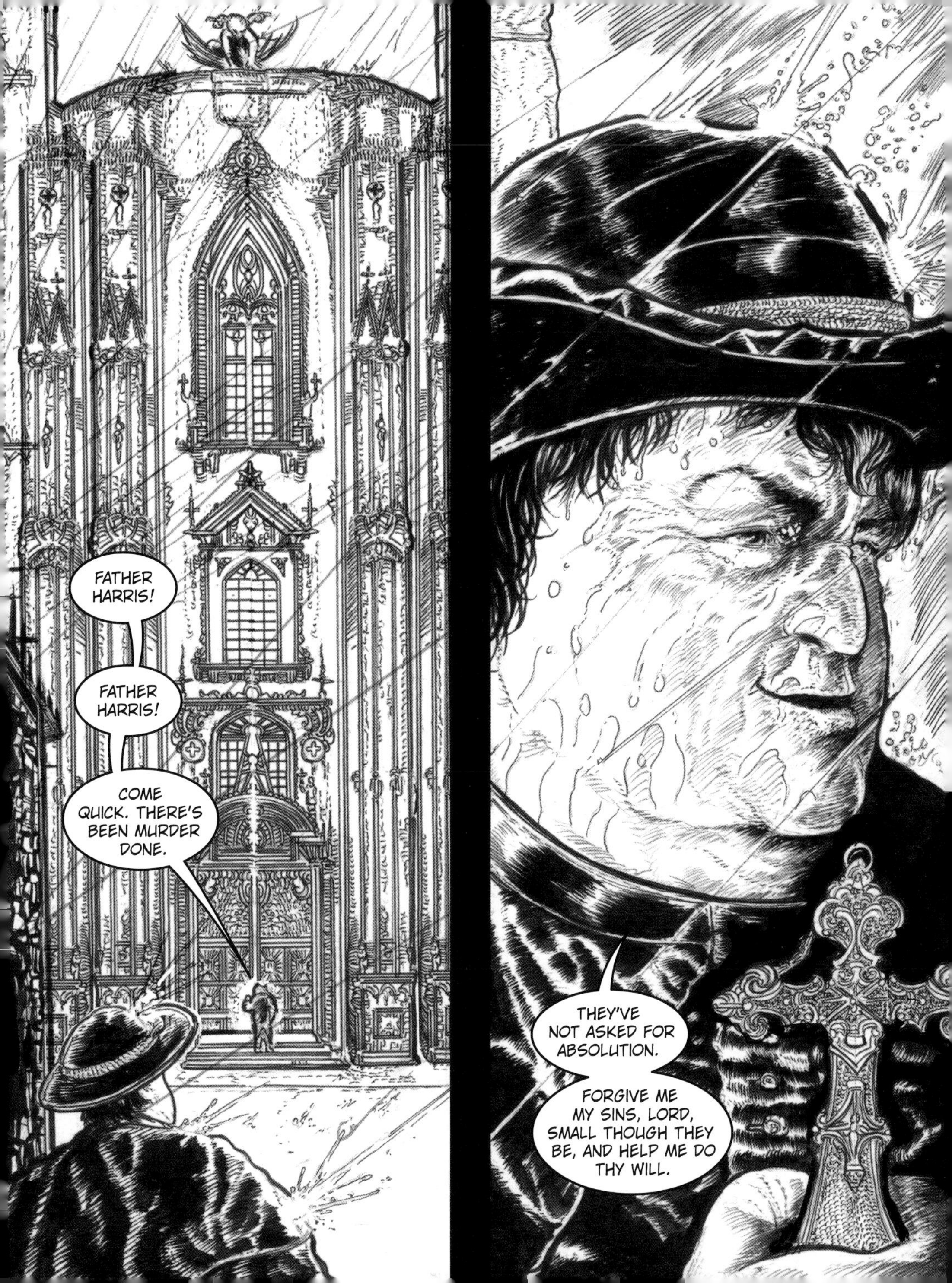
FATHER HARRIS!
FATHER HARRIS!
COME QUICK. THERE'S BEEN MURDER DONE.
THEY'VE NOT ASKED FOR ABSOLUTION.
FORGIVE ME MY SINS, LORD, SMALL THOUGH THEY BE, AND HELP ME DO THY WILL.

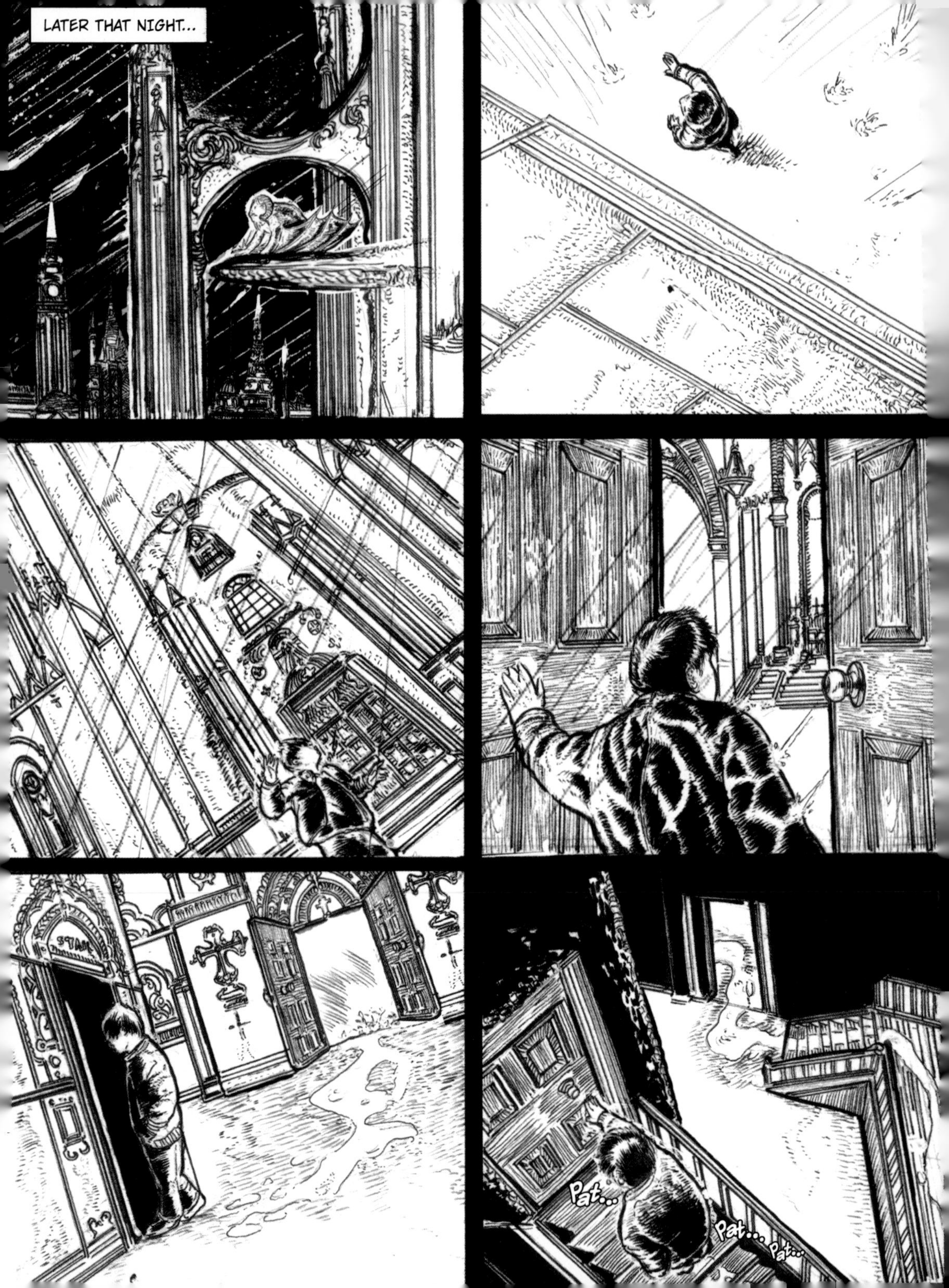
LATER THAT NIGHT...
Pat...
Pat...
Pat...

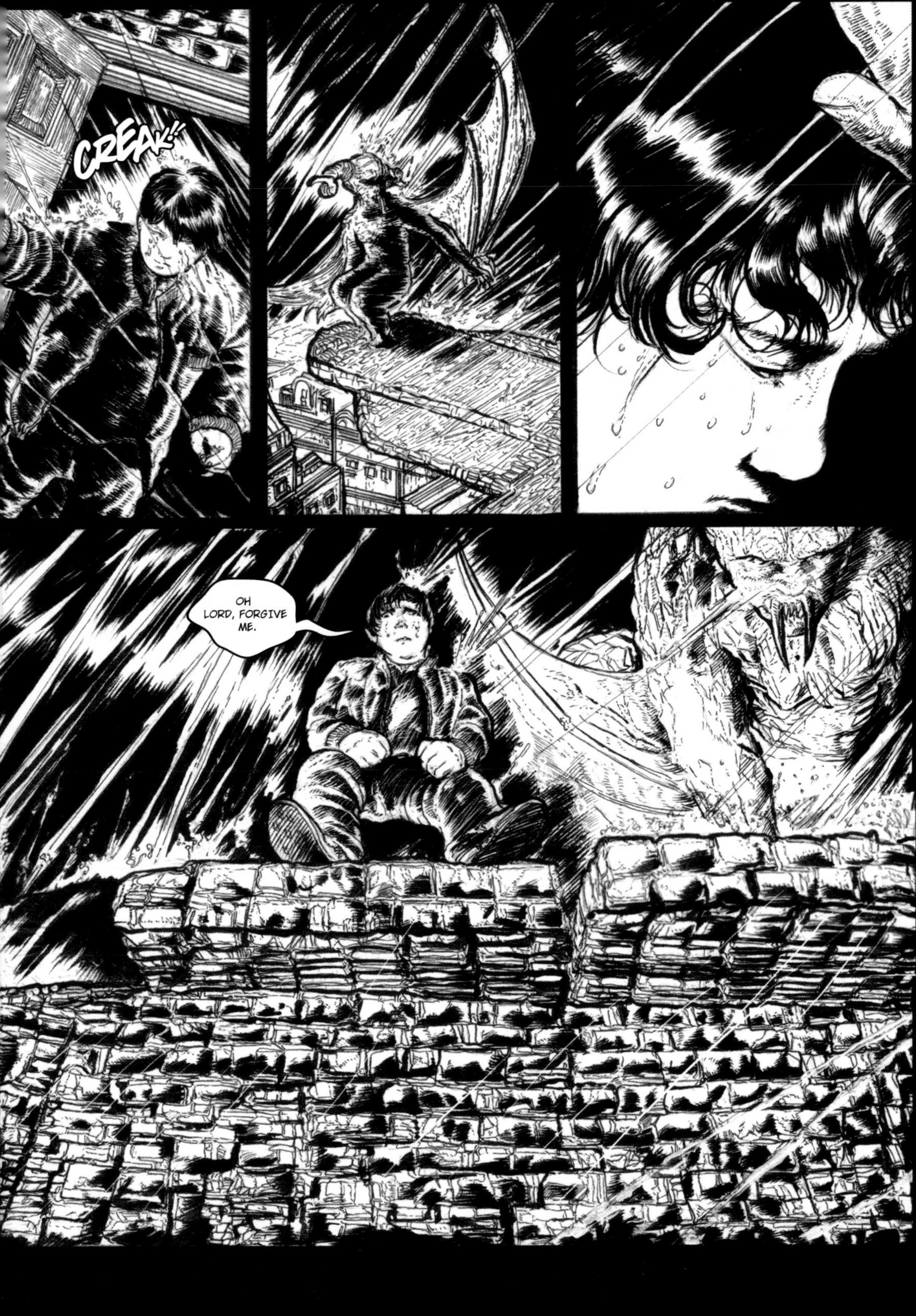
CREAK!!
OH LORD, FORGIVE ME.

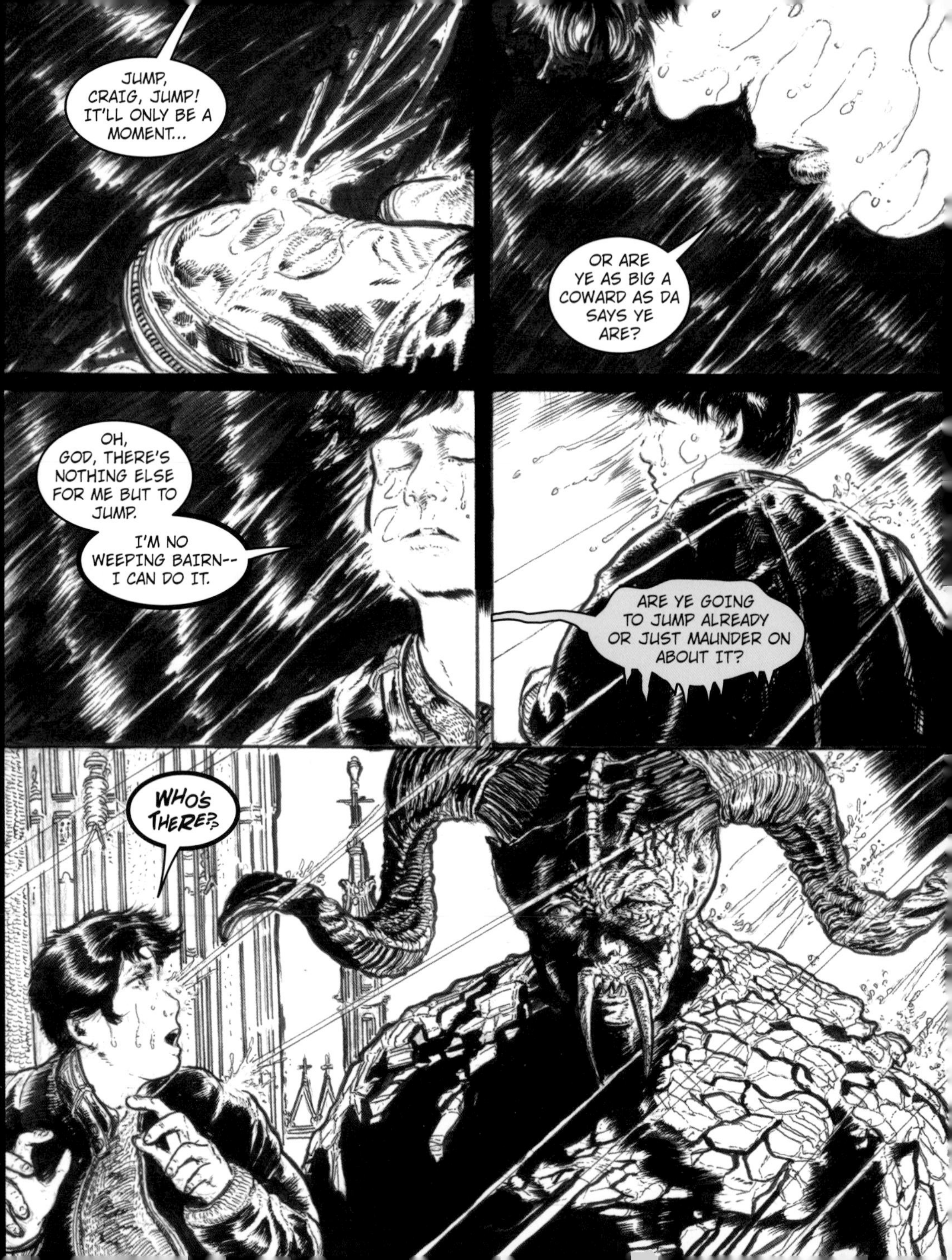
JUMP, CRAIG, JUMP! IT'LL ONLY BE A MOMENT...
OR ARE YE AS BIG A COWARD AS DA SAYS YE ARE?
OH, GOD, THERE'S NOTHING ELSE FOR ME BUT TO JUMP.
I'M NO WEEPING BAIRN-- I CAN DO IT.
ARE YE GOING TO JUMP ALREADY OR JUST MAUNDER ON ABOUT IT?
WHO'S THERE?!

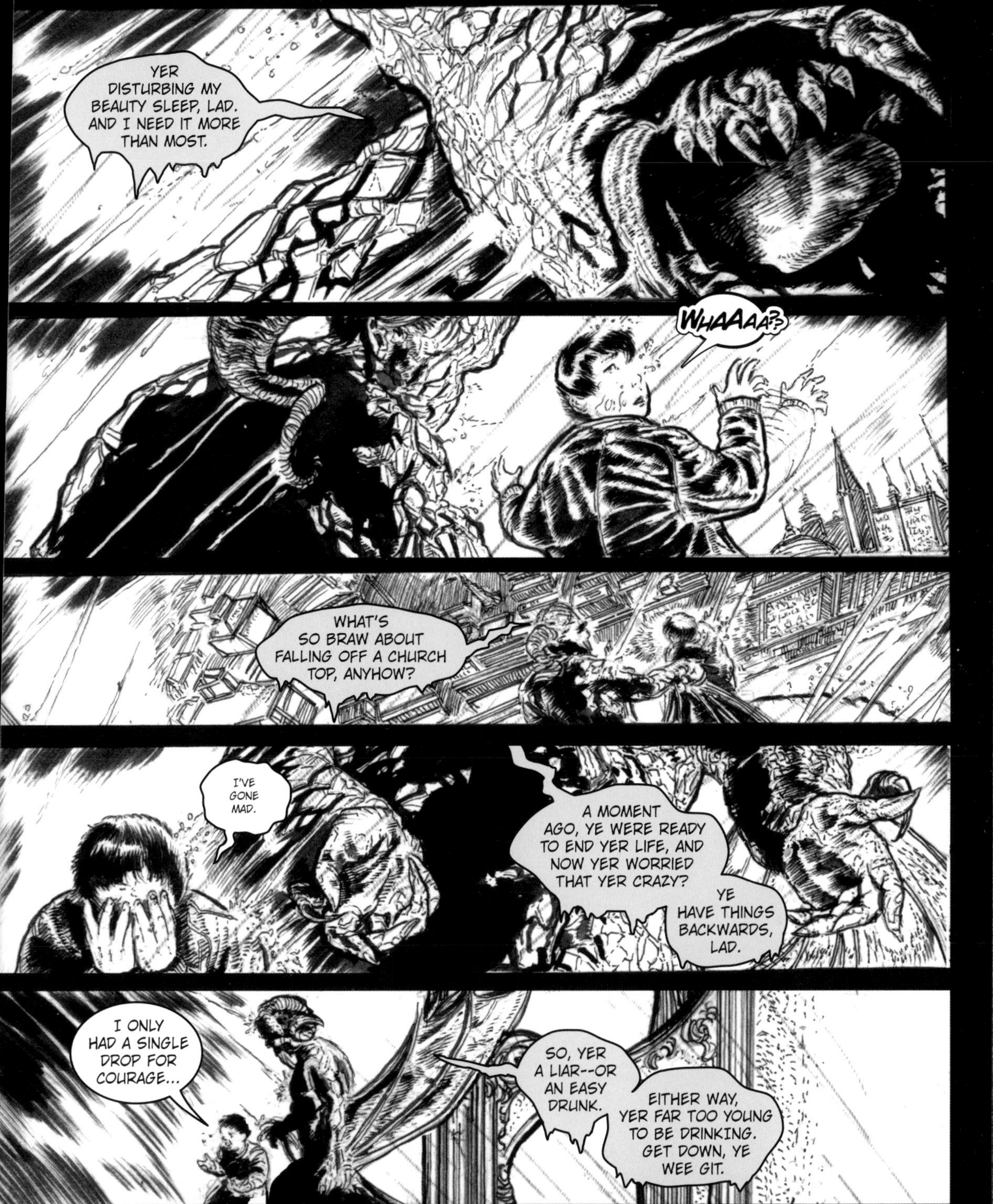
YER DISTURBING MY BEAUTY SLEEP, LAD. AND I NEED IT MORE THAN MOST.
WHAAAA?
WHAT'S SO BRAW ABOUT FALLING OFF A CHURCH TOP, ANYHOW?
I'VE GONE MAD.
A MOMENT AGO, YE WERE READY TO END YER LIFE, AND NOW YER WORRIED THAT YER CRAZY?
YE HAVE THINGS BACKWARDS, LAD.
I ONLY HAD A SINGLE DROP FOR COURAGE...
SO, YER A LIAR--OR AN EASY DRUNK.
EITHER WAY, YER FAR TOO YOUNG TO BE DRINKING. GET DOWN, YE WEE GIT.

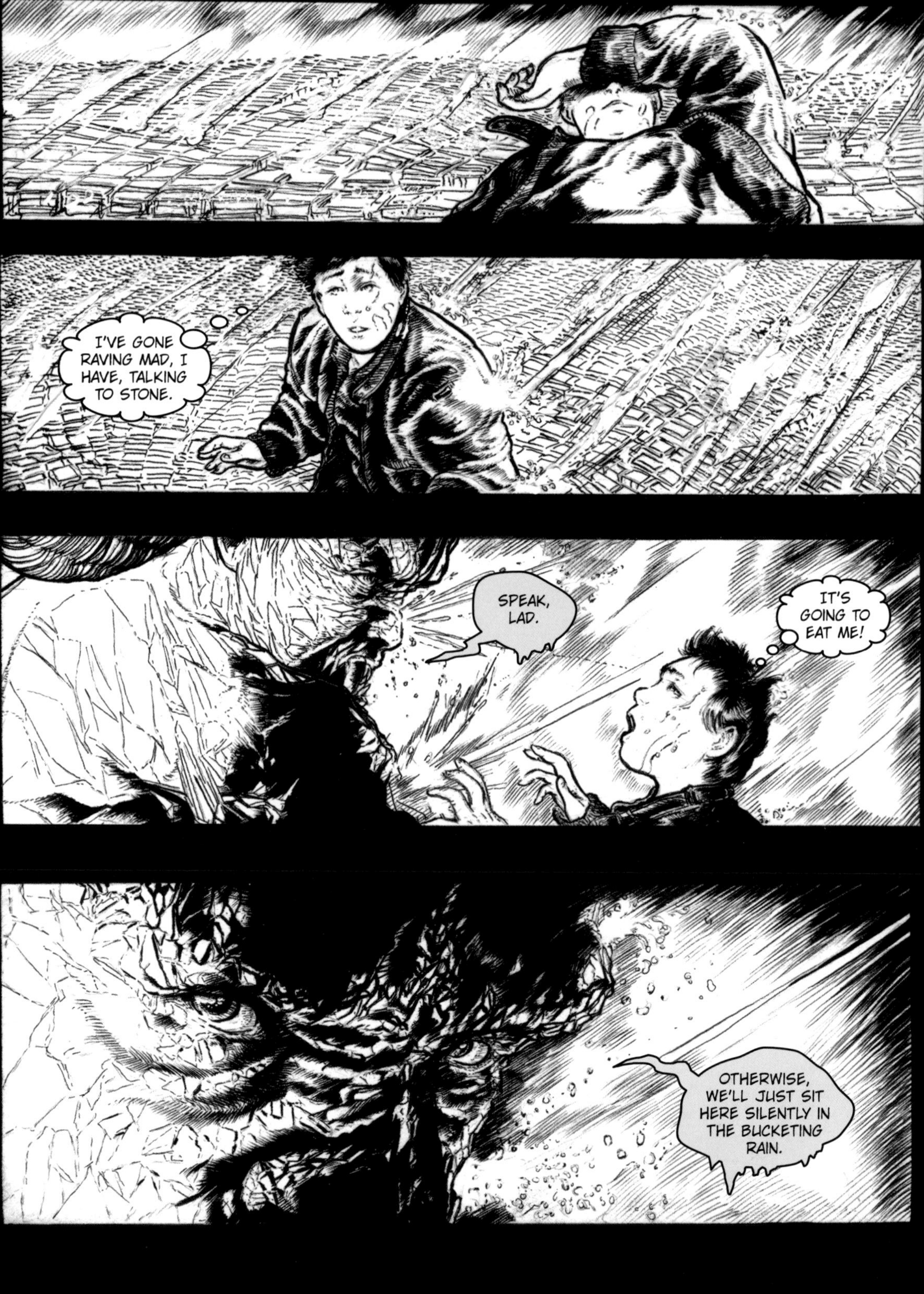
I'VE GONE RAVING MAD, I HAVE, TALKING TO STONE.
SPEAK, LAD.
IT'S GOING TO EAT ME!
OTHERWISE, WE'LL JUST SIT HERE SILENTLY IN THE BUCKETING RAIN.

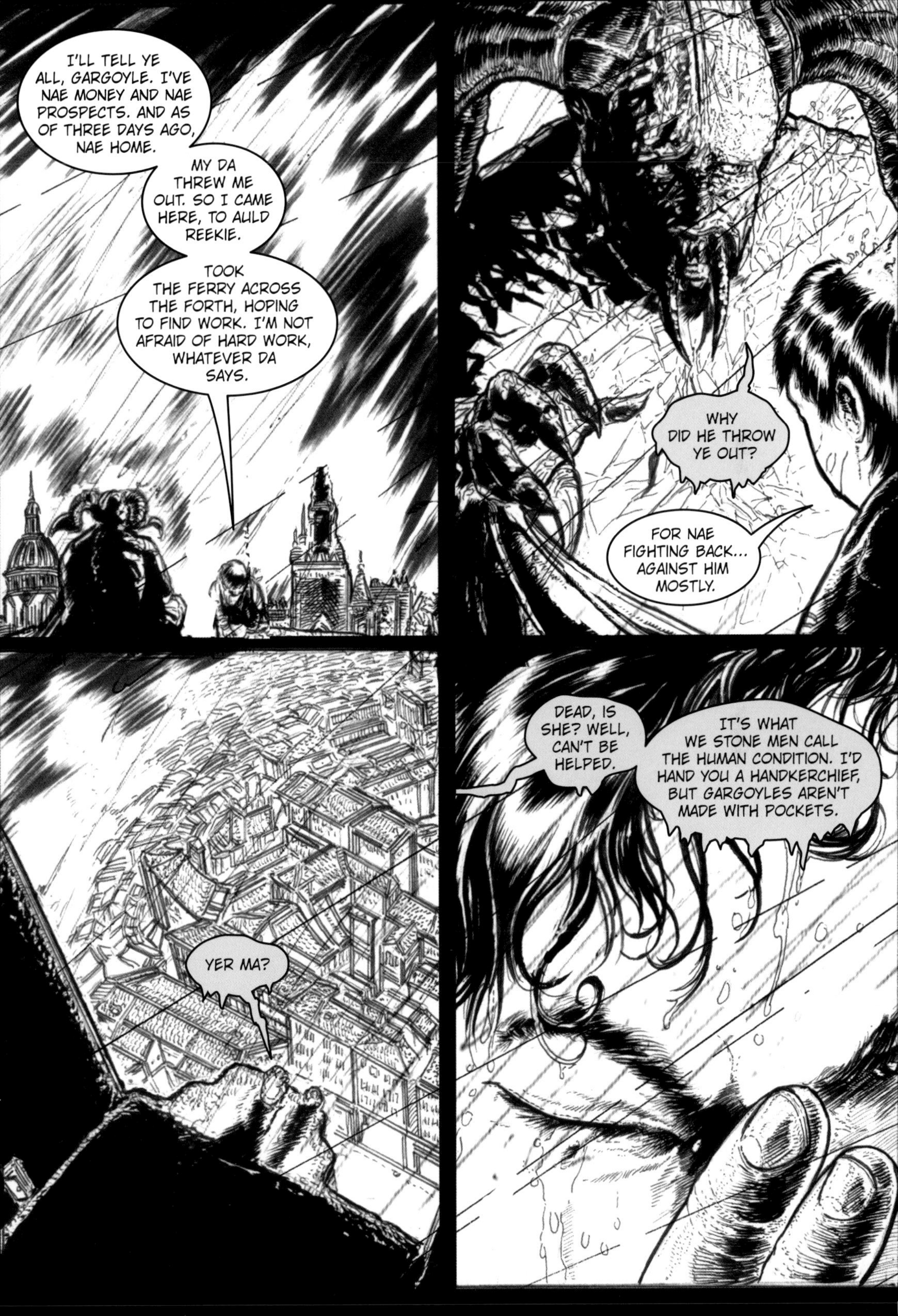
I'LL TELL YE ALL, GARGOYLE. I'VE NAE MONEY AND NAE PROSPECTS. AND AS OF THREE DAYS AGO, NAE HOME.
MY DA THREW ME OUT. SO I CAME HERE, TO AULD REEKIE.
TOOK THE FERRY ACROSS THE FORTH, HOPING TO FIND WORK. I'M NOT AFRAID OF HARD WORK, WHATEVER DA SAYS.
WHY DID HE THROW YE OUT?
FOR NAE FIGHTING BACK... AGAINST HIM MOSTLY.
YER MA?
DEAD, IS SHE? WELL, CAN'T BE HELPED.
IT'S WHAT WE STONE MEN CALL THE HUMAN CONDITION. I'D HAND YOU A HANDKERCHIEF, BUT GARGOYLES AREN'T MADE WITH POCKETS.

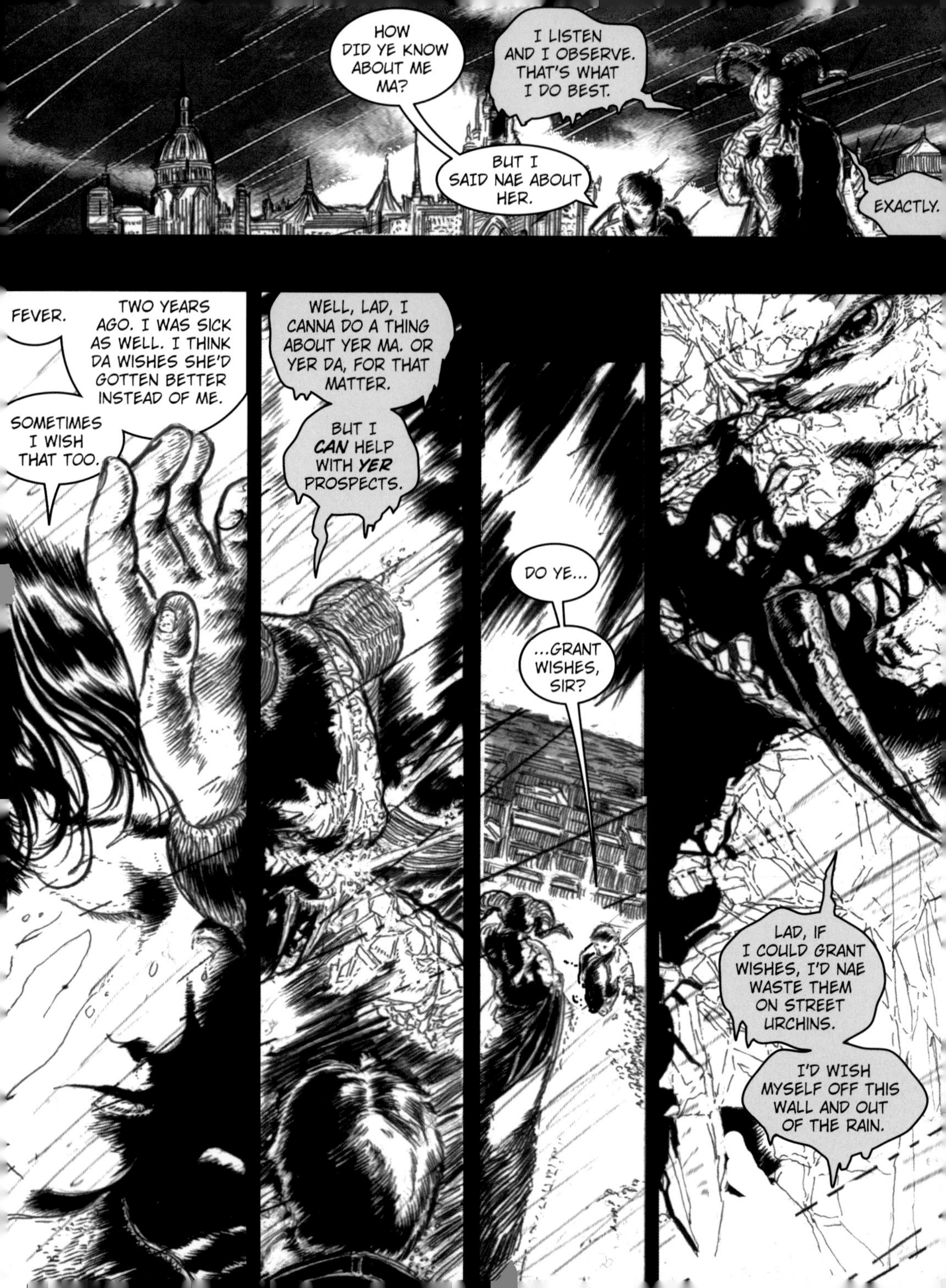
HOW DID YE KNOW ABOUT ME MA?
I LISTEN AND I OBSERVE. THAT'S WHAT I DO BEST.
BUT I SAID NAE ABOUT HER.
EXACTLY.
FEVER.
TWO YEARS AGO. I WAS SICK AS WELL. I THINK DA WISHES SHE'D GOTTEN BETTER INSTEAD OF ME.
SOMETIMES I WISH THAT TOO.
WELL, LAD, I CANNA DO A THING ABOUT YER MA. OR YER DA, FOR THAT MATTER.
BUT I *CAN* HELP WITH *YER* PROSPECTS.
DO YE...
...GRANT WISHES, SIR?
LAD, IF I COULD GRANT WISHES, I'D NAE WASTE THEM ON STREET URCHINS.
I'D WISH MYSELF OFF THIS WALL AND OUT OF THE RAIN.

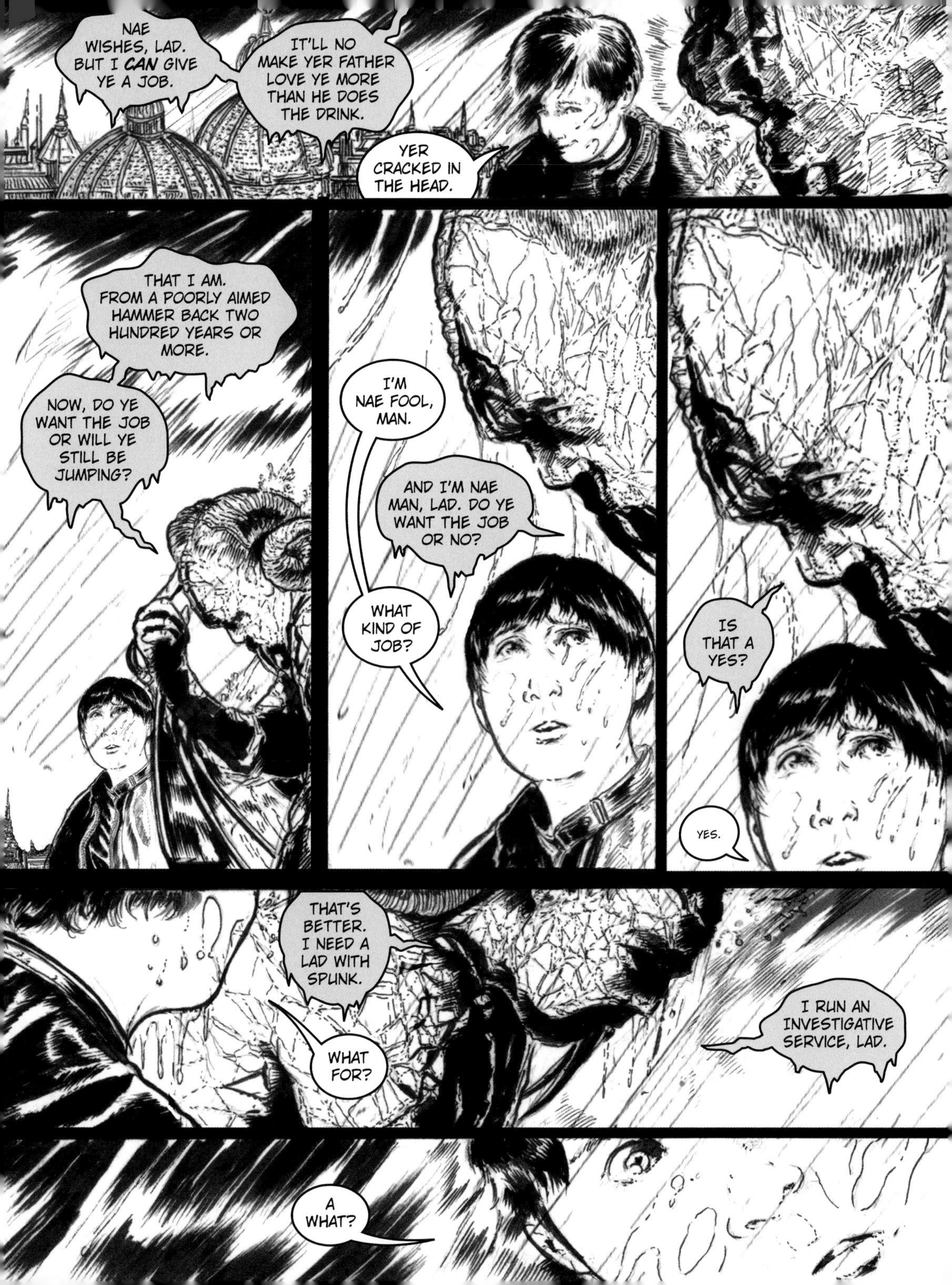
NAE WISHES, LAD. BUT I *CAN* GIVE YE A JOB.
IT'LL NO MAKE YER FATHER LOVE YE MORE THAN HE DOES THE DRINK.
YER CRACKED IN THE HEAD.
THAT I AM. FROM A POORLY AIMED HAMMER BACK TWO HUNDRED YEARS OR MORE.
NOW, DO YE WANT THE JOB OR WILL YE STILL BE JUMPING?
I'M NAE FOOL, MAN.
AND I'M NAE MAN, LAD. DO YE WANT THE JOB OR NO?
WHAT KIND OF JOB?
IS THAT A YES?
YES.
THAT'S BETTER. I NEED A LAD WITH SPUNK.
WHAT FOR?
I RUN AN INVESTIGATIVE SERVICE, LAD.
A WHAT?

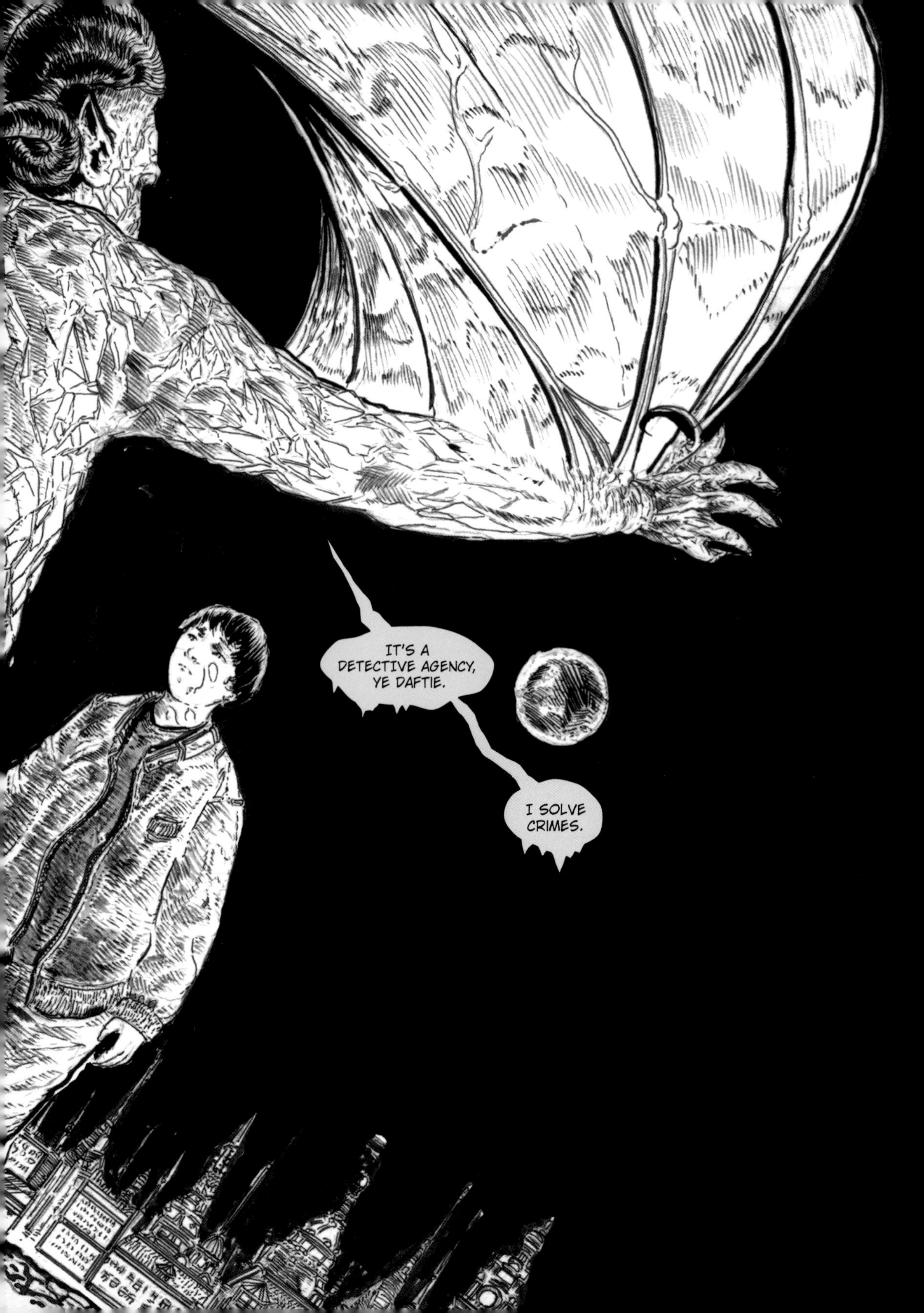
IT'S A DETECTIVE AGENCY, YE DAFTIE.
I SOLVE CRIMES.

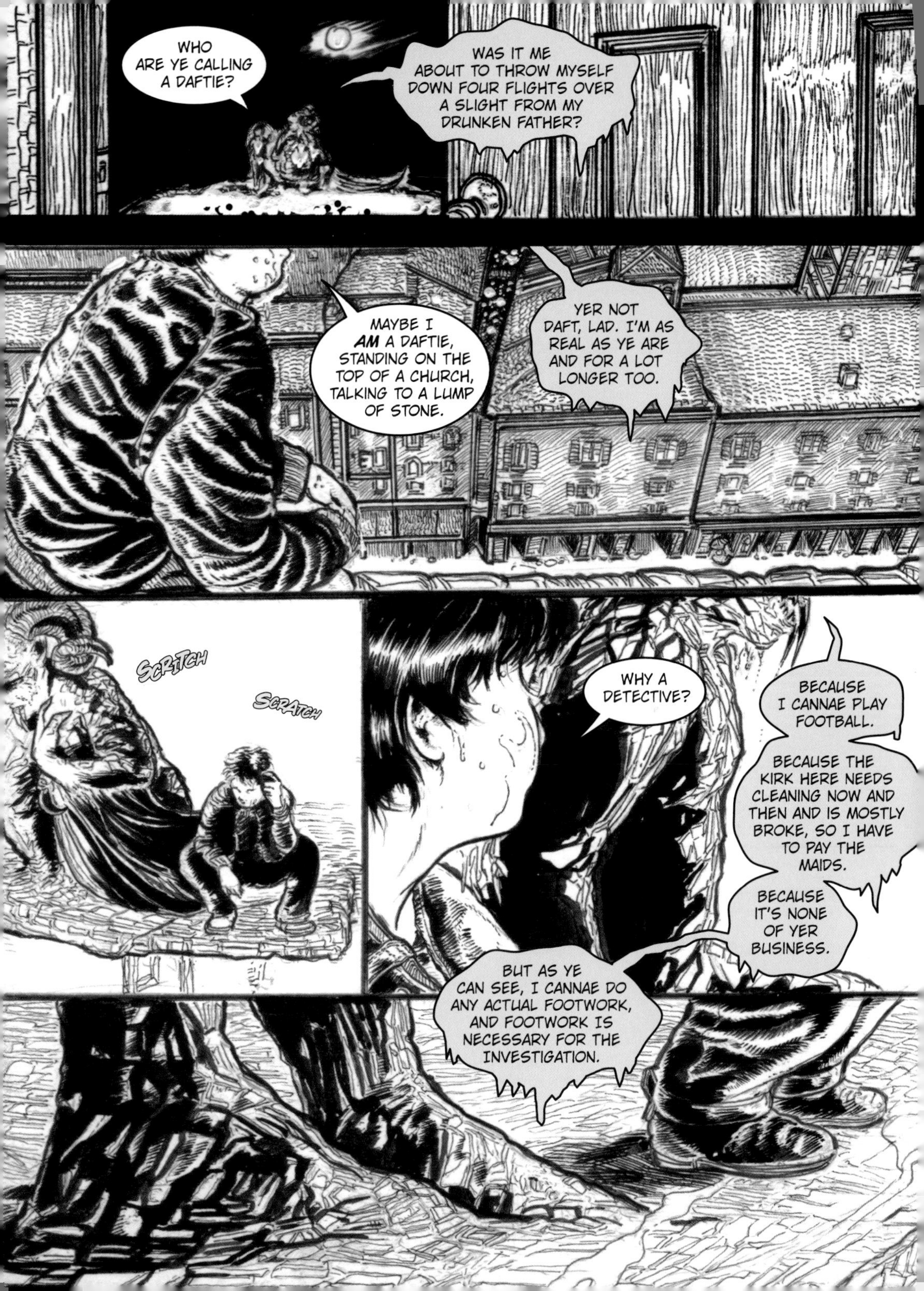
WHO ARE YE CALLING A DAFTIE?
WAS IT ME ABOUT TO THROW MYSELF DOWN FOUR FLIGHTS OVER A SLIGHT FROM MY DRUNKEN FATHER?
MAYBE I **AM** A DAFTIE, STANDING ON THE TOP OF A CHURCH, TALKING TO A LUMP OF STONE.
YER NOT DAFT, LAD. I'M AS REAL AS YE ARE AND FOR A LOT LONGER TOO.
SCRITCH
SCRATCH
WHY A DETECTIVE?
BECAUSE I CANNAE PLAY FOOTBALL.
BECAUSE THE KIRK HERE NEEDS CLEANING NOW AND THEN AND IS MOSTLY BROKE, SO I HAVE TO PAY THE MAIDS.
BECAUSE IT'S NONE OF YER BUSINESS.
BUT AS YE CAN SEE, I CANNAE DO ANY ACTUAL FOOTWORK, AND FOOTWORK IS NECESSARY FOR THE INVESTIGATION.

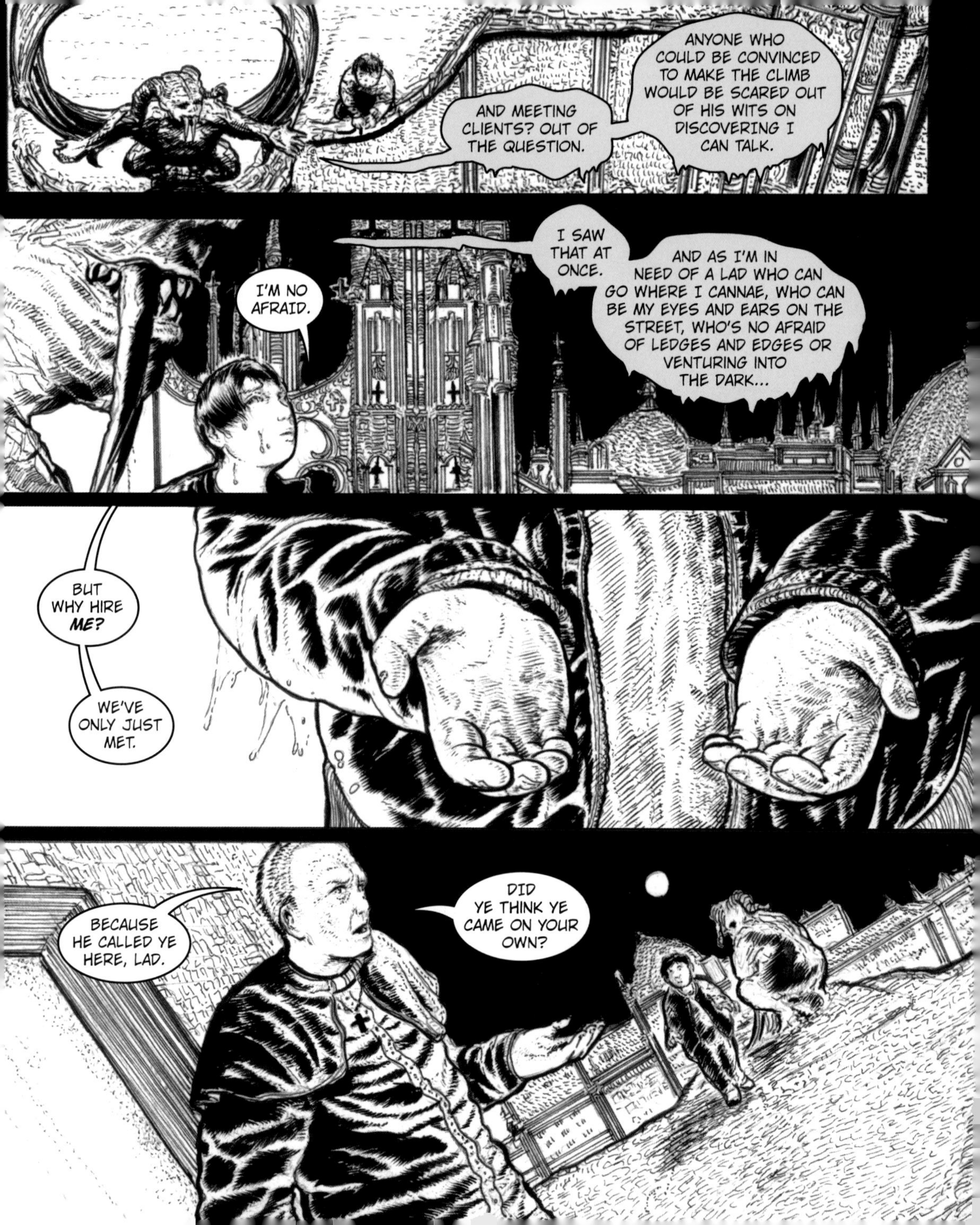
ANYONE WHO COULD BE CONVINCED TO MAKE THE CLIMB WOULD BE SCARED OUT OF HIS WITS ON DISCOVERING I CAN TALK.
AND MEETING CLIENTS? OUT OF THE QUESTION.
I'M NO AFRAID.
I SAW THAT AT ONCE.
AND AS I'M IN NEED OF A LAD WHO CAN GO WHERE I CANNAE, WHO CAN BE MY EYES AND EARS ON THE STREET, WHO'S NO AFRAID OF LEDGES AND EDGES OR VENTURING INTO THE DARK...
BUT WHY HIRE *ME?*
WE'VE ONLY JUST MET.
BECAUSE HE CALLED YE HERE, LAD.
DID YE THINK YE CAME ON YOUR OWN?

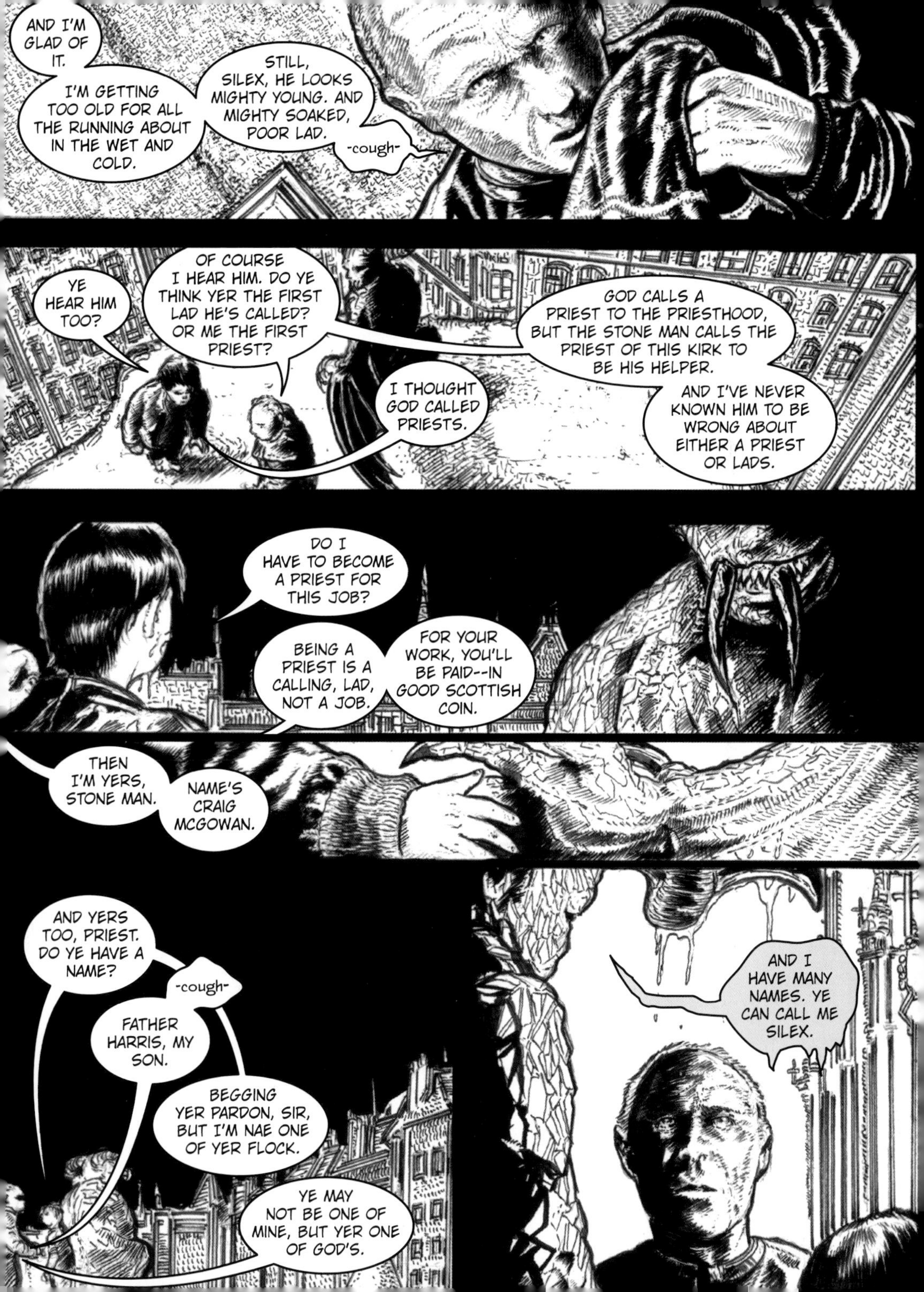
AND I'M GLAD OF IT.
I'M GETTING TOO OLD FOR ALL THE RUNNING ABOUT IN THE WET AND COLD.
STILL, SILEX, HE LOOKS MIGHTY YOUNG. AND MIGHTY SOAKED, POOR LAD.
-cough-
YE HEAR HIM TOO?
OF COURSE I HEAR HIM. DO YE THINK YER THE FIRST LAD HE'S CALLED? OR ME THE FIRST PRIEST?
I THOUGHT GOD CALLED PRIESTS.
GOD CALLS A PRIEST TO THE PRIESTHOOD, BUT THE STONE MAN CALLS THE PRIEST OF THIS KIRK TO BE HIS HELPER.
AND I'VE NEVER KNOWN HIM TO BE WRONG ABOUT EITHER A PRIEST OR LADS.
DO I HAVE TO BECOME A PRIEST FOR THIS JOB?
BEING A PRIEST IS A CALLING, LAD, NOT A JOB.
FOR YOUR WORK, YOU'LL BE PAID--IN GOOD SCOTTISH COIN.
THEN I'M YERS, STONE MAN.
NAME'S CRAIG MCGOWAN.
AND YERS TOO, PRIEST. DO YE HAVE A NAME?
-cough-
FATHER HARRIS, MY SON.
BEGGING YER PARDON, SIR, BUT I'M NAE ONE OF YER FLOCK.
YE MAY NOT BE ONE OF MINE, BUT YER ONE OF GOD'S.
AND I HAVE MANY NAMES. YE CAN CALL ME SILEX.

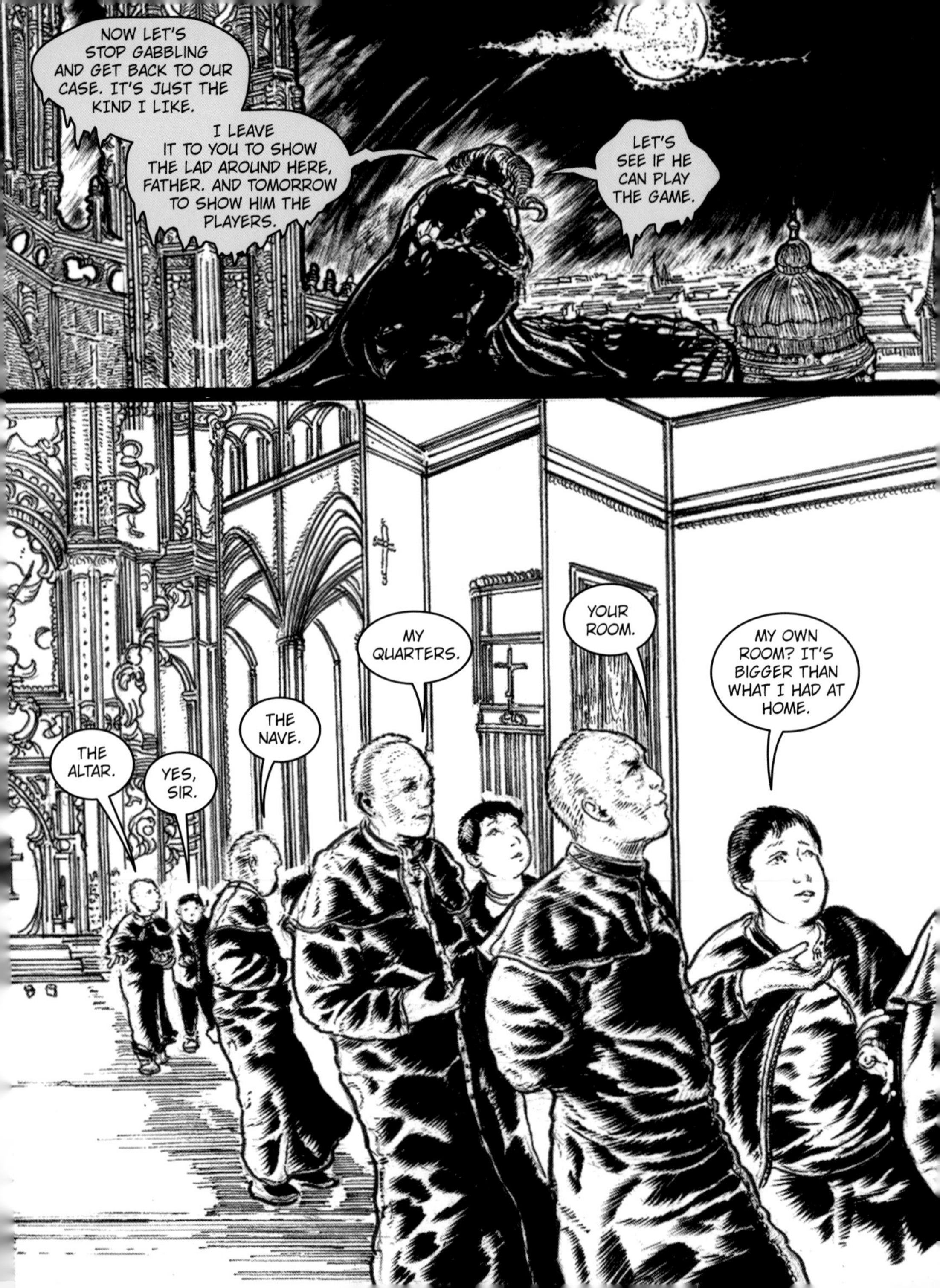
NOW LET'S STOP GABBLING AND GET BACK TO OUR CASE. IT'S JUST THE KIND I LIKE.
I LEAVE IT TO YOU TO SHOW THE LAD AROUND HERE, FATHER. AND TOMORROW TO SHOW HIM THE PLAYERS.
LET'S SEE IF HE CAN PLAY THE GAME.
THE ALTAR.
YES, SIR.
THE NAVE.
MY QUARTERS.
YOUR ROOM.
MY OWN ROOM? IT'S BIGGER THAN WHAT I HAD AT HOME.

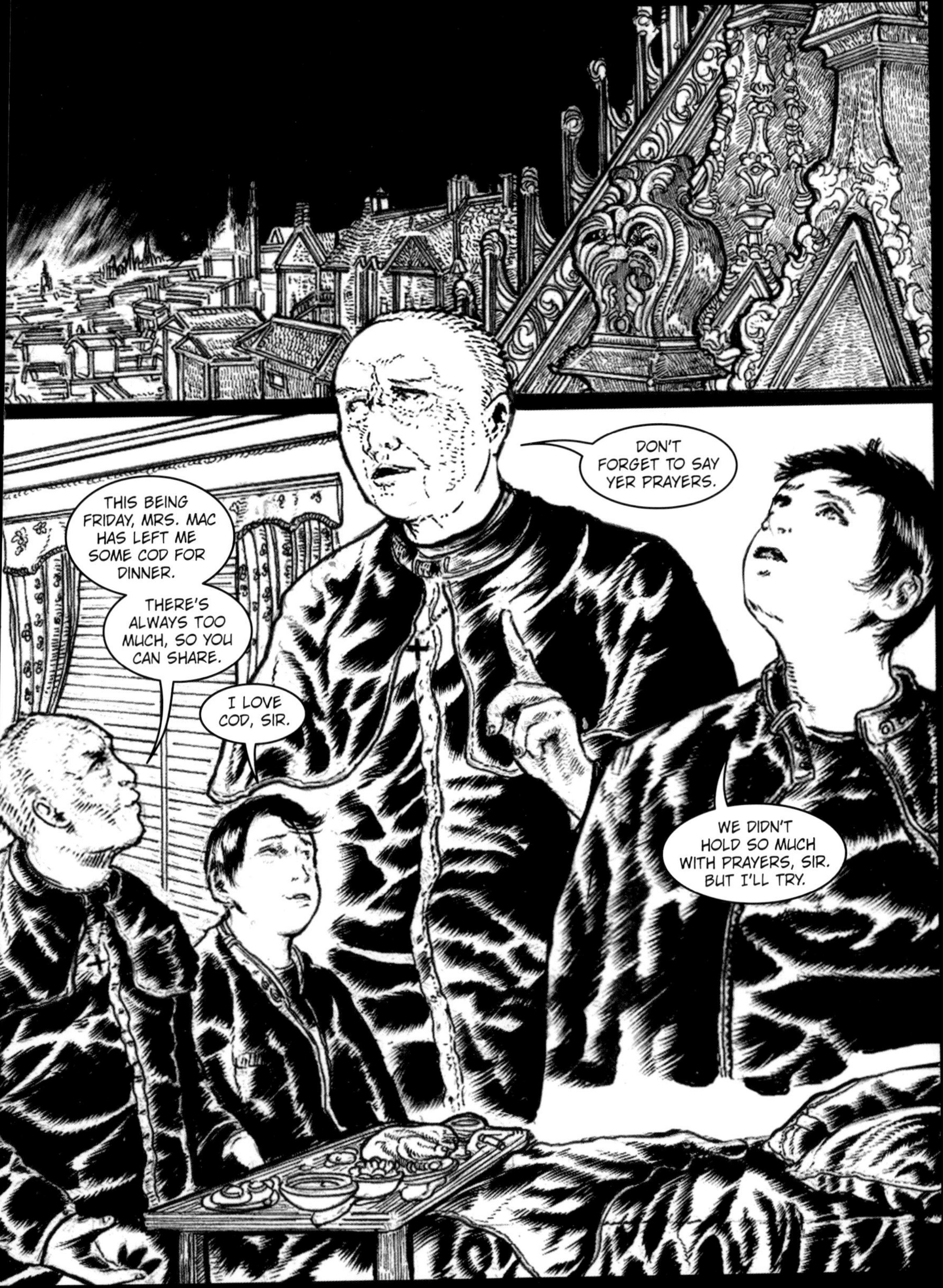
THIS BEING FRIDAY, MRS. MAC HAS LEFT ME SOME COD FOR DINNER.
THERE'S ALWAYS TOO MUCH, SO YOU CAN SHARE.
DON'T FORGET TO SAY YER PRAYERS.
I LOVE COD, SIR.
WE DIDN'T HOLD SO MUCH WITH PRAYERS, SIR. BUT I'LL TRY.

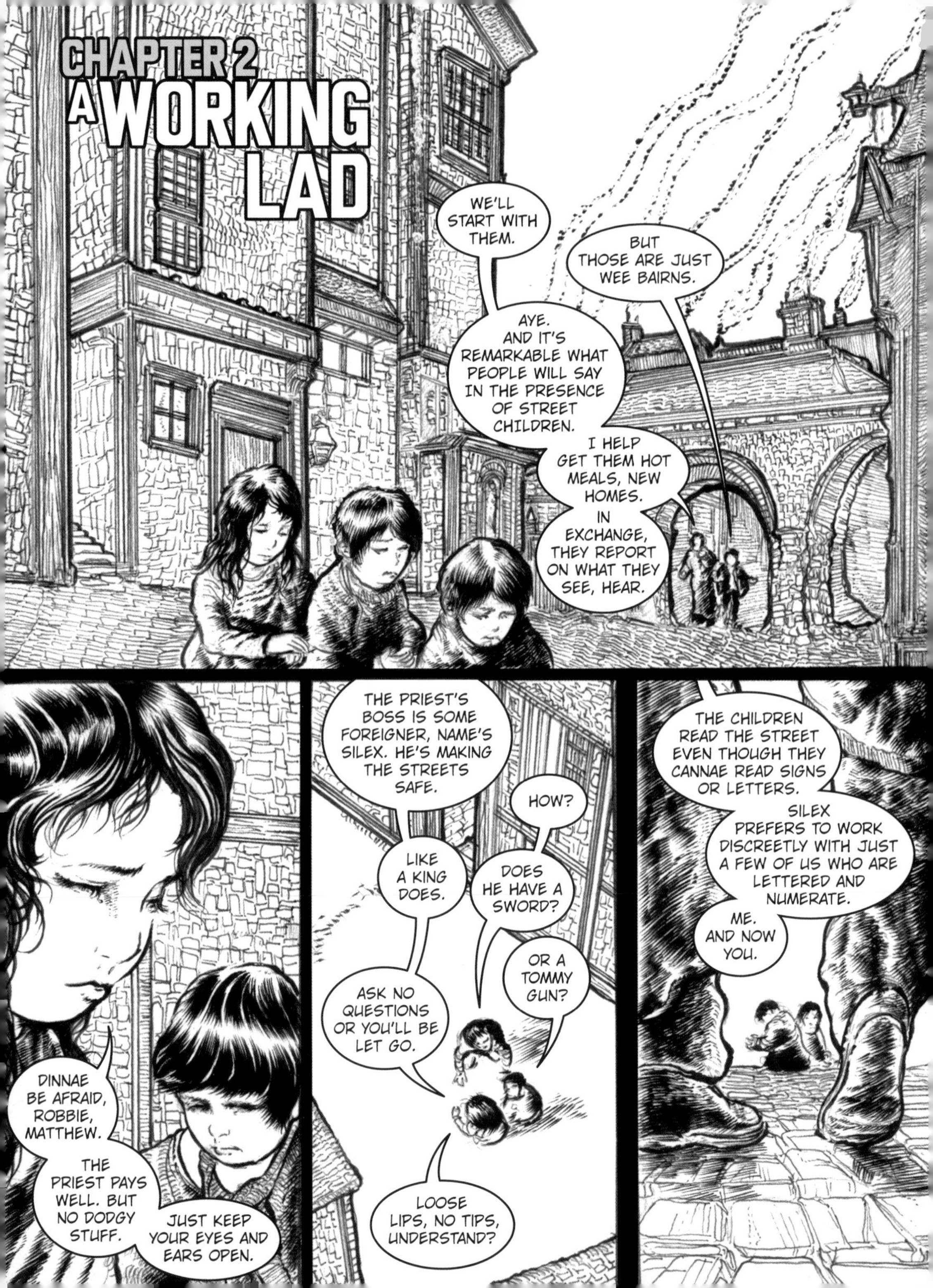
CHAPTER 2
A WORKING LAD
WE'LL START WITH THEM.
BUT THOSE ARE JUST WEE BAIRNS.
AYE. AND IT'S REMARKABLE WHAT PEOPLE WILL SAY IN THE PRESENCE OF STREET CHILDREN.
I HELP GET THEM HOT MEALS, NEW HOMES.
IN EXCHANGE, THEY REPORT ON WHAT THEY SEE, HEAR.
DINNAE BE AFRAID, ROBBIE, MATTHEW.
THE PRIEST PAYS WELL. BUT NO DODGY STUFF.
JUST KEEP YOUR EYES AND EARS OPEN.
THE PRIEST'S BOSS IS SOME FOREIGNER, NAME'S SILEX. HE'S MAKING THE STREETS SAFE.
HOW?
LIKE A KING DOES.
DOES HE HAVE A SWORD?
OR A TOMMY GUN?
ASK NO QUESTIONS OR YOU'LL BE LET GO.
LOOSE LIPS, NO TIPS, UNDERSTAND?
THE CHILDREN READ THE STREET EVEN THOUGH THEY CANNAE READ SIGNS OR LETTERS.
SILEX PREFERS TO WORK DISCREETLY WITH JUST A FEW OF US WHO ARE LETTERED AND NUMERATE.
ME. AND NOW YOU.

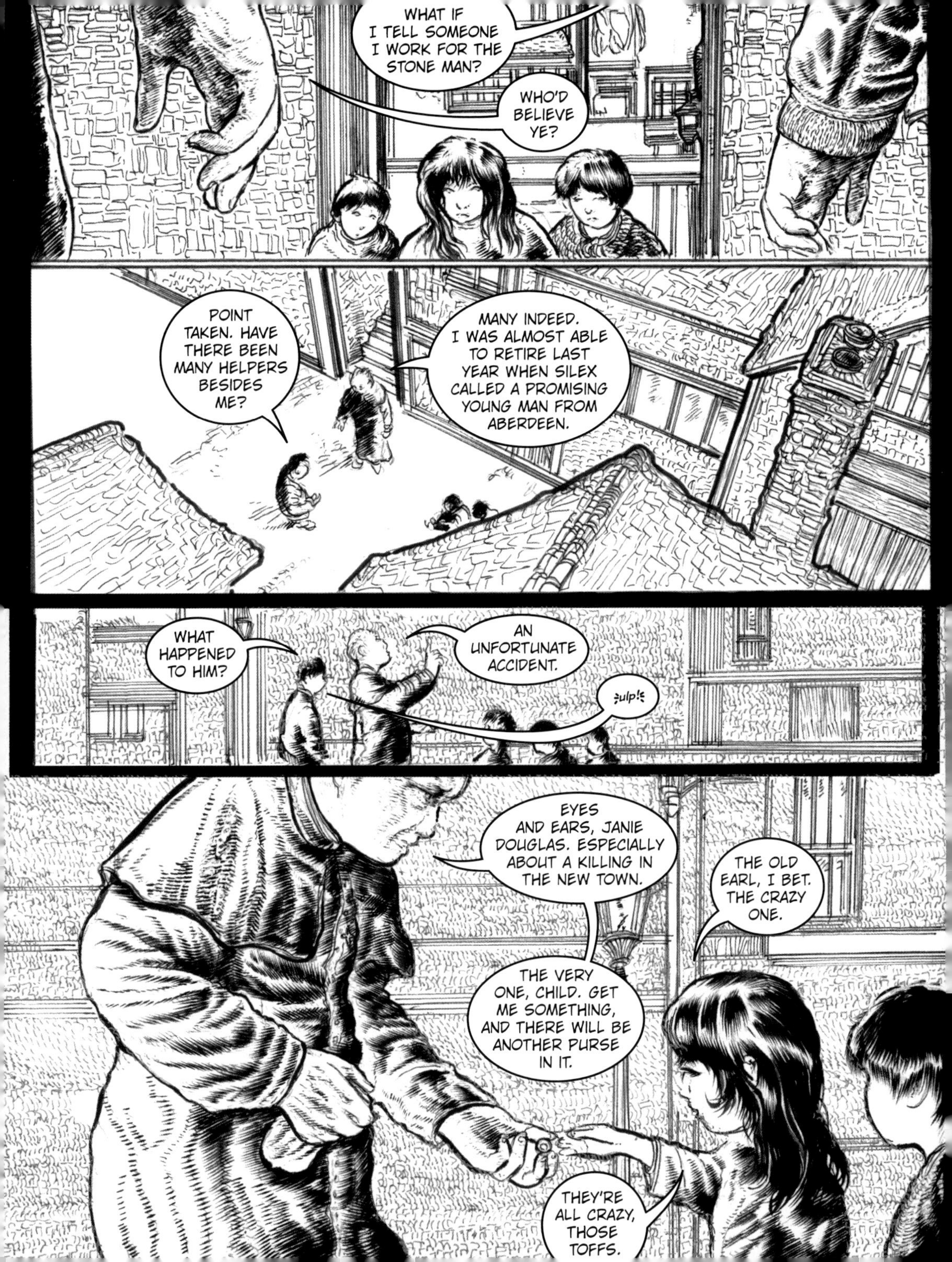
WHAT IF I TELL SOMEONE I WORK FOR THE STONE MAN?
WHO'D BELIEVE YE?
POINT TAKEN. HAVE THERE BEEN MANY HELPERS BESIDES ME?
MANY INDEED. I WAS ALMOST ABLE TO RETIRE LAST YEAR WHEN SILEX CALLED A PROMISING YOUNG MAN FROM ABERDEEN.
WHAT HAPPENED TO HIM?
AN UNFORTUNATE ACCIDENT.
ulp!
EYES AND EARS, JANIE DOUGLAS. ESPECIALLY ABOUT A KILLING IN THE NEW TOWN.
THE OLD EARL, I BET. THE CRAZY ONE.
THE VERY ONE, CHILD. GET ME SOMETHING, AND THERE WILL BE ANOTHER PURSE IN IT.
THEY'RE ALL CRAZY, THOSE TOFFS.

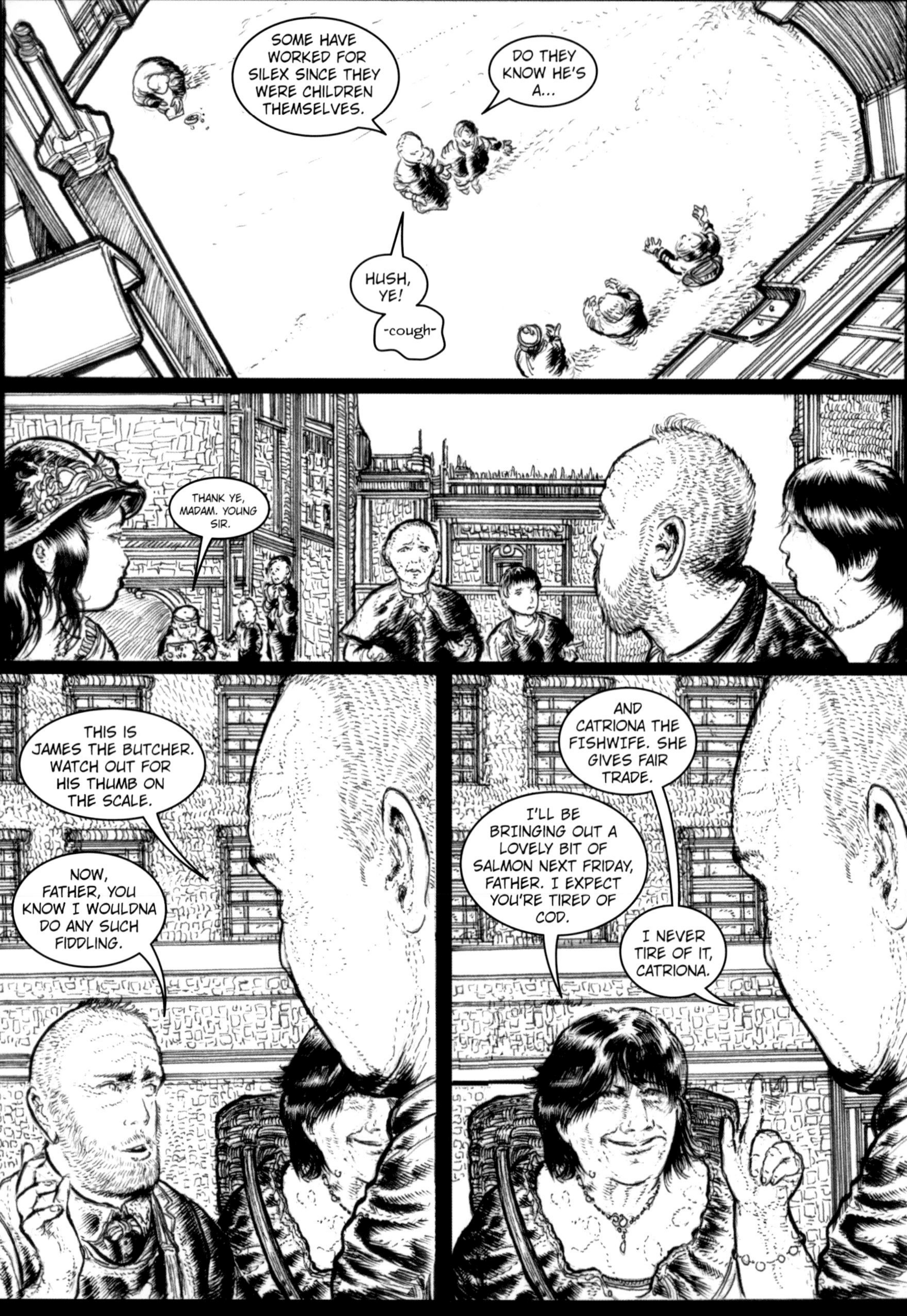
SOME HAVE WORKED FOR SILEX SINCE THEY WERE CHILDREN THEMSELVES.
DO THEY KNOW HE'S A...
HUSH, YE!
-cough-
THANK YE, MADAM. YOUNG SIR.
THIS IS JAMES THE BUTCHER. WATCH OUT FOR HIS THUMB ON THE SCALE.
NOW, FATHER, YOU KNOW I WOULDNA DO ANY SUCH FIDDLING.
AND CATRIONA THE FISHWIFE. SHE GIVES FAIR TRADE.
I'LL BE BRINGING OUT A LOVELY BIT OF SALMON NEXT FRIDAY, FATHER. I EXPECT YOU'RE TIRED OF COD.
I NEVER TIRE OF IT, CATRIONA.

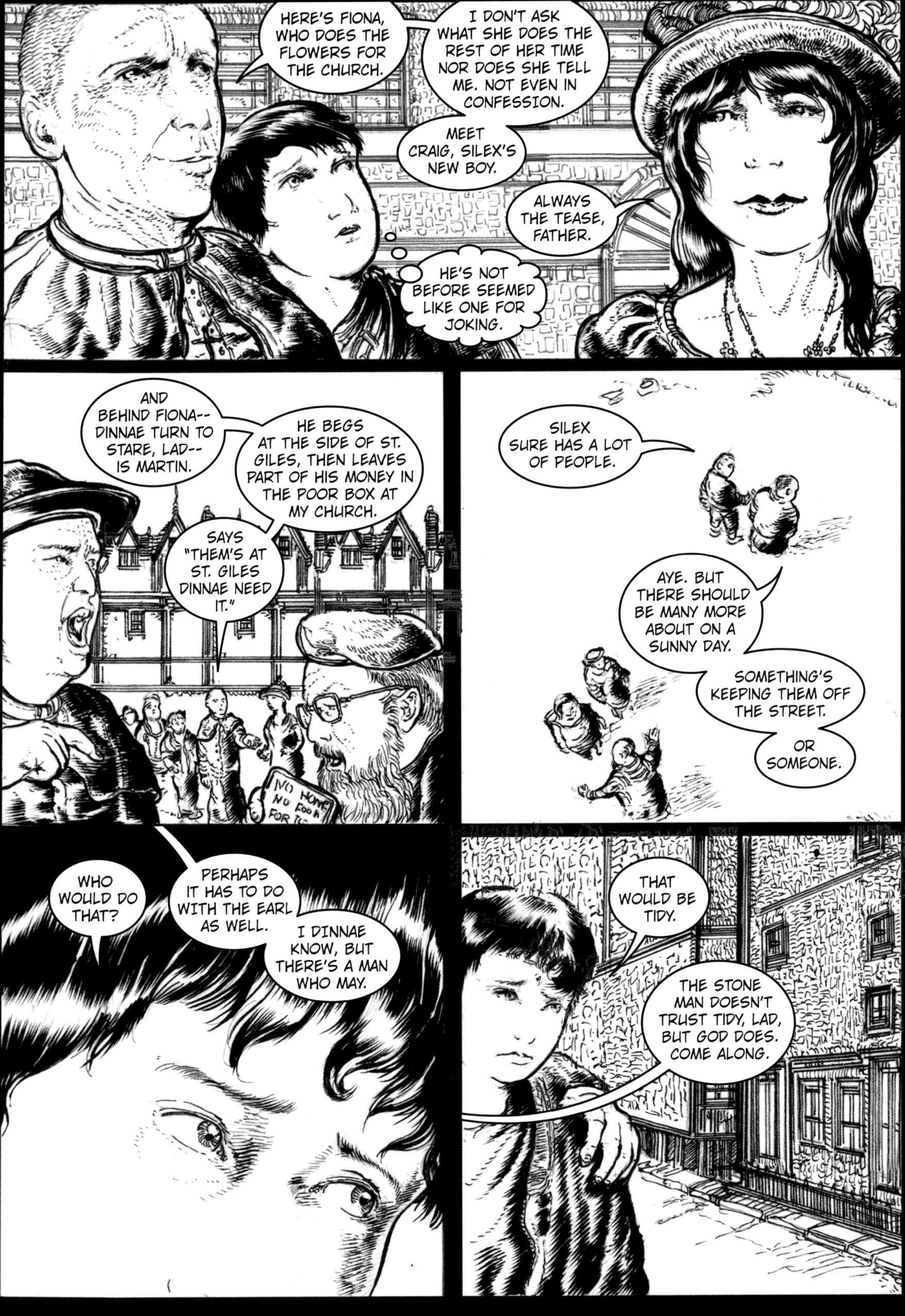
HERE'S FIONA, WHO DOES THE FLOWERS FOR THE CHURCH.
I DON'T ASK WHAT SHE DOES THE REST OF HER TIME NOR DOES SHE TELL ME. NOT EVEN IN CONFESSION.
MEET CRAIG, SILEX'S NEW BOY.
ALWAYS THE TEASE, FATHER.
HE'S NOT BEFORE SEEMED LIKE ONE FOR JOKING.
AND BEHIND FIONA-- DINNAE TURN TO STARE, LAD-- IS MARTIN.
HE BEGS AT THE SIDE OF ST. GILES, THEN LEAVES PART OF HIS MONEY IN THE POOR BOX AT MY CHURCH.
SAYS "THEM'S AT ST. GILES DINNAE NEED IT."
SILEX SURE HAS A LOT OF PEOPLE.
AYE. BUT THERE SHOULD BE MANY MORE ABOUT ON A SUNNY DAY.
SOMETHING'S KEEPING THEM OFF THE STREET.
OR SOMEONE.
WHO WOULD DO THAT?
PERHAPS IT HAS TO DO WITH THE EARL AS WELL.
I DINNAE KNOW, BUT THERE'S A MAN WHO MAY.
THAT WOULD BE TIDY.
THE STONE MAN DOESN'T TRUST TIDY, LAD, BUT GOD DOES. COME ALONG.

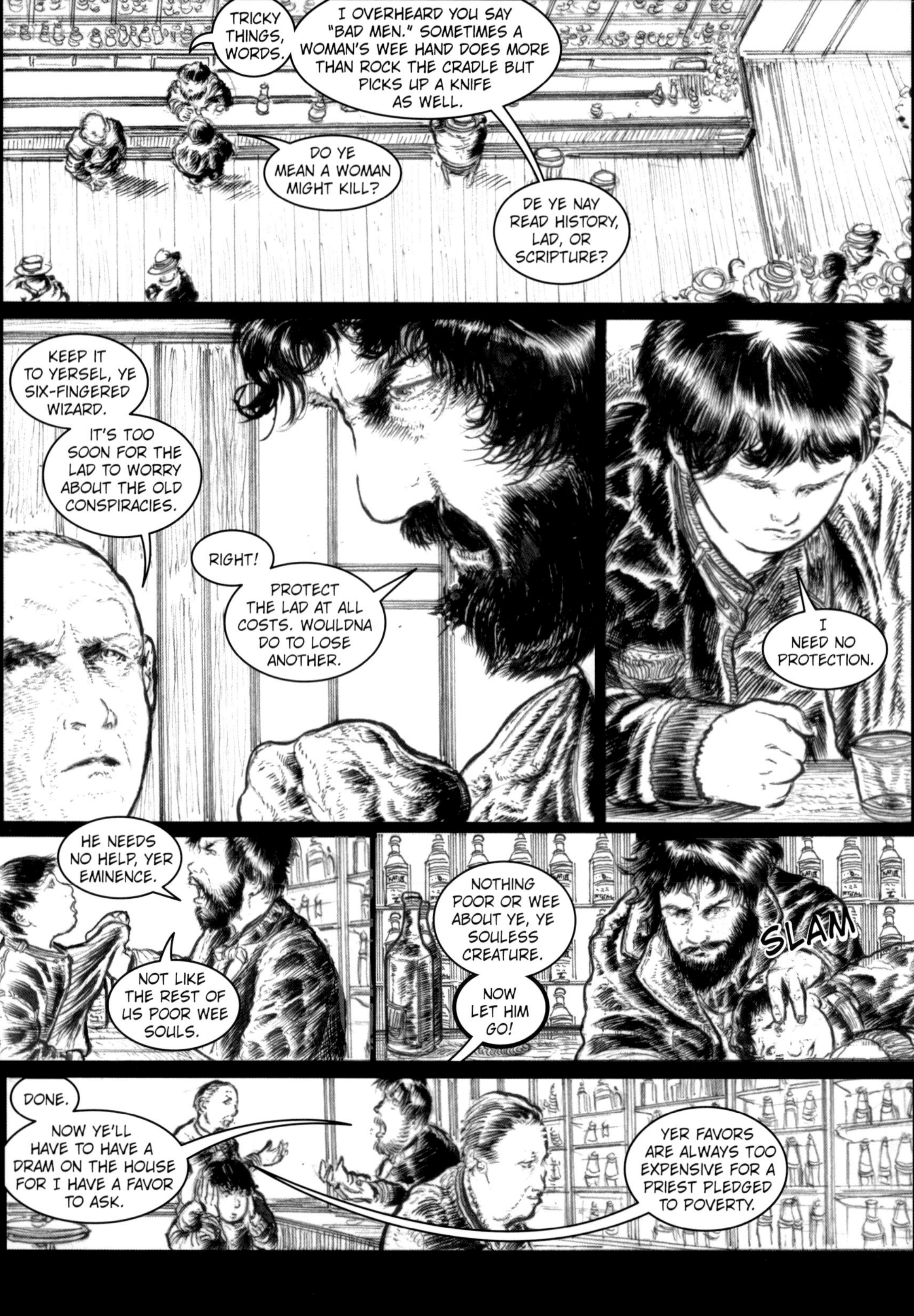
TRICKY THINGS, WORDS.
I OVERHEARD YOU SAY "BAD MEN." SOMETIMES A WOMAN'S WEE HAND DOES MORE THAN ROCK THE CRADLE BUT PICKS UP A KNIFE AS WELL.
DO YE MEAN A WOMAN MIGHT KILL?
DE YE NAY READ HISTORY, LAD, OR SCRIPTURE?
KEEP IT TO YERSEL, YE SIX-FINGERED WIZARD.
IT'S TOO SOON FOR THE LAD TO WORRY ABOUT THE OLD CONSPIRACIES.
RIGHT!
PROTECT THE LAD AT ALL COSTS. WOULDNA DO TO LOSE ANOTHER.
I NEED NO PROTECTION.
HE NEEDS NO HELP, YER EMINENCE.
NOT LIKE THE REST OF US POOR WEE SOULS.
NOTHING POOR OR WEE ABOUT YE, YE SOULESS CREATURE.
NOW LET HIM GO!
SLAM
DONE.
NOW YE'LL HAVE TO HAVE A DRAM ON THE HOUSE FOR I HAVE A FAVOR TO ASK.
YER FAVORS ARE ALWAYS TOO EXPENSIVE FOR A PRIEST PLEDGED TO POVERTY.

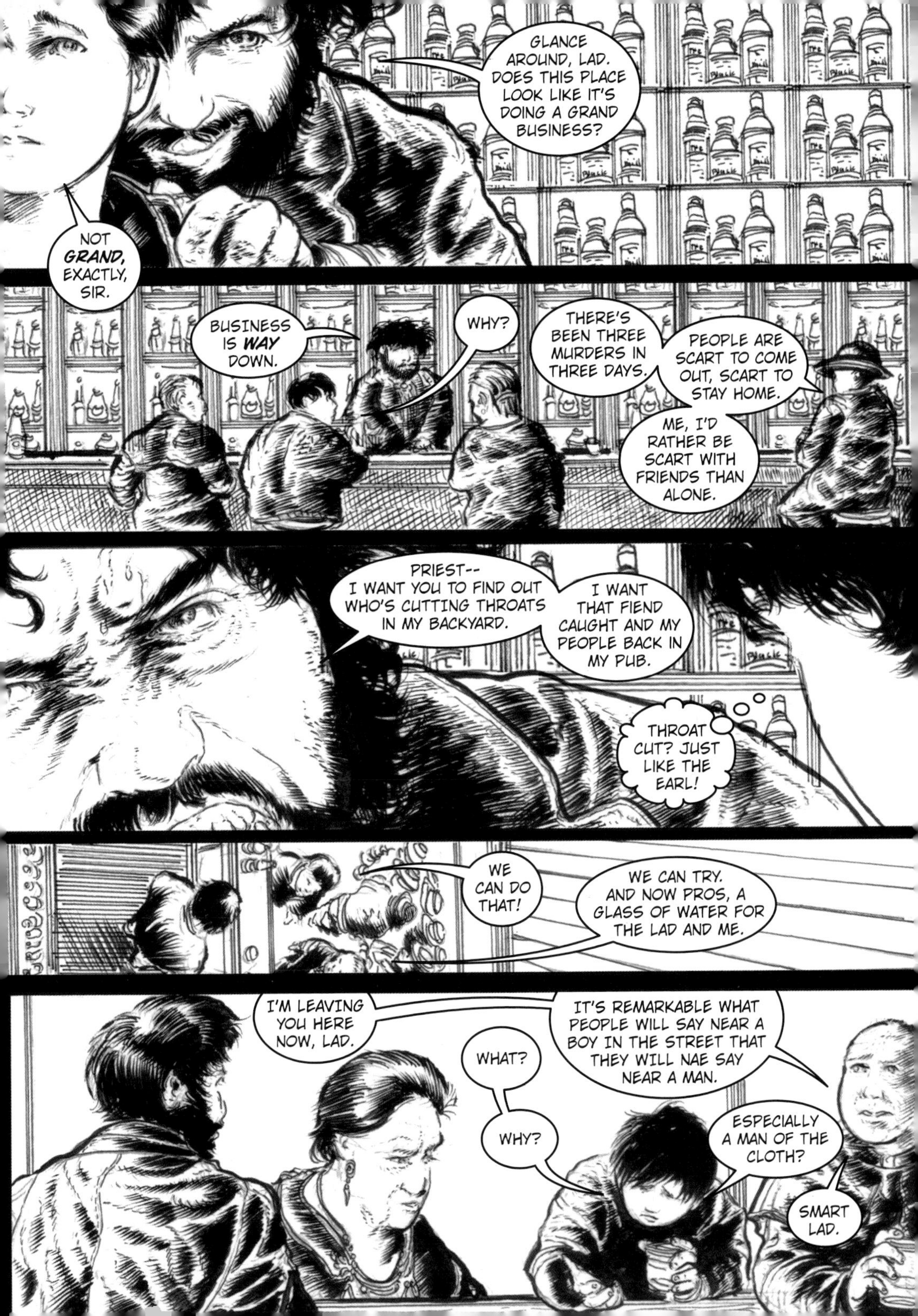
GLANCE AROUND, LAD. DOES THIS PLACE LOOK LIKE IT'S DOING A GRAND BUSINESS?
NOT GRAND, EXACTLY, SIR.
BUSINESS IS WAY DOWN.
WHY?
THERE'S BEEN THREE MURDERS IN THREE DAYS.
PEOPLE ARE SCART TO COME OUT, SCART TO STAY HOME.
ME, I'D RATHER BE SCART WITH FRIENDS THAN ALONE.
PRIEST-- I WANT YOU TO FIND OUT WHO'S CUTTING THROATS IN MY BACKYARD.
I WANT THAT FIEND CAUGHT AND MY PEOPLE BACK IN MY PUB.
THROAT CUT? JUST LIKE THE EARL!
WE CAN DO THAT!
WE CAN TRY. AND NOW PROS, A GLASS OF WATER FOR THE LAD AND ME.
I'M LEAVING YOU HERE NOW, LAD.
IT'S REMARKABLE WHAT PEOPLE WILL SAY NEAR A BOY IN THE STREET THAT THEY WILL NAE SAY NEAR A MAN.
WHAT?
WHY?
ESPECIALLY A MAN OF THE CLOTH?
SMART LAD.

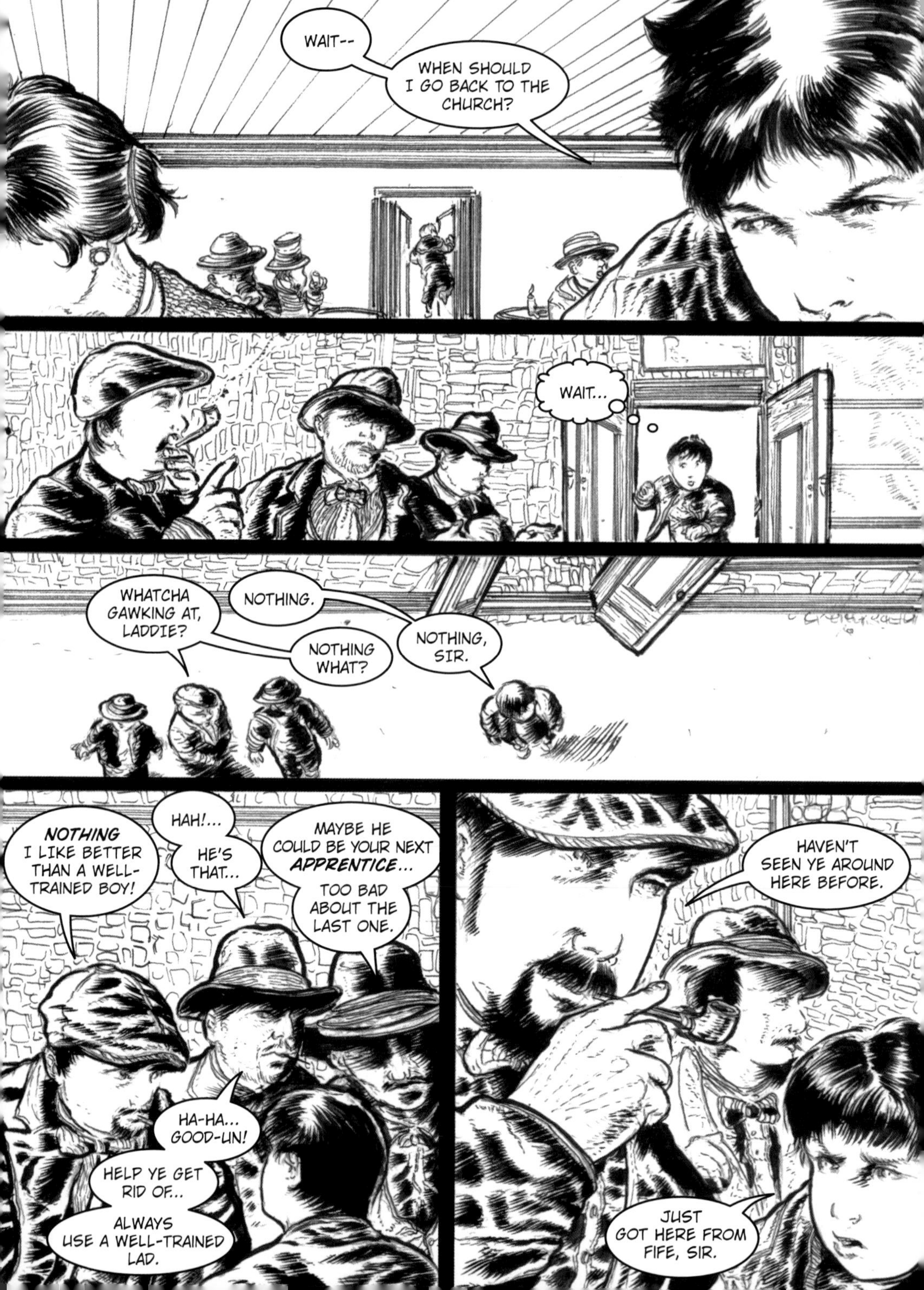
WAIT--
WHEN SHOULD I GO BACK TO THE CHURCH?
WAIT...
WHATCHA GAWKING AT, LADDIE?
NOTHING.
NOTHING WHAT?
NOTHING, SIR.
NOTHING I LIKE BETTER THAN A WELL-TRAINED BOY!
HAH!...
HE'S THAT...
MAYBE HE COULD BE YOUR NEXT APPRENTICE...
TOO BAD ABOUT THE LAST ONE.
HA-HA... GOOD-UN!
HELP YE GET RID OF...
ALWAYS USE A WELL-TRAINED LAD.
HAVEN'T SEEN YE AROUND HERE BEFORE.
JUST GOT HERE FROM FIFE, SIR.

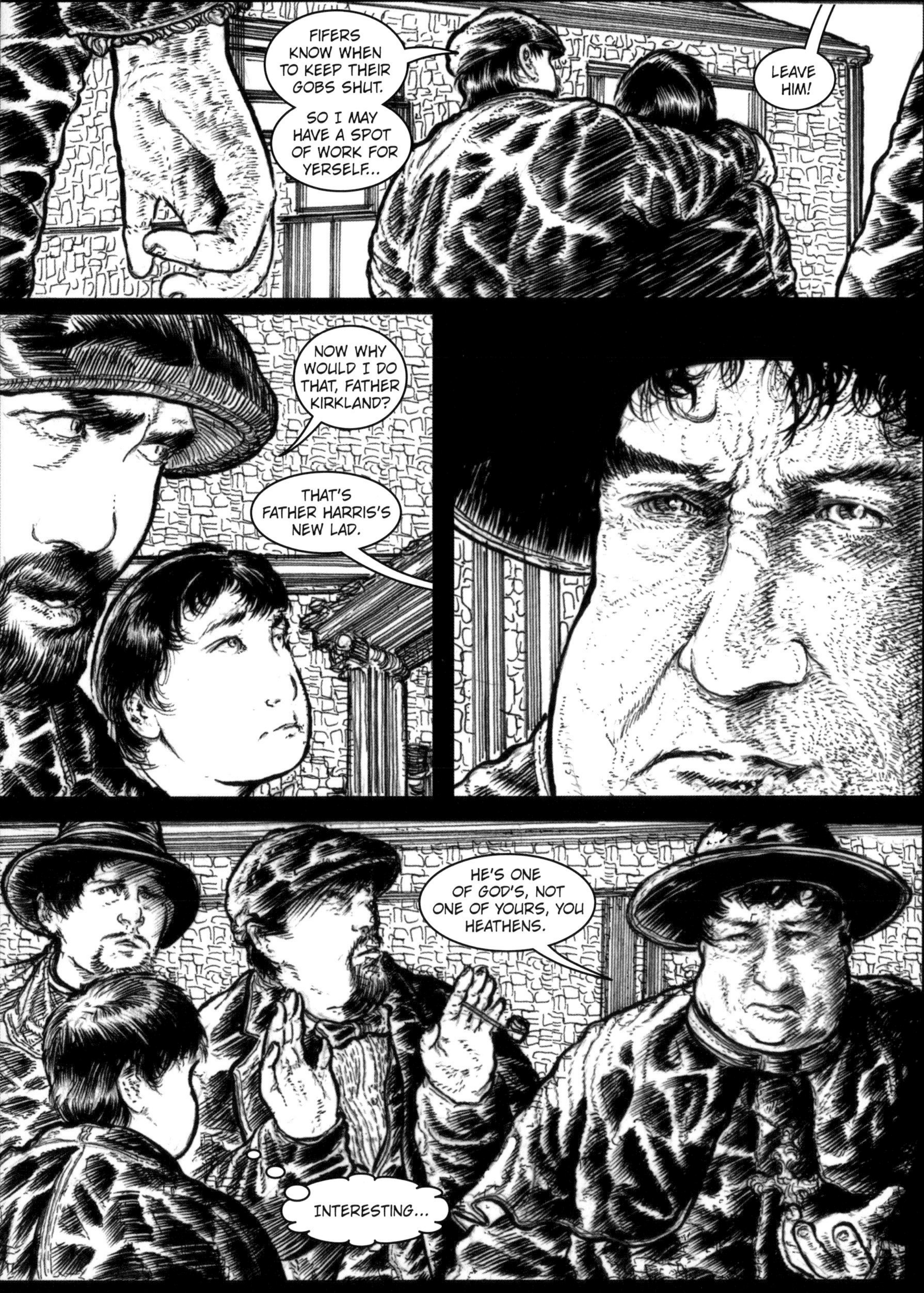
FIFERS KNOW WHEN TO KEEP THEIR GOBS SHUT.
SO I MAY HAVE A SPOT OF WORK FOR YERSELF...
LEAVE HIM!
NOW WHY WOULD I DO THAT, FATHER KIRKLAND?
THAT'S FATHER HARRIS'S NEW LAD.
HE'S ONE OF GOD'S, NOT ONE OF YOURS, YOU HEATHENS.
INTERESTING...

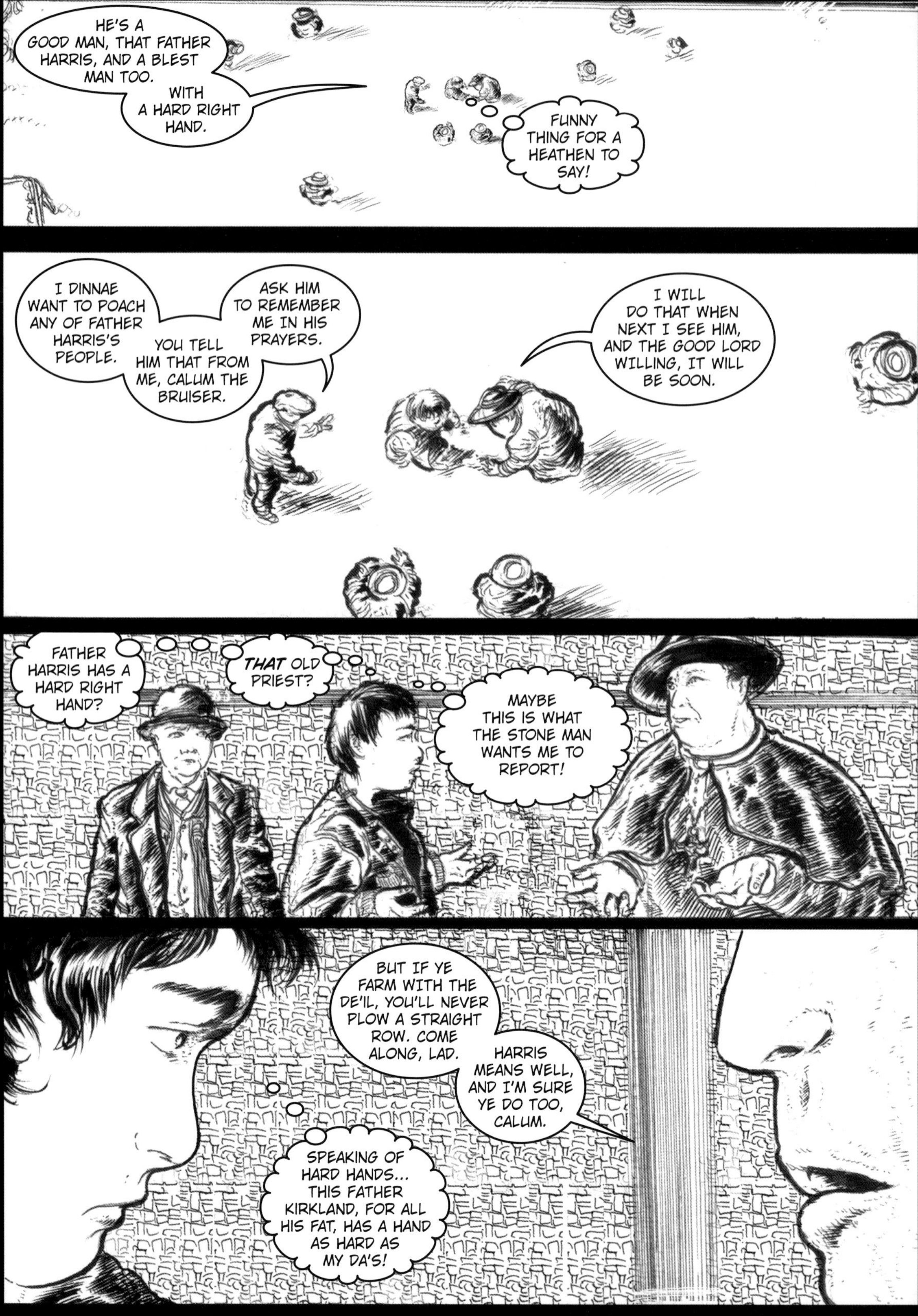
HE'S A GOOD MAN, THAT FATHER HARRIS, AND A BLEST MAN TOO.
WITH A HARD RIGHT HAND.
FUNNY THING FOR A HEATHEN TO SAY!
I DINNAE WANT TO POACH ANY OF FATHER HARRIS'S PEOPLE.
YOU TELL HIM THAT FROM ME, CALUM THE BRUISER.
ASK HIM TO REMEMBER ME IN HIS PRAYERS.
I WILL DO THAT WHEN NEXT I SEE HIM, AND THE GOOD LORD WILLING, IT WILL BE SOON.
FATHER HARRIS HAS A HARD RIGHT HAND?
THAT OLD PRIEST?
MAYBE THIS IS WHAT THE STONE MAN WANTS ME TO REPORT!
HARRIS MEANS WELL, AND I'M SURE YE DO TOO, CALUM.
BUT IF YE FARM WITH THE DE'IL, YOU'LL NEVER PLOW A STRAIGHT ROW. COME ALONG, LAD.
SPEAKING OF HARD HANDS... THIS FATHER KIRKLAND, FOR ALL HIS FAT, HAS A HAND AS HARD AS MY DA'S!

CHAPTER 3
WORKING THE EARL'S CASE

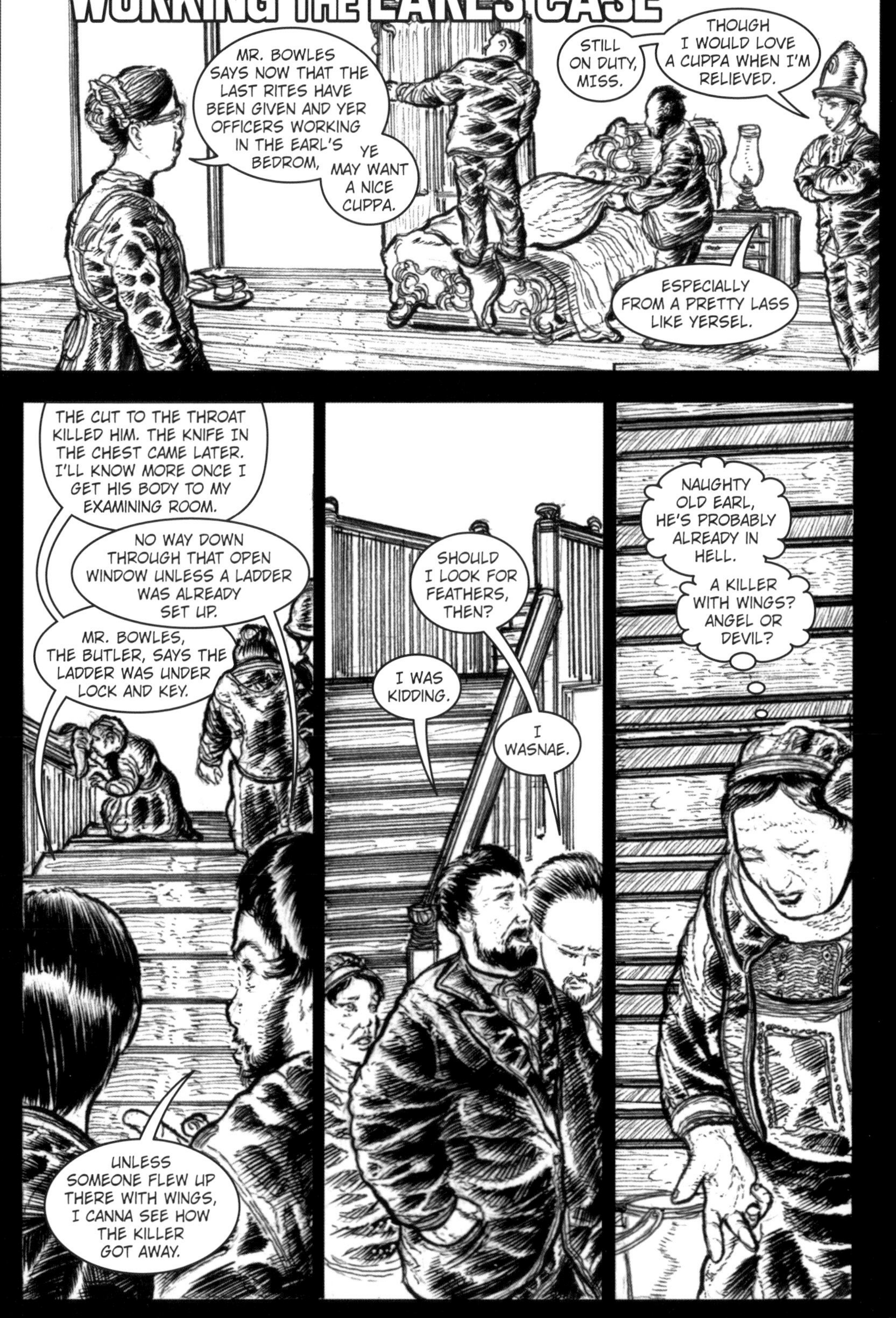

MR. BOWLES SAYS NOW THAT THE LAST RITES HAVE BEEN GIVEN AND YER OFFICERS WORKING IN THE EARL'S BEDROM,
YE MAY WANT A NICE CUPPA.
STILL ON DUTY, MISS.
THOUGH I WOULD LOVE A CUPPA WHEN I'M RELIEVED.
ESPECIALLY FROM A PRETTY LASS LIKE YERSEL.
THE CUT TO THE THROAT KILLED HIM. THE KNIFE IN THE CHEST CAME LATER. I'LL KNOW MORE ONCE I GET HIS BODY TO MY EXAMINING ROOM.
NO WAY DOWN THROUGH THAT OPEN WINDOW UNLESS A LADDER WAS ALREADY SET UP.
MR. BOWLES, THE BUTLER, SAYS THE LADDER WAS UNDER LOCK AND KEY.
UNLESS SOMEONE FLEW UP THERE WITH WINGS, I CANNA SEE HOW THE KILLER GOT AWAY.
SHOULD I LOOK FOR FEATHERS, THEN?
I WAS KIDDING.
I WASNAE.
NAUGHTY OLD EARL, HE'S PROBABLY ALREADY IN HELL.
A KILLER WITH WINGS? ANGEL OR DEVIL?

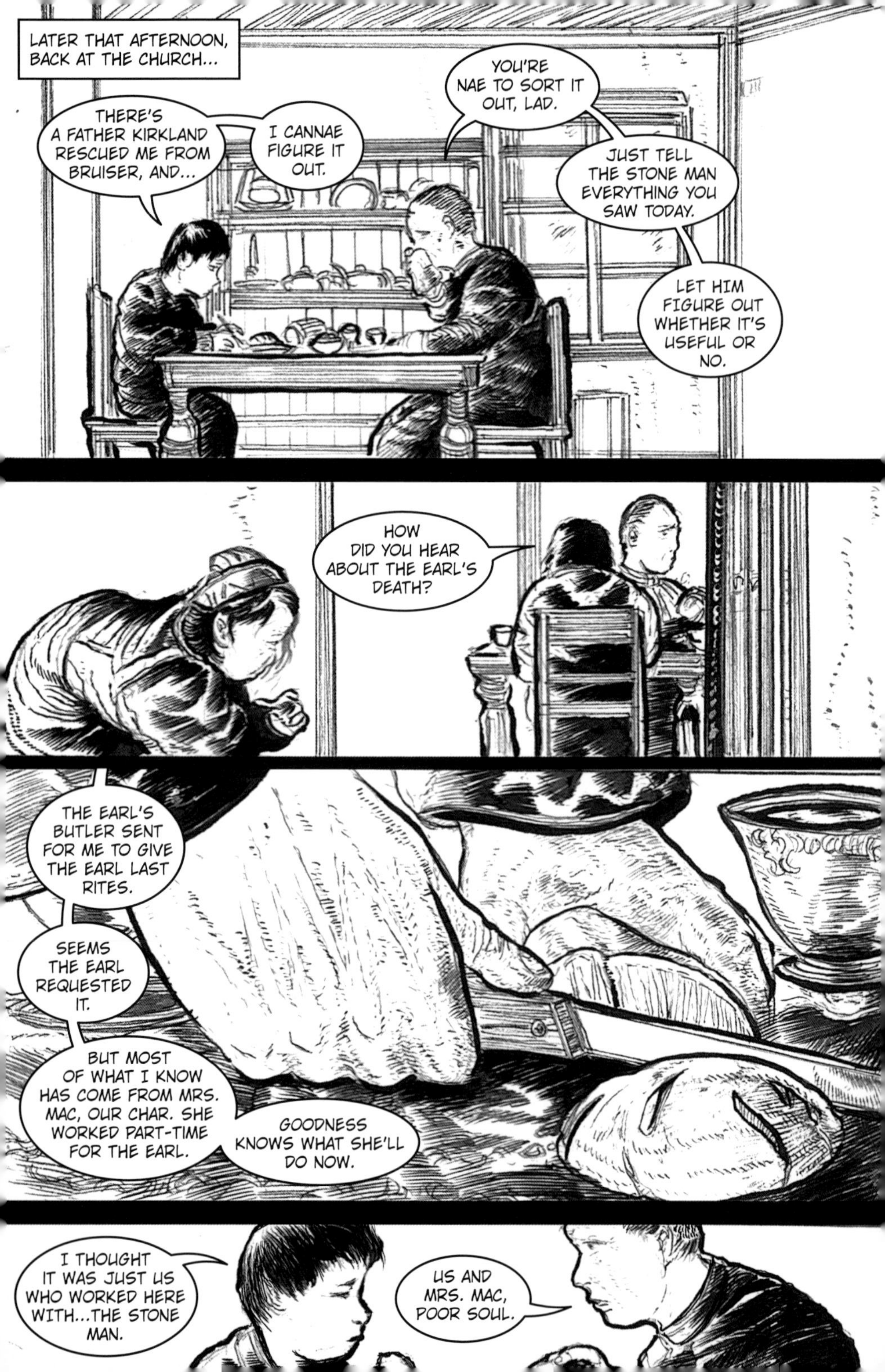

LATER THAT AFTERNOON, BACK AT THE CHURCH...
THERE'S A FATHER KIRKLAND RESCUED ME FROM BRUISER, AND...
I CANNAE FIGURE IT OUT.
YOU'RE NAE TO SORT IT OUT, LAD.
JUST TELL THE STONE MAN EVERYTHING YOU SAW TODAY.
LET HIM FIGURE OUT WHETHER IT'S USEFUL OR NO.
HOW DID YOU HEAR ABOUT THE EARL'S DEATH?
THE EARL'S BUTLER SENT FOR ME TO GIVE THE EARL LAST RITES.
SEEMS THE EARL REQUESTED IT.
BUT MOST OF WHAT I KNOW HAS COME FROM MRS. MAC, OUR CHAR. SHE WORKED PART-TIME FOR THE EARL.
GOODNESS KNOWS WHAT SHE'LL DO NOW.
I THOUGHT IT WAS JUST US WHO WORKED HERE WITH...THE STONE MAN.
US AND MRS. MAC, POOR SOUL.

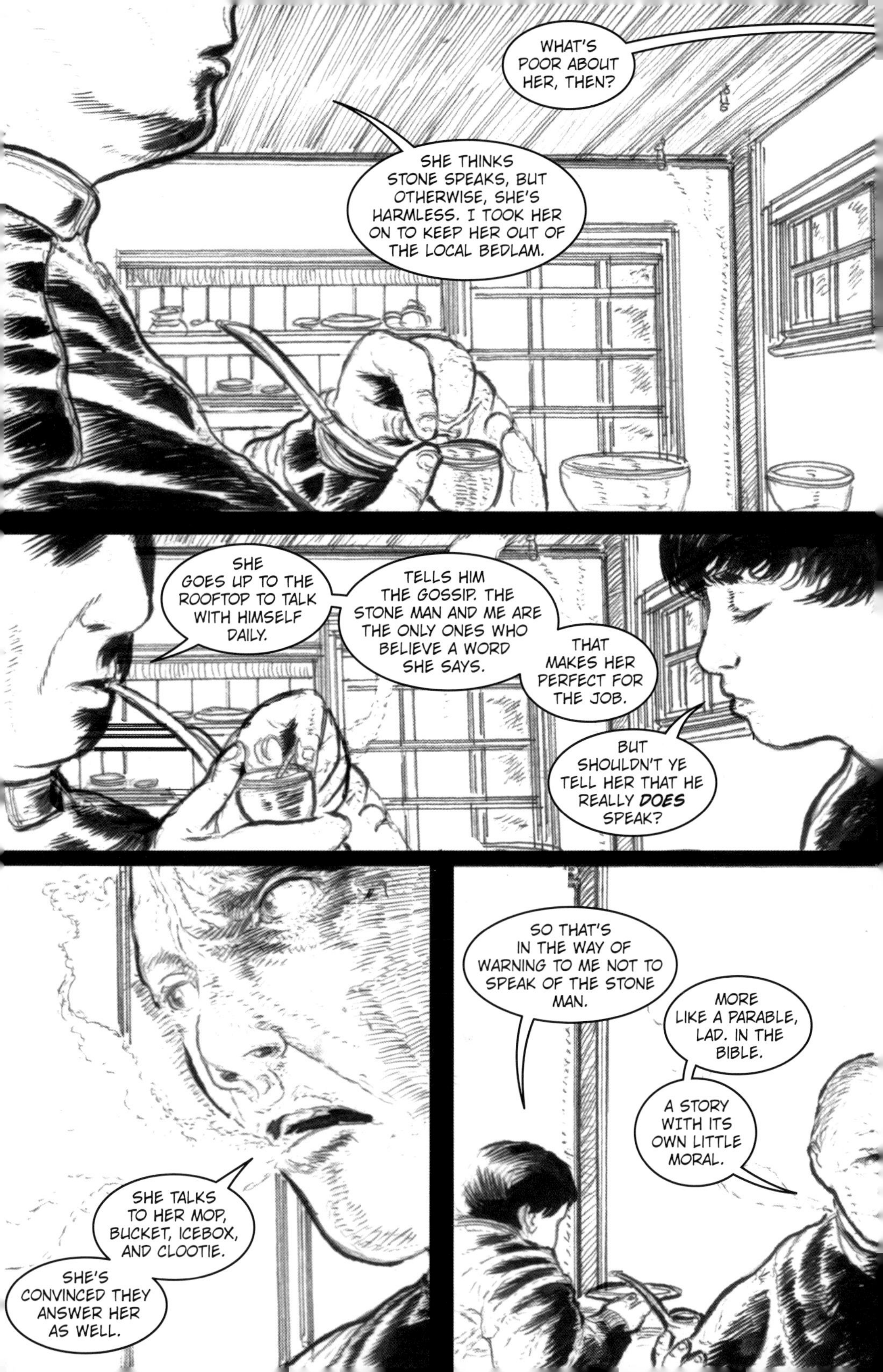
WHAT'S POOR ABOUT HER, THEN?
SHE THINKS STONE SPEAKS, BUT OTHERWISE, SHE'S HARMLESS. I TOOK HER ON TO KEEP HER OUT OF THE LOCAL BEDLAM.
SHE GOES UP TO THE ROOFTOP TO TALK WITH HIMSELF DAILY.
TELLS HIM THE GOSSIP. THE STONE MAN AND ME ARE THE ONLY ONES WHO BELIEVE A WORD SHE SAYS.
THAT MAKES HER PERFECT FOR THE JOB.
BUT SHOULDN'T YE TELL HER THAT HE REALLY **DOES** SPEAK?
SHE TALKS TO HER MOP, BUCKET, ICEBOX, AND CLOOTIE.
SHE'S CONVINCED THEY ANSWER HER AS WELL.
SO THAT'S IN THE WAY OF WARNING TO ME NOT TO SPEAK OF THE STONE MAN.
MORE LIKE A PARABLE, LAD. IN THE BIBLE.
A STORY WITH ITS OWN LITTLE MORAL.

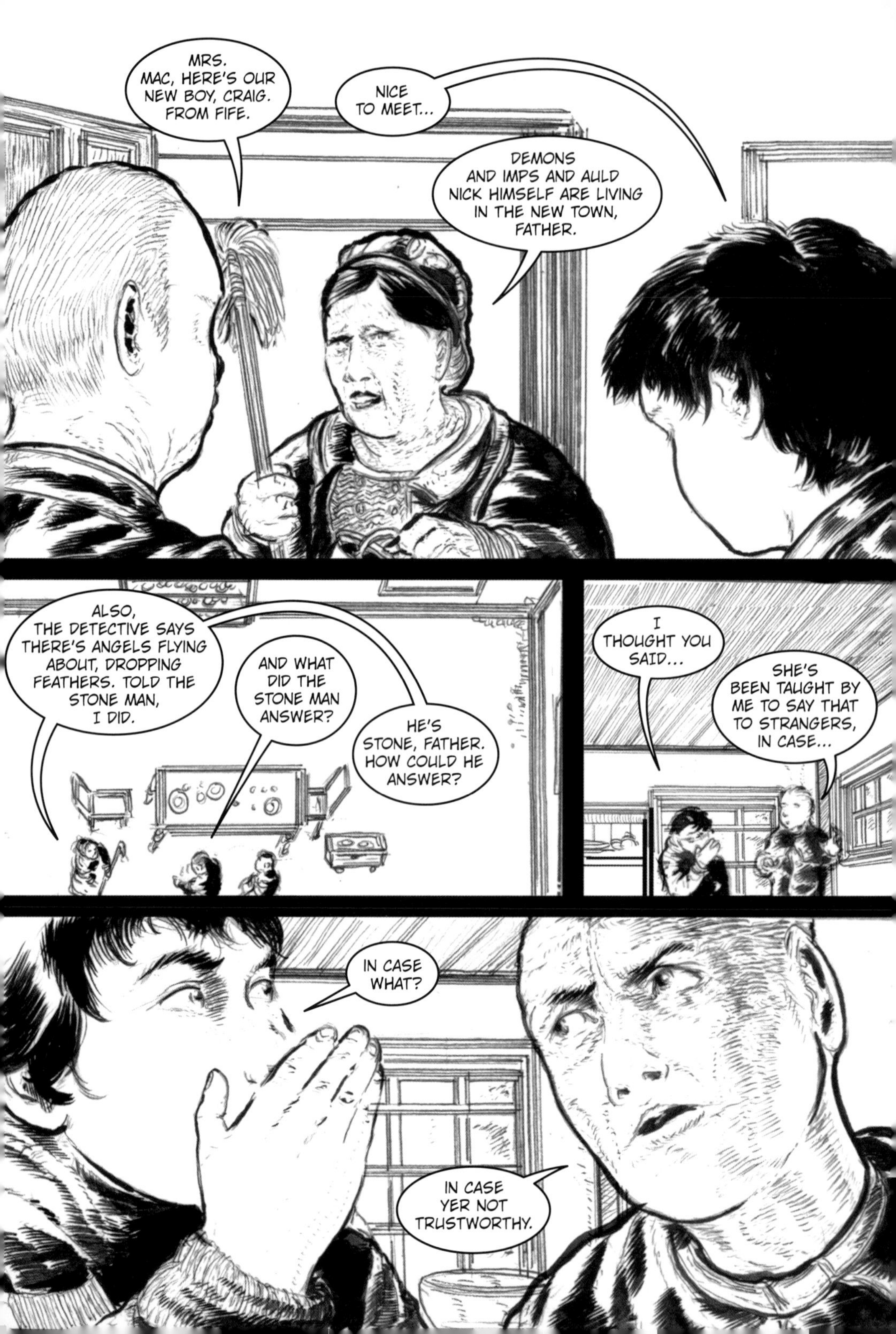

MRS. MAC, HERE'S OUR NEW BOY, CRAIG. FROM FIFE.
NICE TO MEET...
DEMONS AND IMPS AND AULD NICK HIMSELF ARE LIVING IN THE NEW TOWN, FATHER.
ALSO, THE DETECTIVE SAYS THERE'S ANGELS FLYING ABOUT, DROPPING FEATHERS. TOLD THE STONE MAN, I DID.
AND WHAT DID THE STONE MAN ANSWER?
HE'S STONE, FATHER. HOW COULD HE ANSWER?
I THOUGHT YOU SAID...
SHE'S BEEN TAUGHT BY ME TO SAY THAT TO STRANGERS, IN CASE...
IN CASE WHAT?
IN CASE YER NOT TRUSTWORTHY.

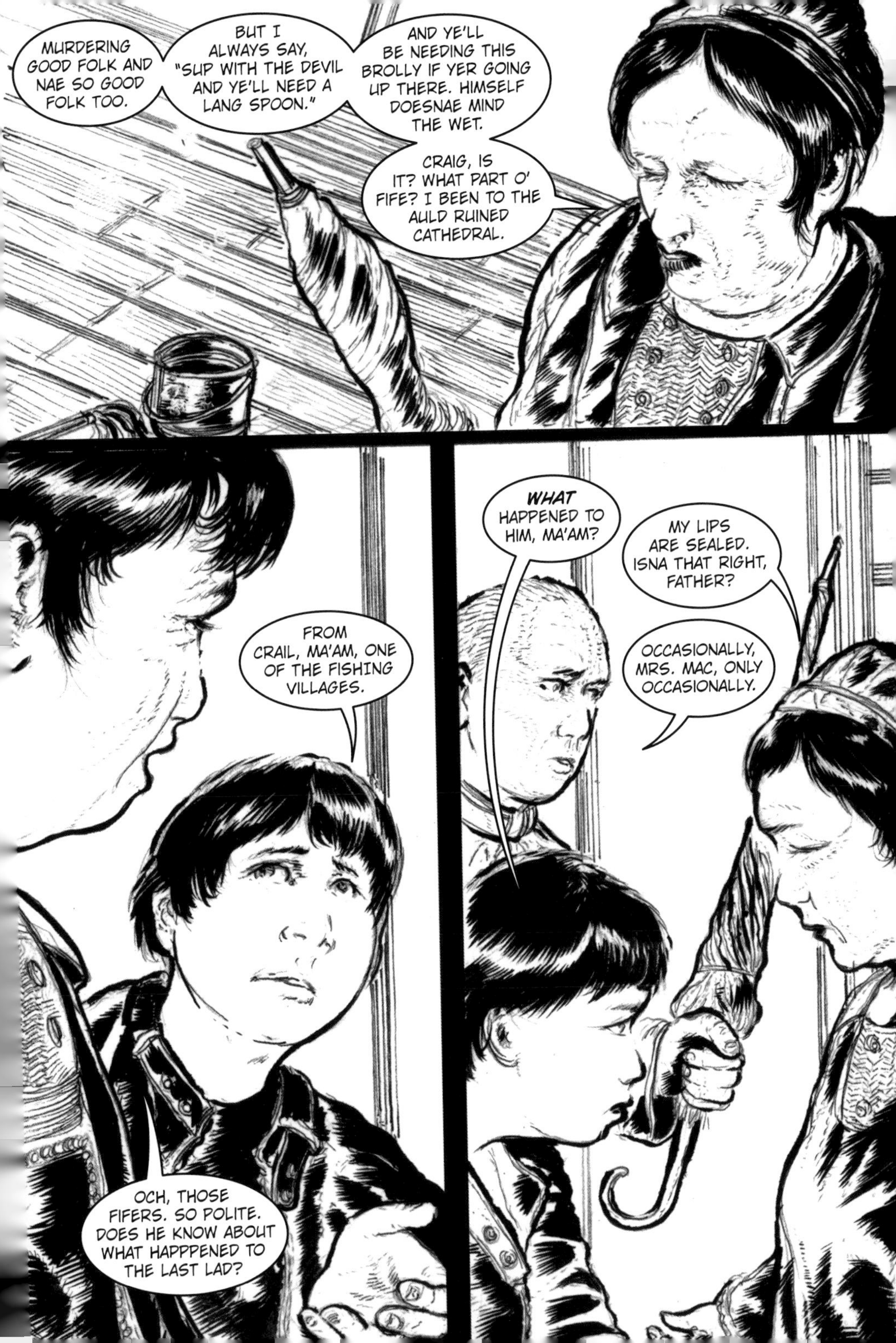
MURDERING GOOD FOLK AND NAE SO GOOD FOLK TOO.
BUT I ALWAYS SAY, "SUP WITH THE DEVIL AND YE'LL NEED A LANG SPOON."
AND YE'LL BE NEEDING THIS BROLLY IF YER GOING UP THERE. HIMSELF DOESNAE MIND THE WET.
CRAIG, IS IT? WHAT PART O' FIFE? I BEEN TO THE AULD RUINED CATHEDRAL.
FROM CRAIL, MA'AM, ONE OF THE FISHING VILLAGES.
OCH, THOSE FIFERS. SO POLITE. DOES HE KNOW ABOUT WHAT HAPPPENED TO THE LAST LAD?
WHAT HAPPENED TO HIM, MA'AM?
MY LIPS ARE SEALED. ISNA THAT RIGHT, FATHER?
OCCASIONALLY, MRS. MAC, ONLY OCCASIONALLY.

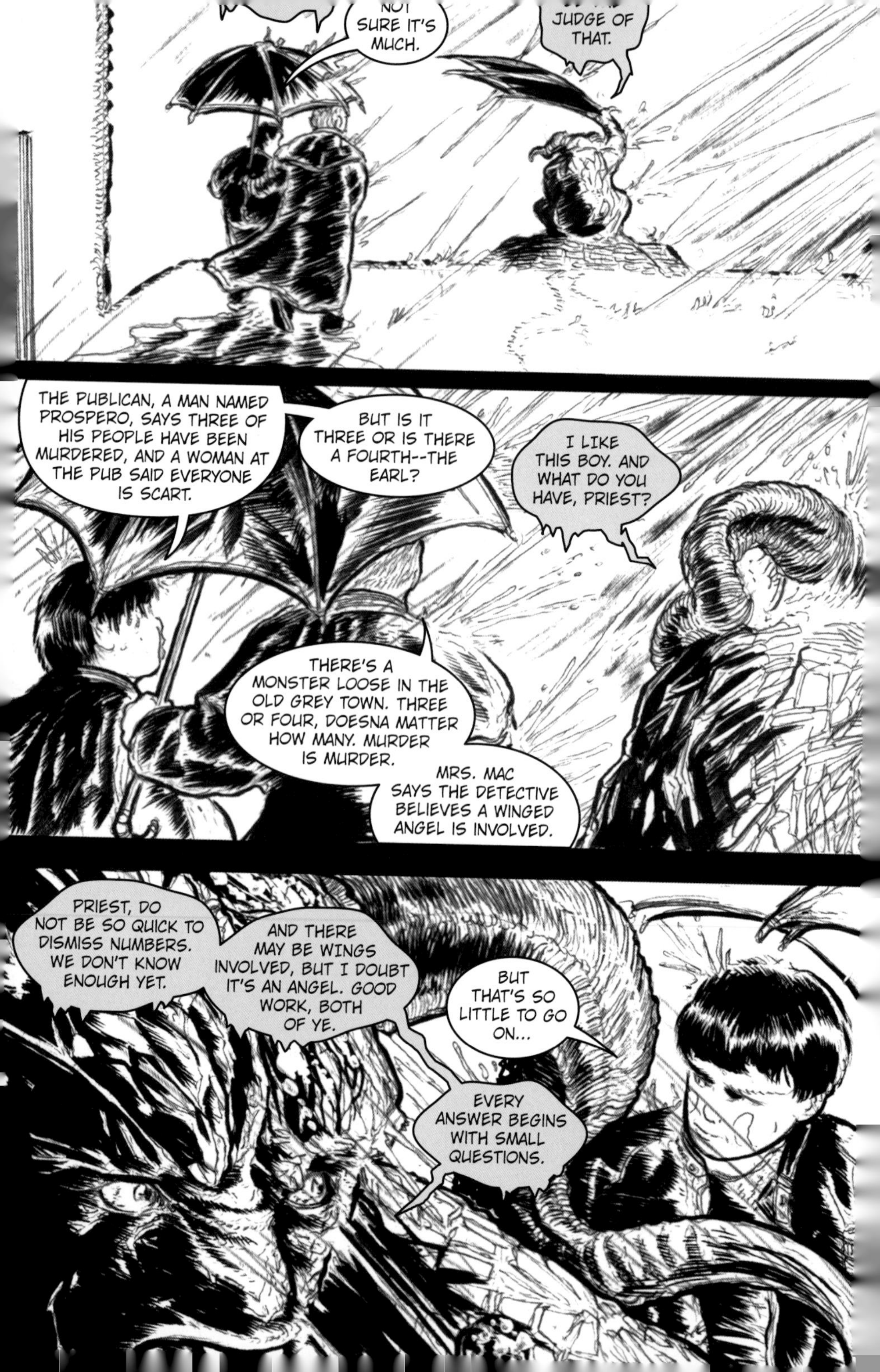
NOT SURE IT'S MUCH.
JUDGE OF THAT.
THE PUBLICAN, A MAN NAMED PROSPERO, SAYS THREE OF HIS PEOPLE HAVE BEEN MURDERED, AND A WOMAN AT THE PUB SAID EVERYONE IS SCART.
BUT IS IT THREE OR IS THERE A FOURTH--THE EARL?
I LIKE THIS BOY. AND WHAT DO YOU HAVE, PRIEST?
THERE'S A MONSTER LOOSE IN THE OLD GREY TOWN. THREE OR FOUR, DOESNA MATTER HOW MANY. MURDER IS MURDER.
MRS. MAC SAYS THE DETECTIVE BELIEVES A WINGED ANGEL IS INVOLVED.
PRIEST, DO NOT BE SO QUICK TO DISMISS NUMBERS. WE DON'T KNOW ENOUGH YET.
AND THERE MAY BE WINGS INVOLVED, BUT I DOUBT IT'S AN ANGEL. GOOD WORK, BOTH OF YE.
BUT THAT'S SO LITTLE TO GO ON...
EVERY ANSWER BEGINS WITH SMALL QUESTIONS.

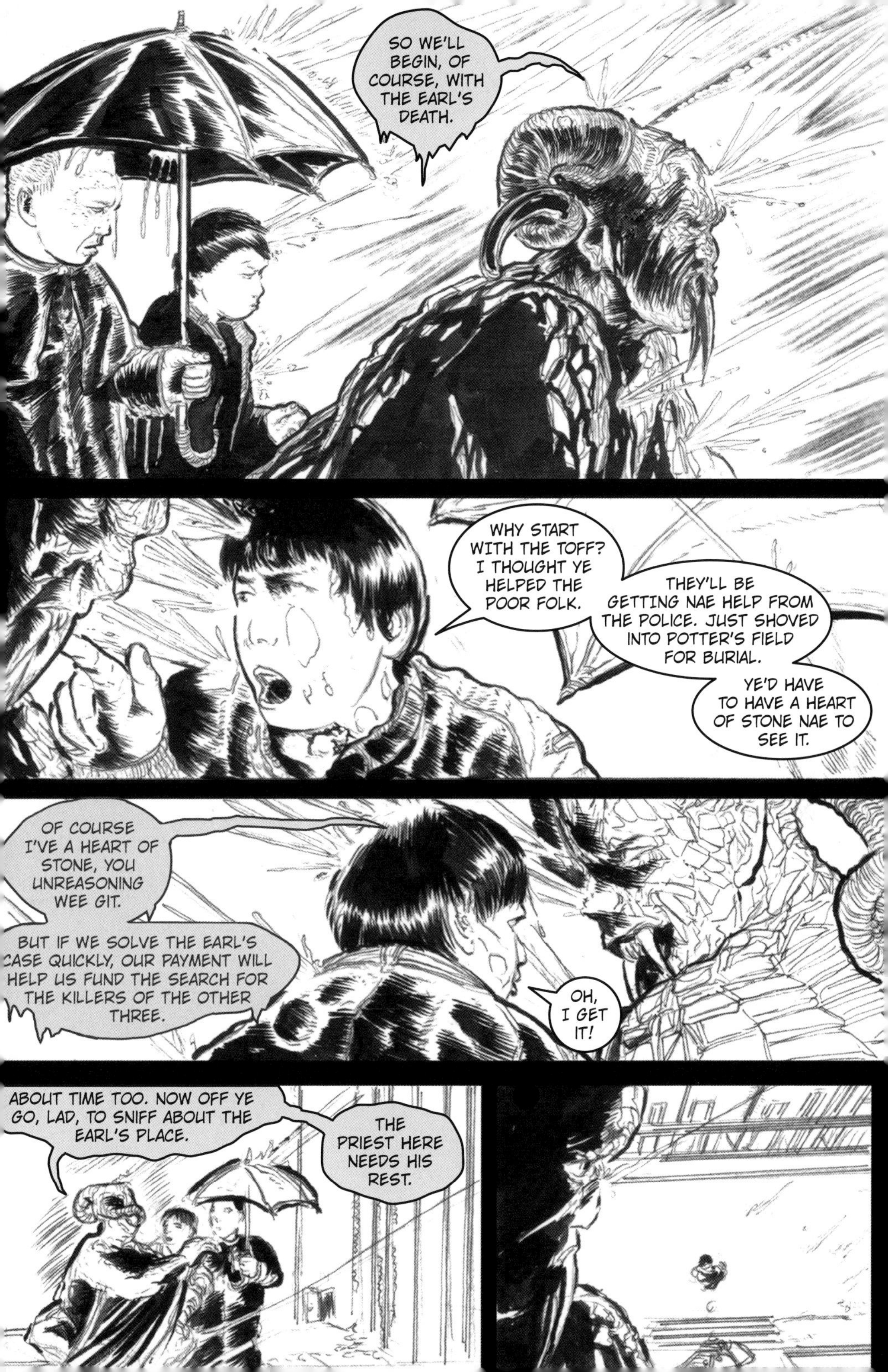
SO WE'LL BEGIN, OF COURSE, WITH THE EARL'S DEATH.
WHY START WITH THE TOFF? I THOUGHT YE HELPED THE POOR FOLK.
THEY'LL BE GETTING NAE HELP FROM THE POLICE. JUST SHOVED INTO POTTER'S FIELD FOR BURIAL.
YE'D HAVE TO HAVE A HEART OF STONE NAE TO SEE IT.
OF COURSE I'VE A HEART OF STONE, YOU UNREASONING WEE GIT.
BUT IF WE SOLVE THE EARL'S CASE QUICKLY, OUR PAYMENT WILL HELP US FUND THE SEARCH FOR THE KILLERS OF THE OTHER THREE.
OH, I GET IT!
ABOUT TIME TOO. NOW OFF YE GO, LAD, TO SNIFF ABOUT THE EARL'S PLACE.
THE PRIEST HERE NEEDS HIS REST.

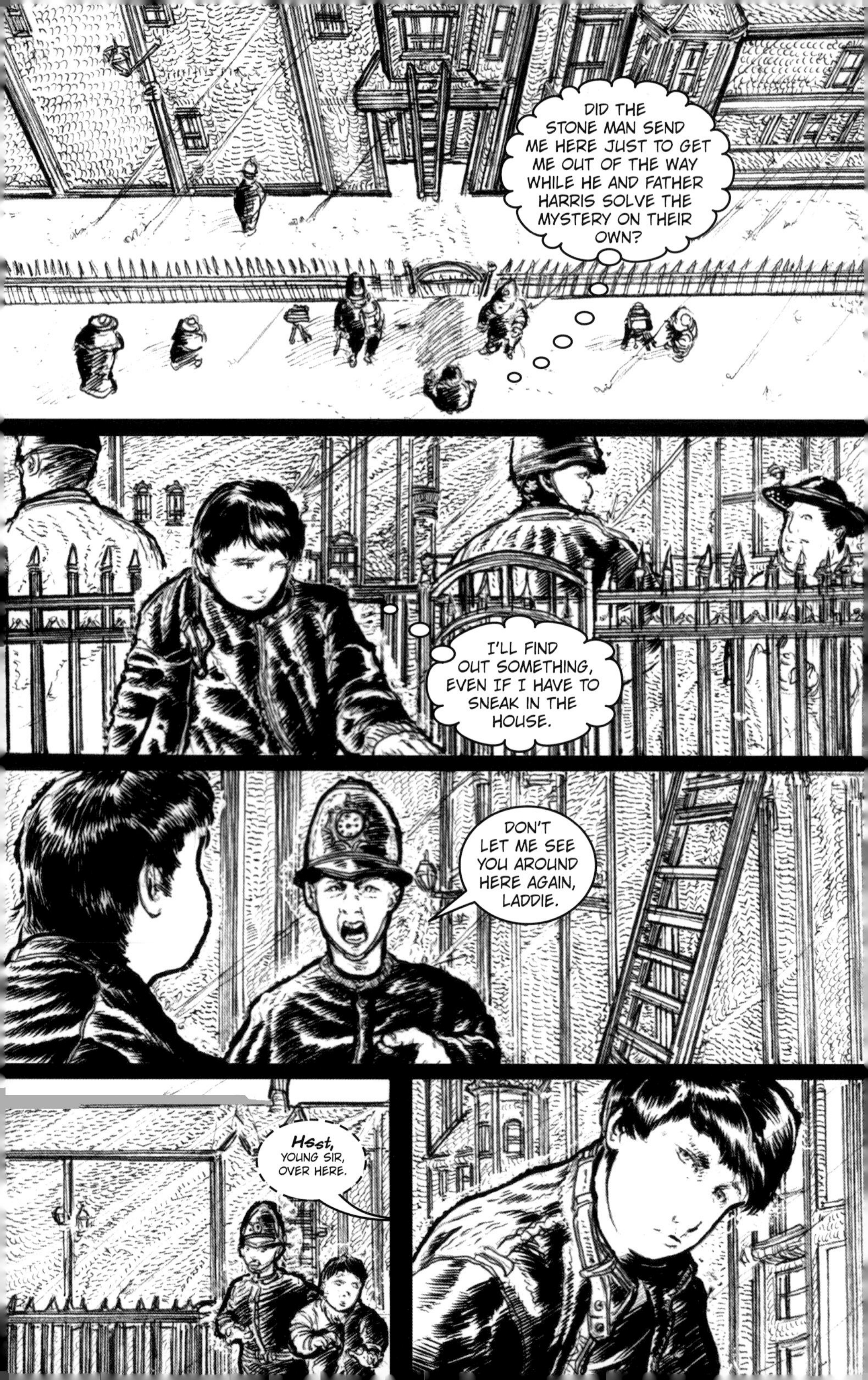
DID THE STONE MAN SEND ME HERE JUST TO GET ME OUT OF THE WAY WHILE HE AND FATHER HARRIS SOLVE THE MYSTERY ON THEIR OWN?
I'LL FIND OUT SOMETHING, EVEN IF I HAVE TO SNEAK IN THE HOUSE.
DON'T LET ME SEE YOU AROUND HERE AGAIN, LADDIE.
Hsst, YOUNG SIR, OVER HERE.

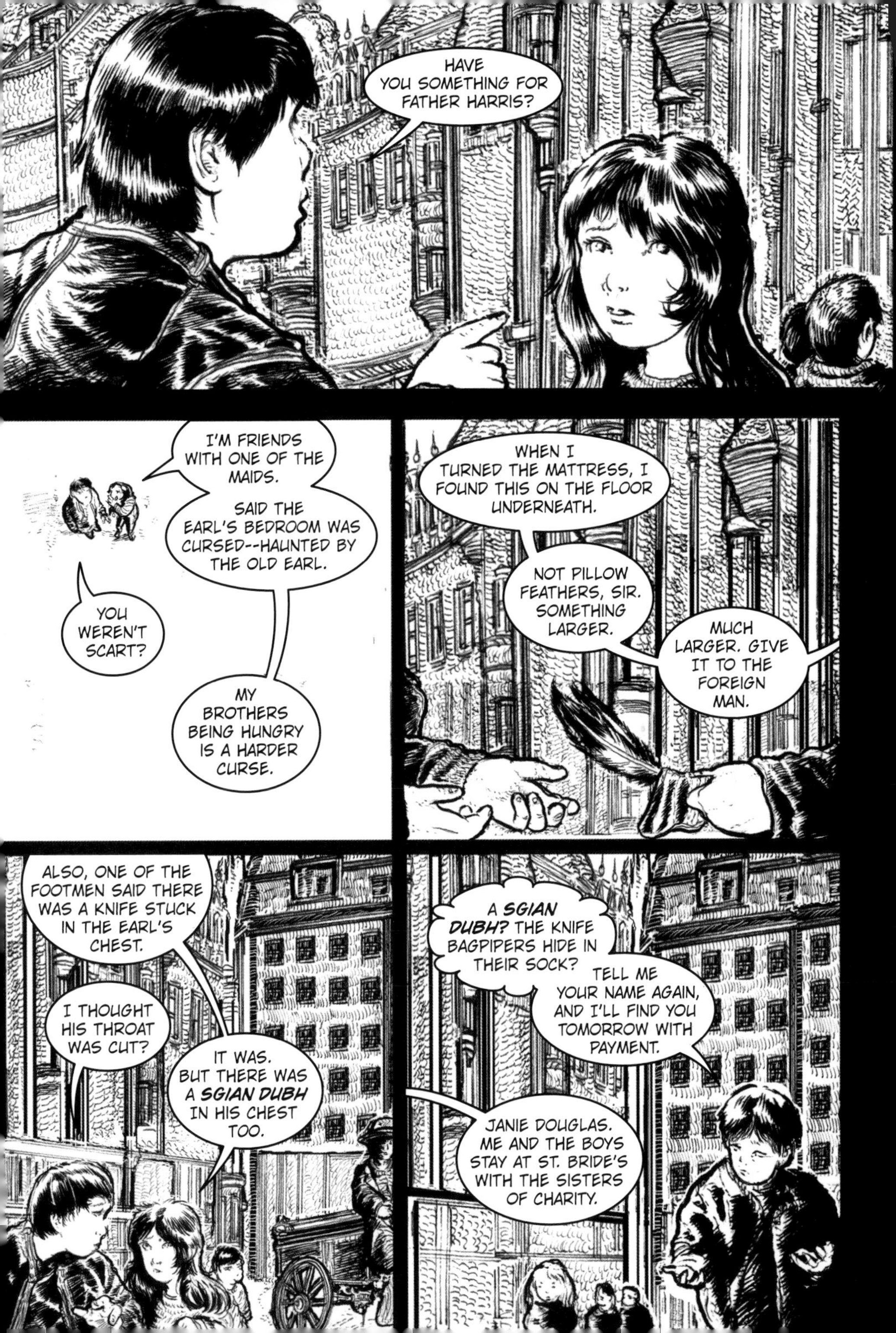
HAVE YOU SOMETHING FOR FATHER HARRIS?
I'M FRIENDS WITH ONE OF THE MAIDS.
SAID THE EARL'S BEDROOM WAS CURSED--HAUNTED BY THE OLD EARL.
YOU WEREN'T SCART?
MY BROTHERS BEING HUNGRY IS A HARDER CURSE.
WHEN I TURNED THE MATTRESS, I FOUND THIS ON THE FLOOR UNDERNEATH.
NOT PILLOW FEATHERS, SIR. SOMETHING LARGER.
MUCH LARGER. GIVE IT TO THE FOREIGN MAN.
ALSO, ONE OF THE FOOTMEN SAID THERE WAS A KNIFE STUCK IN THE EARL'S CHEST.
I THOUGHT HIS THROAT WAS CUT?
IT WAS. BUT THERE WAS A ***SGIAN DUBH*** IN HIS CHEST TOO.
A ***SGIAN DUBH?*** THE KNIFE BAGPIPERS HIDE IN THEIR SOCK?
TELL ME YOUR NAME AGAIN, AND I'LL FIND YOU TOMORROW WITH PAYMENT.
JANIE DOUGLAS. ME AND THE BOYS STAY AT ST. BRIDE'S WITH THE SISTERS OF CHARITY.

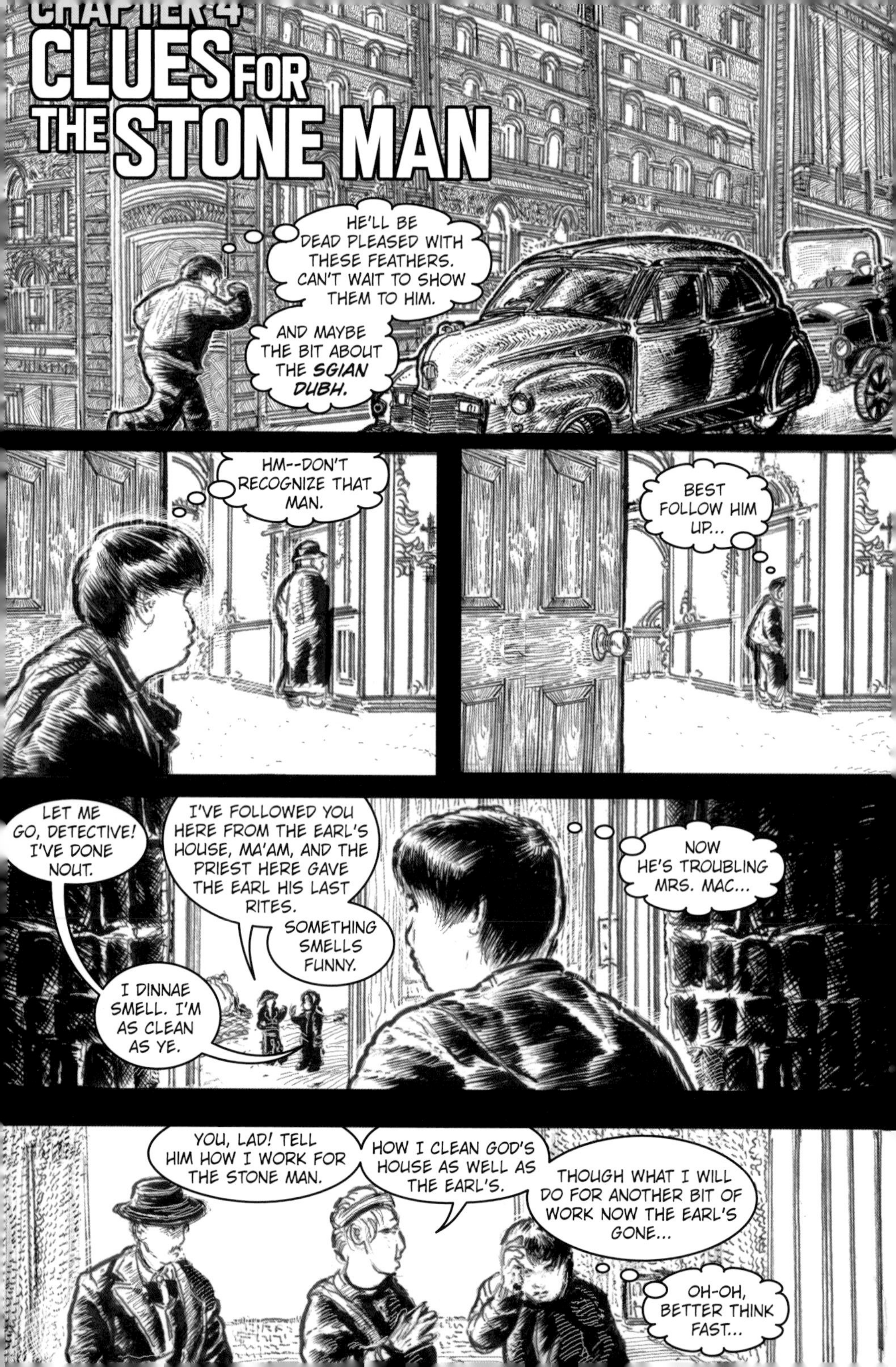
CHAPTER 4
CLUES FOR THE STONE MAN
HE'LL BE DEAD PLEASED WITH THESE FEATHERS. CAN'T WAIT TO SHOW THEM TO HIM.
AND MAYBE THE BIT ABOUT THE *SGIAN DUBH.*
HM--DON'T RECOGNIZE THAT MAN.
BEST FOLLOW HIM UP...
LET ME GO, DETECTIVE! I'VE DONE NOUT.
I'VE FOLLOWED YOU HERE FROM THE EARL'S HOUSE, MA'AM, AND THE PRIEST HERE GAVE THE EARL HIS LAST RITES.
SOMETHING SMELLS FUNNY.
I DINNAE SMELL. I'M AS CLEAN AS YE.
NOW HE'S TROUBLING MRS. MAC...
YOU, LAD! TELL HIM HOW I WORK FOR THE STONE MAN.
HOW I CLEAN GOD'S HOUSE AS WELL AS THE EARL'S.
THOUGH WHAT I WILL DO FOR ANOTHER BIT OF WORK NOW THE EARL'S GONE...
OH-OH, BETTER THINK FAST...

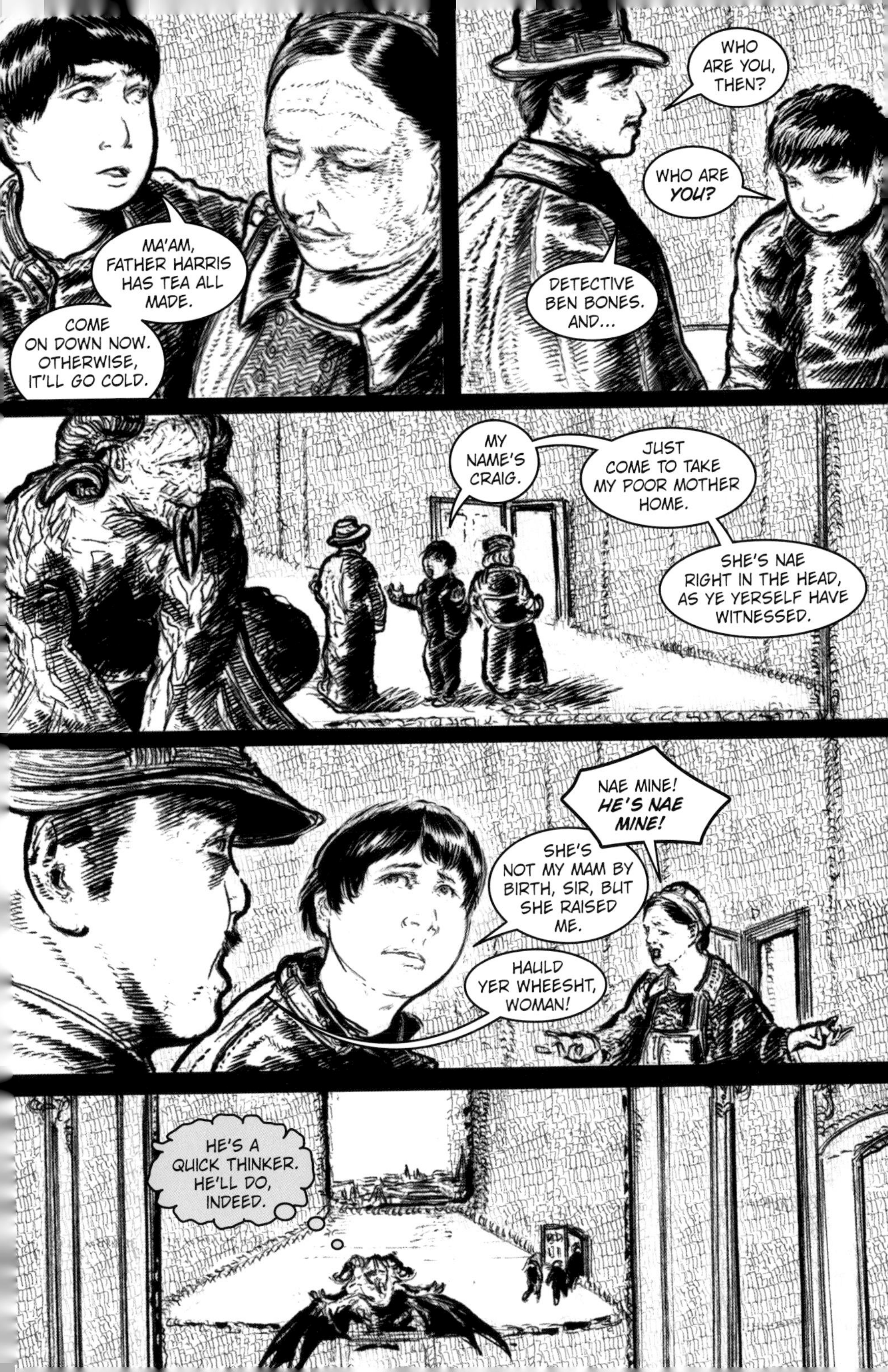
MA'AM, FATHER HARRIS HAS TEA ALL MADE.
COME ON DOWN NOW. OTHERWISE, IT'LL GO COLD.
WHO ARE YOU, THEN?
WHO ARE *YOU?*
DETECTIVE BEN BONES. AND...
MY NAME'S CRAIG.
JUST COME TO TAKE MY POOR MOTHER HOME.
SHE'S NAE RIGHT IN THE HEAD, AS YE YERSELF HAVE WITNESSED.
NAE MINE! ***HE'S NAE MINE!***
SHE'S NOT MY MAM BY BIRTH, SIR, BUT SHE RAISED ME.
HAULD YER WHEESHT, WOMAN!
HE'S A QUICK THINKER. HE'LL DO, INDEED.

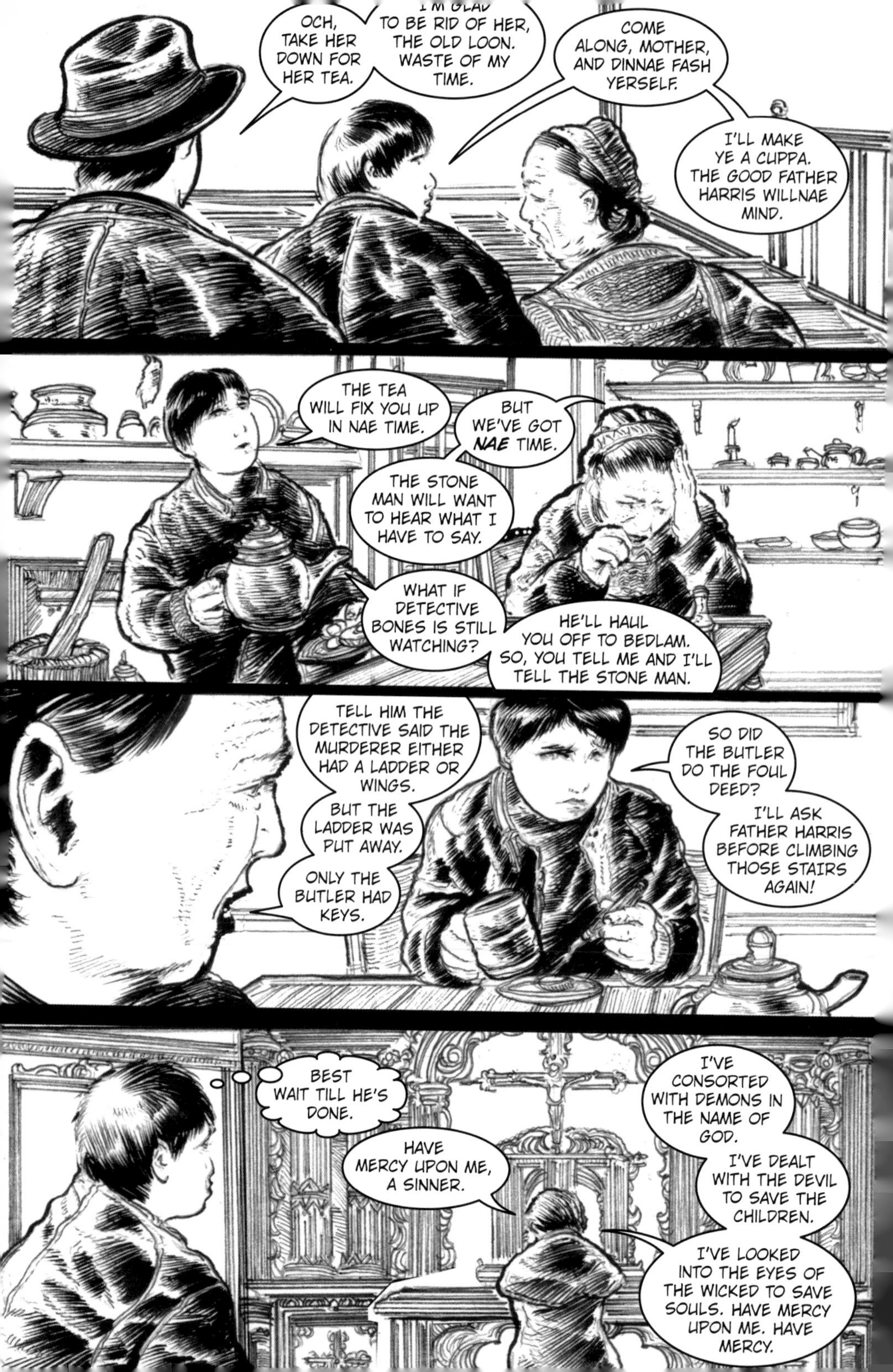
OCH, TAKE HER DOWN FOR HER TEA.
TO BE RID OF HER, THE OLD LOON. WASTE OF MY TIME.
COME ALONG, MOTHER, AND DINNAE FASH YERSELF.
I'LL MAKE YE A CUPPA. THE GOOD FATHER HARRIS WILLNAE MIND.
THE TEA WILL FIX YOU UP IN NAE TIME.
BUT WE'VE GOT NAE TIME.
THE STONE MAN WILL WANT TO HEAR WHAT I HAVE TO SAY.
WHAT IF DETECTIVE BONES IS STILL WATCHING?
HE'LL HAUL YOU OFF TO BEDLAM. SO, YOU TELL ME AND I'LL TELL THE STONE MAN.
TELL HIM THE DETECTIVE SAID THE MURDERER EITHER HAD A LADDER OR WINGS.
BUT THE LADDER WAS PUT AWAY.
ONLY THE BUTLER HAD KEYS.
SO DID THE BUTLER DO THE FOUL DEED?
I'LL ASK FATHER HARRIS BEFORE CLIMBING THOSE STAIRS AGAIN!
BEST WAIT TILL HE'S DONE.
HAVE MERCY UPON ME, A SINNER.
I'VE CONSORTED WITH DEMONS IN THE NAME OF GOD.
I'VE DEALT WITH THE DEVIL TO SAVE THE CHILDREN.
I'VE LOOKED INTO THE EYES OF THE WICKED TO SAVE SOULS. HAVE MERCY UPON ME. HAVE MERCY.

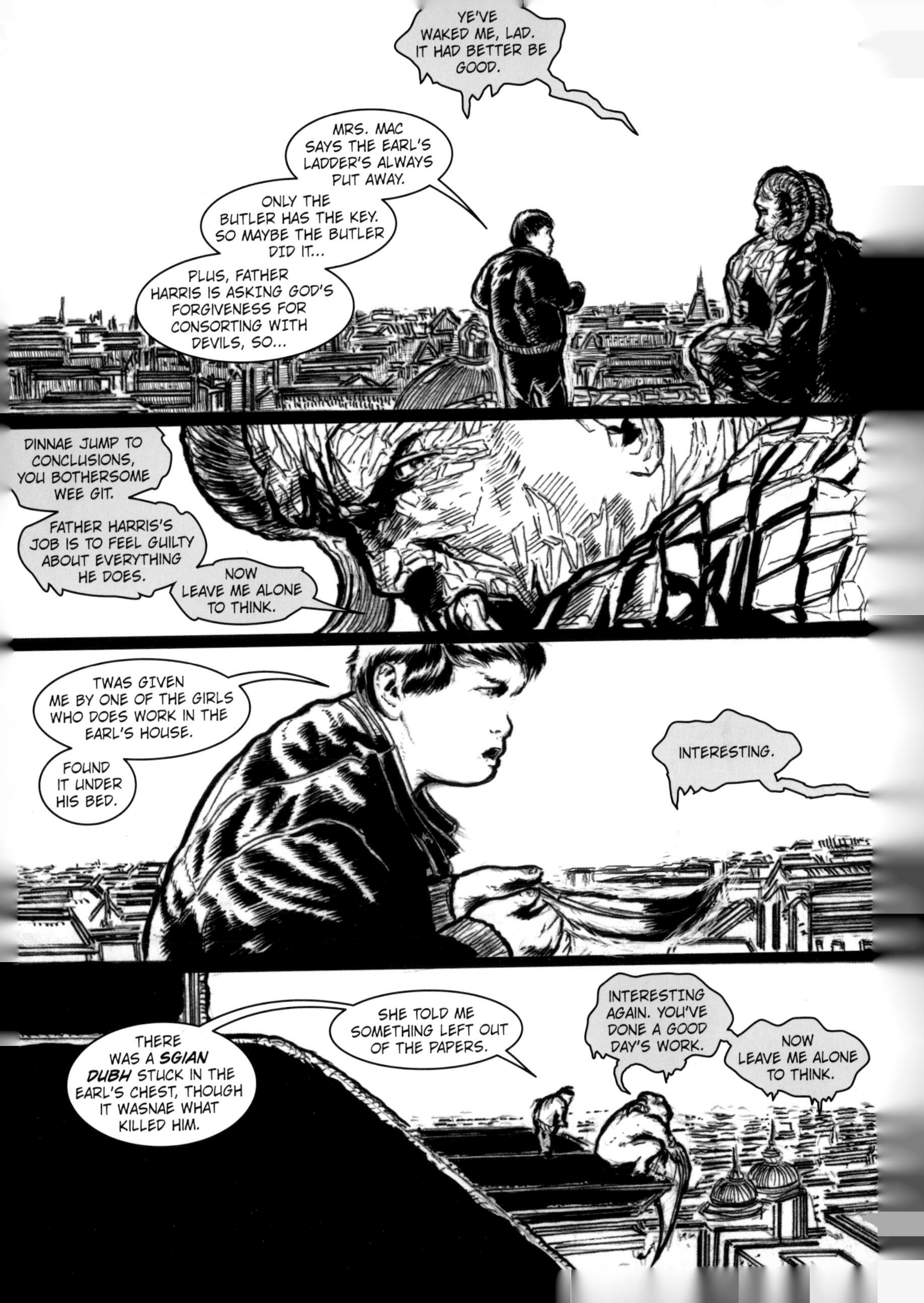
YE'VE WAKED ME, LAD. IT HAD BETTER BE GOOD.
MRS. MAC SAYS THE EARL'S LADDER'S ALWAYS PUT AWAY.
ONLY THE BUTLER HAS THE KEY. SO MAYBE THE BUTLER DID IT...
PLUS, FATHER HARRIS IS ASKING GOD'S FORGIVENESS FOR CONSORTING WITH DEVILS, SO...
DINNAE JUMP TO CONCLUSIONS, YOU BOTHERSOME WEE GIT.
FATHER HARRIS'S JOB IS TO FEEL GUILTY ABOUT EVERYTHING HE DOES.
NOW LEAVE ME ALONE TO THINK.
TWAS GIVEN ME BY ONE OF THE GIRLS WHO DOES WORK IN THE EARL'S HOUSE.
FOUND IT UNDER HIS BED.
INTERESTING.
SHE TOLD ME SOMETHING LEFT OUT OF THE PAPERS.
THERE WAS A ***SGIAN DUBH*** STUCK IN THE EARL'S CHEST, THOUGH IT WASNAE WHAT KILLED HIM.
INTERESTING AGAIN. YOU'VE DONE A GOOD DAY'S WORK.
NOW LEAVE ME ALONE TO THINK.

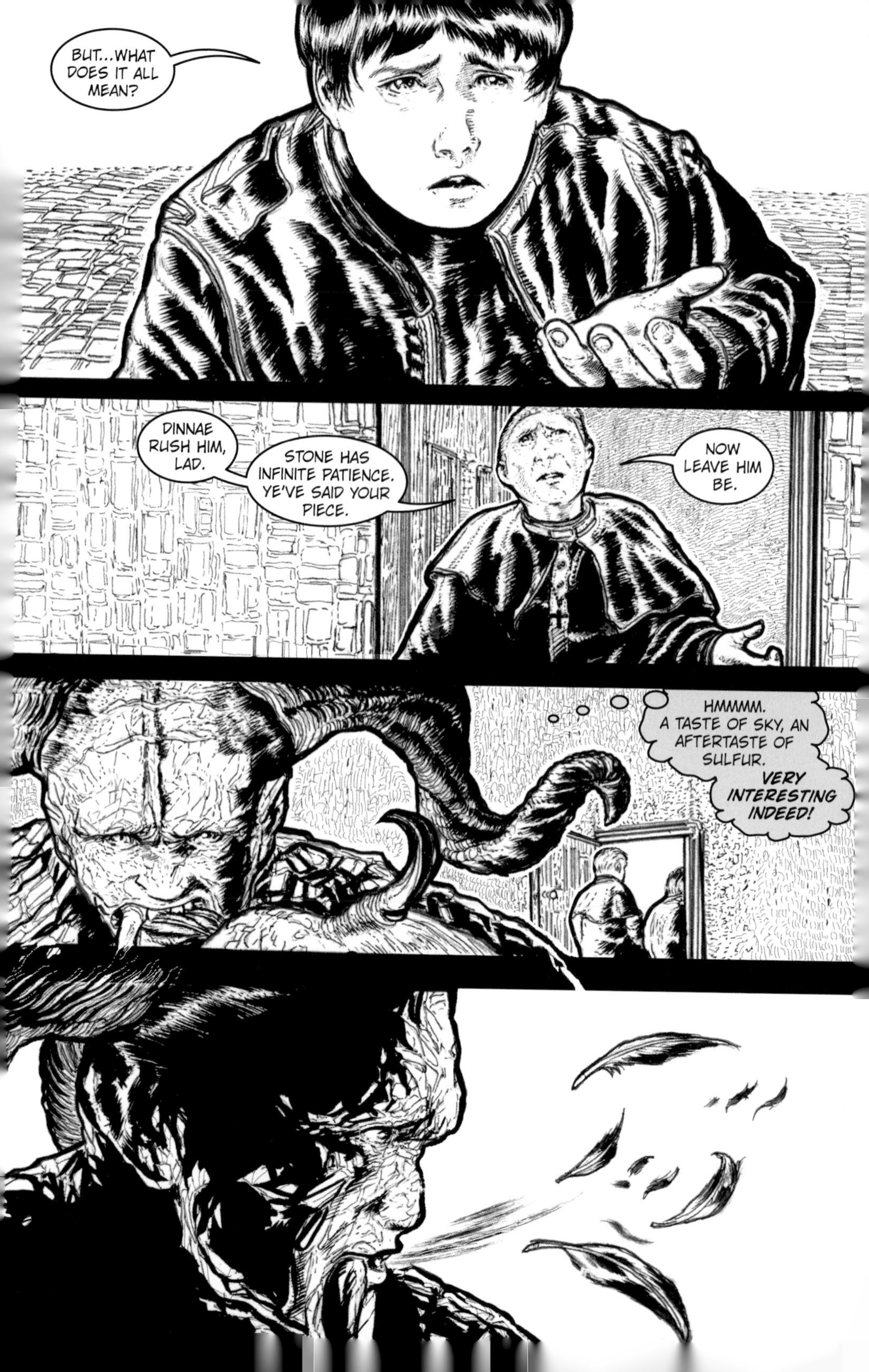
BUT...WHAT DOES IT ALL MEAN?
DINNAE RUSH HIM, LAD.
STONE HAS INFINITE PATIENCE. YE'VE SAID YOUR PIECE.
NOW LEAVE HIM BE.
HMMMM. A TASTE OF SKY, AN AFTERTASTE OF SULFUR. VERY INTERESTING INDEED!

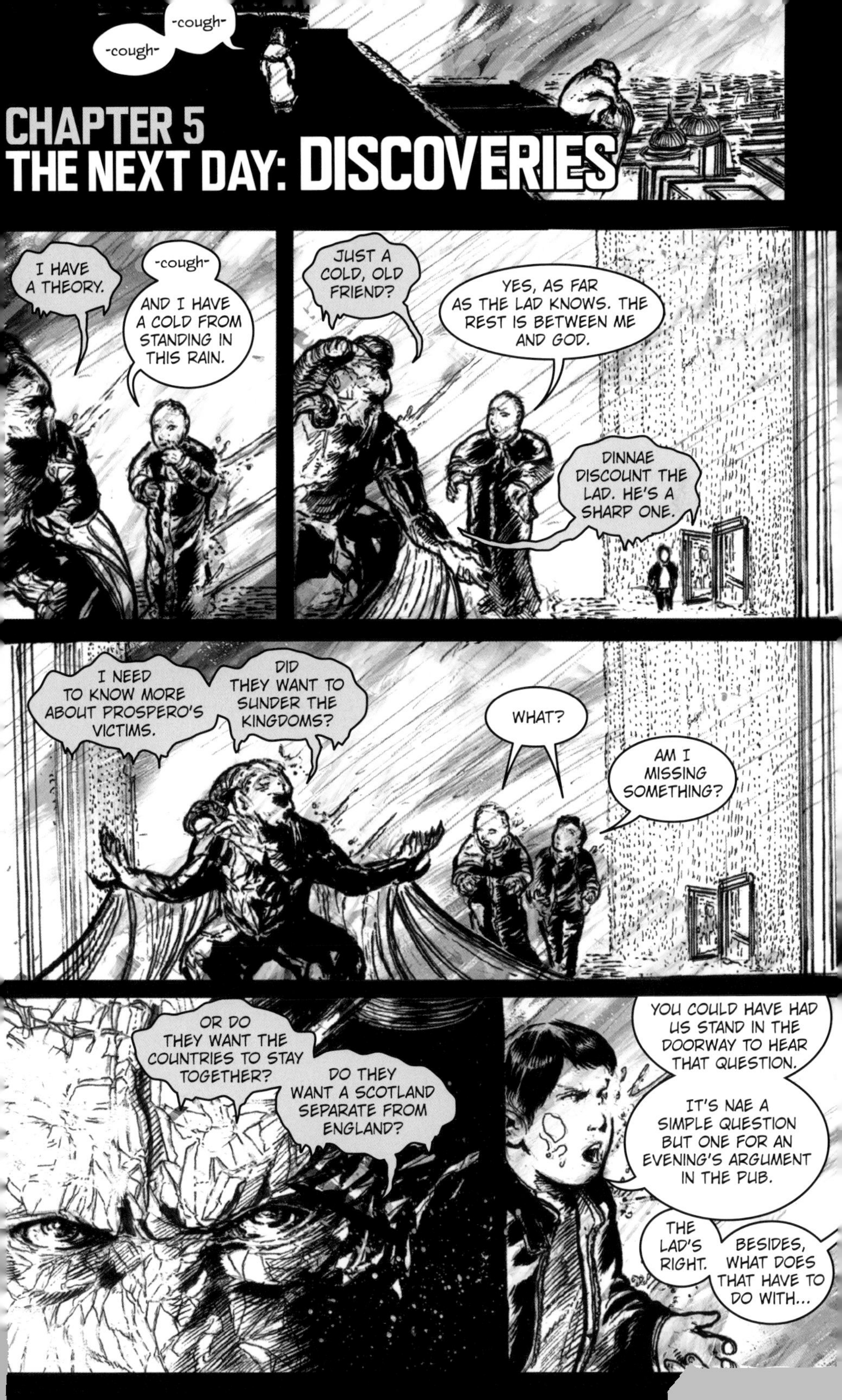
-cough-
-cough-
CHAPTER 5
THE NEXT DAY: DISCOVERIES
I HAVE A THEORY.
-cough-
AND I HAVE A COLD FROM STANDING IN THIS RAIN.
JUST A COLD, OLD FRIEND?
YES, AS FAR AS THE LAD KNOWS. THE REST IS BETWEEN ME AND GOD.
DINNAE DISCOUNT THE LAD. HE'S A SHARP ONE.
I NEED TO KNOW MORE ABOUT PROSPERO'S VICTIMS.
DID THEY WANT TO SUNDER THE KINGDOMS?
WHAT?
AM I MISSING SOMETHING?
OR DO THEY WANT THE COUNTRIES TO STAY TOGETHER?
DO THEY WANT A SCOTLAND SEPARATE FROM ENGLAND?
YOU COULD HAVE HAD US STAND IN THE DOORWAY TO HEAR THAT QUESTION.
IT'S NAE A SIMPLE QUESTION BUT ONE FOR AN EVENING'S ARGUMENT IN THE PUB.
THE LAD'S RIGHT.
BESIDES, WHAT DOES THAT HAVE TO DO WITH...

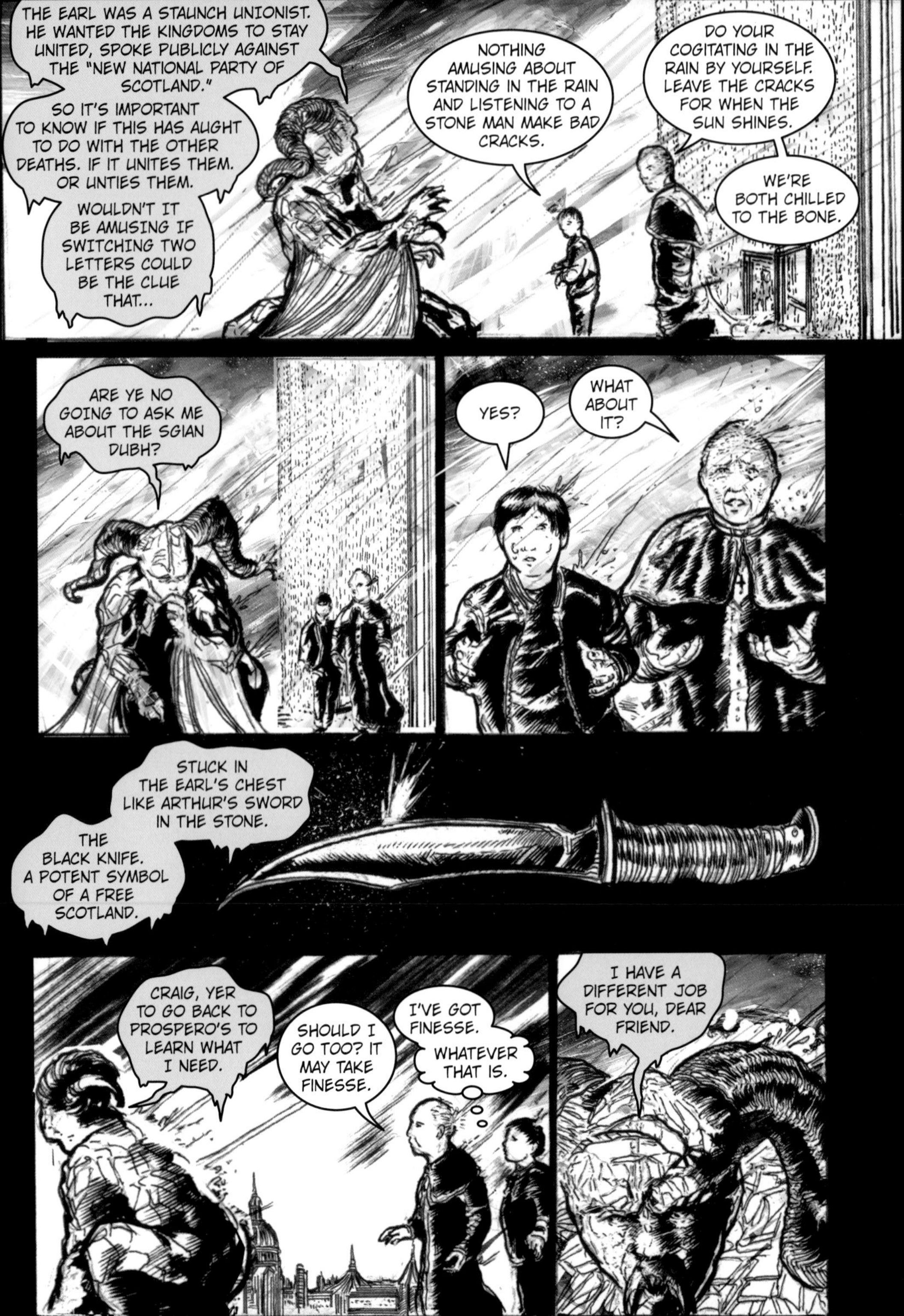
THE EARL WAS A STAUNCH UNIONIST. HE WANTED THE KINGDOMS TO STAY UNITED, SPOKE PUBLICLY AGAINST THE "NEW NATIONAL PARTY OF SCOTLAND."
SO IT'S IMPORTANT TO KNOW IF THIS HAS AUGHT TO DO WITH THE OTHER DEATHS. IF IT UNITES THEM. OR UNTIES THEM.
WOULDN'T IT BE AMUSING IF SWITCHING TWO LETTERS COULD BE THE CLUE THAT...
NOTHING AMUSING ABOUT STANDING IN THE RAIN AND LISTENING TO A STONE MAN MAKE BAD CRACKS.
DO YOUR COGITATING IN THE RAIN BY YOURSELF. LEAVE THE CRACKS FOR WHEN THE SUN SHINES.
WE'RE BOTH CHILLED TO THE BONE.
ARE YE NO GOING TO ASK ME ABOUT THE SGIAN DUBH?
YES?
WHAT ABOUT IT?
STUCK IN THE EARL'S CHEST LIKE ARTHUR'S SWORD IN THE STONE.
THE BLACK KNIFE. A POTENT SYMBOL OF A FREE SCOTLAND.
CRAIG, YER TO GO BACK TO PROSPERO'S TO LEARN WHAT I NEED.
SHOULD I GO TOO? IT MAY TAKE FINESSE.
I'VE GOT FINESSE.
WHATEVER THAT IS.
I HAVE A DIFFERENT JOB FOR YOU, DEAR FRIEND.

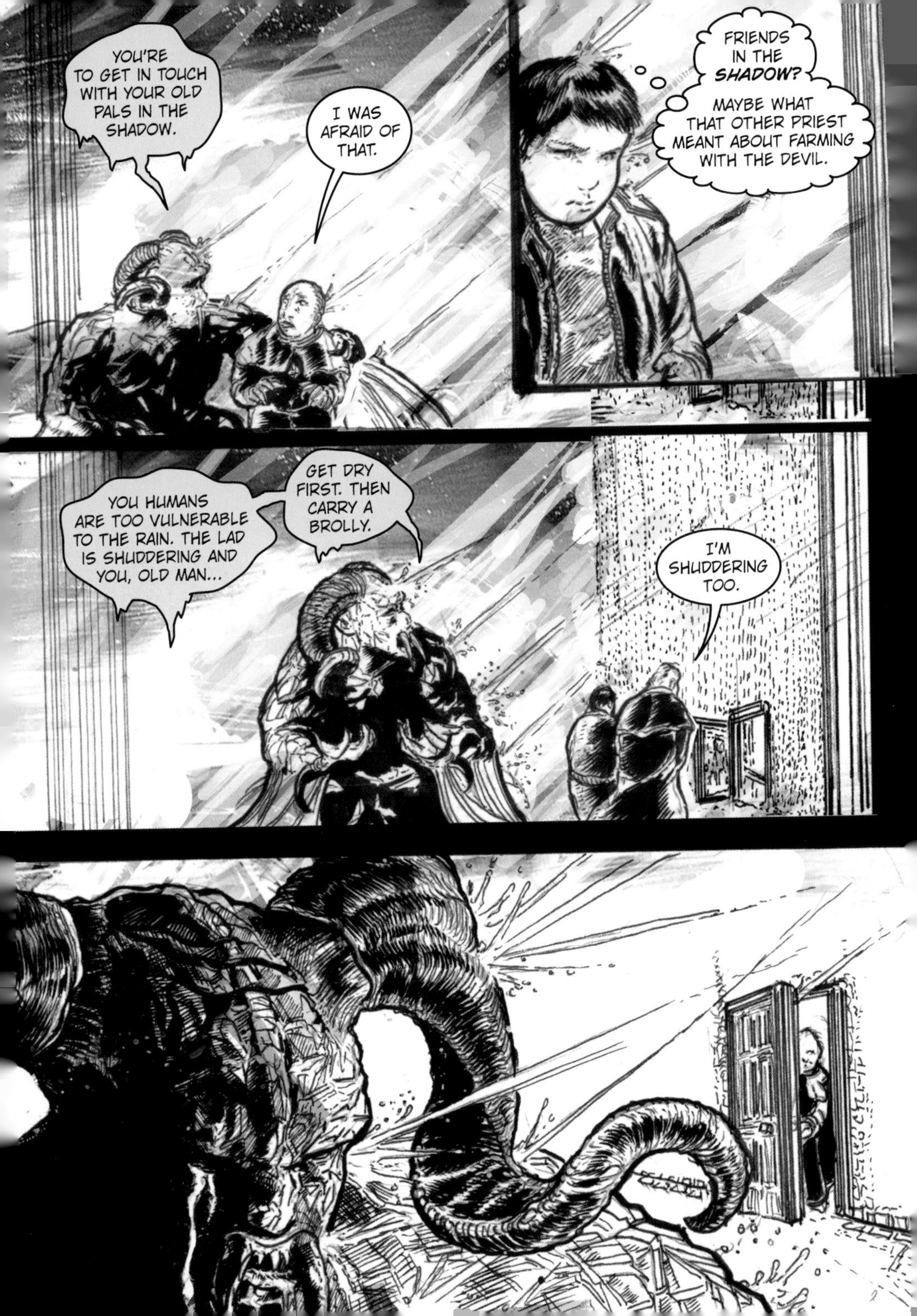
YOU'RE TO GET IN TOUCH WITH YOUR OLD PALS IN THE SHADOW.
I WAS AFRAID OF THAT.
FRIENDS IN THE *SHADOW?*
MAYBE WHAT THAT OTHER PRIEST MEANT ABOUT FARMING WITH THE DEVIL.
YOU HUMANS ARE TOO VULNERABLE TO THE RAIN. THE LAD IS SHUDDERING AND YOU, OLD MAN...
GET DRY FIRST. THEN CARRY A BROLLY.
I'M SHUDDERING TOO.

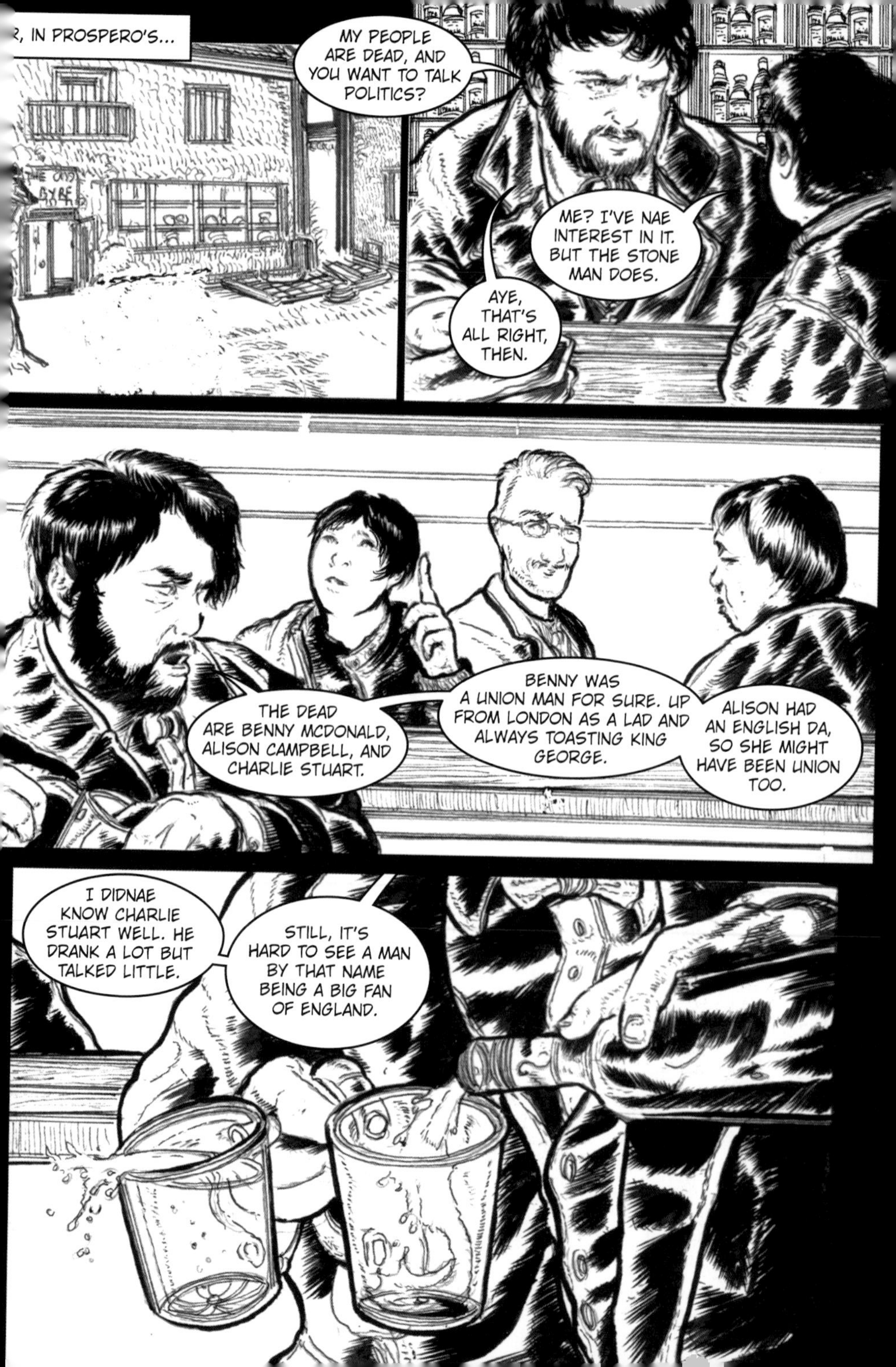
R, IN PROSPERO'S...
MY PEOPLE ARE DEAD, AND YOU WANT TO TALK POLITICS?
ME? I'VE NAE INTEREST IN IT. BUT THE STONE MAN DOES.
AYE, THAT'S ALL RIGHT, THEN.
THE DEAD ARE BENNY MCDONALD, ALISON CAMPBELL, AND CHARLIE STUART.
BENNY WAS A UNION MAN FOR SURE. UP FROM LONDON AS A LAD AND ALWAYS TOASTING KING GEORGE.
ALISON HAD AN ENGLISH DA, SO SHE MIGHT HAVE BEEN UNION TOO.
I DIDNAE KNOW CHARLIE STUART WELL. HE DRANK A LOT BUT TALKED LITTLE.
STILL, IT'S HARD TO SEE A MAN BY THAT NAME BEING A BIG FAN OF ENGLAND.

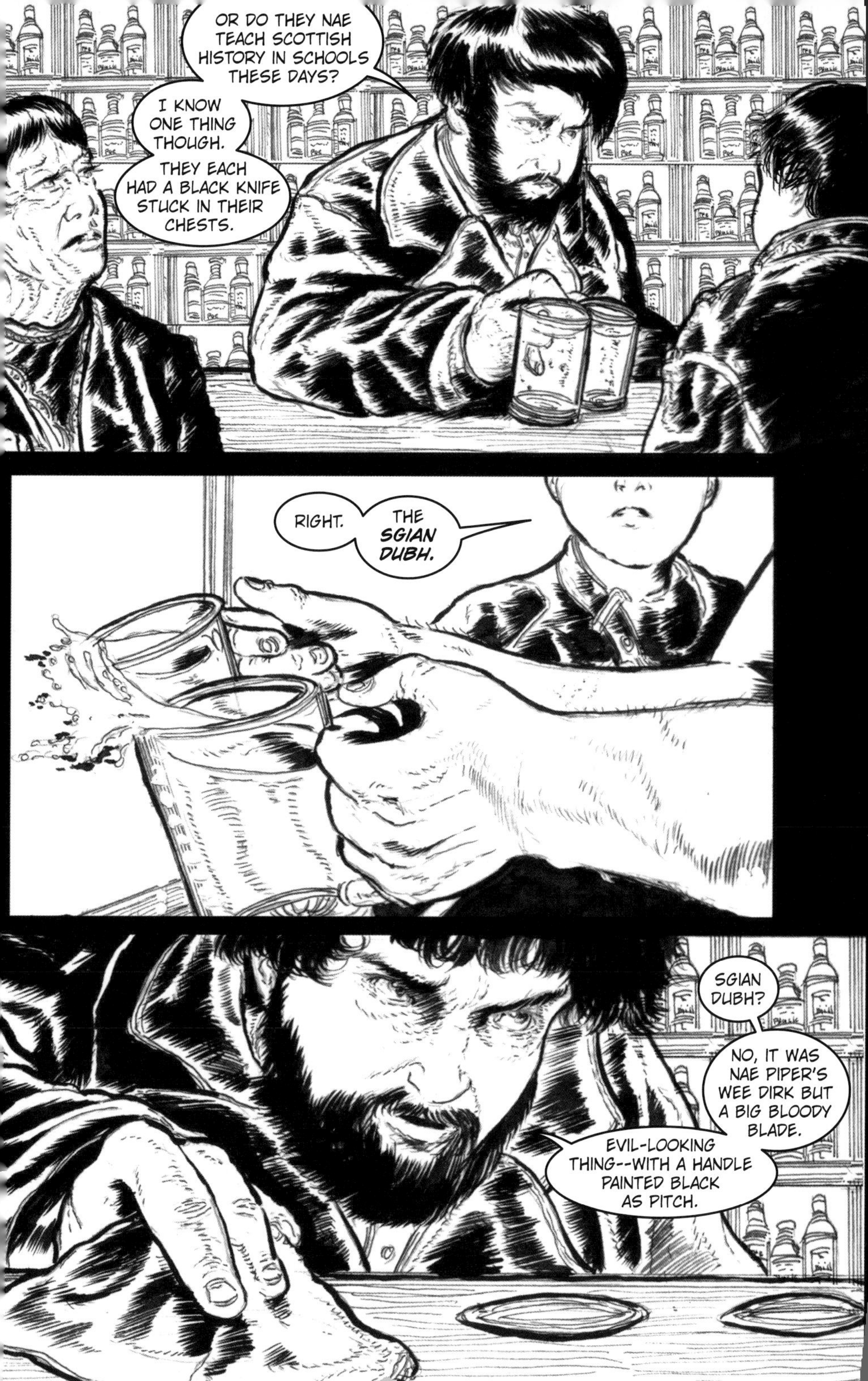
OR DO THEY NAE TEACH SCOTTISH HISTORY IN SCHOOLS THESE DAYS?
I KNOW ONE THING THOUGH.
THEY EACH HAD A BLACK KNIFE STUCK IN THEIR CHESTS.
RIGHT.
THE *SGIAN DUBH.*
SGIAN DUBH?
NO, IT WAS NAE PIPER'S WEE DIRK BUT A BIG BLOODY BLADE.
EVIL-LOOKING THING--WITH A HANDLE PAINTED BLACK AS PITCH.

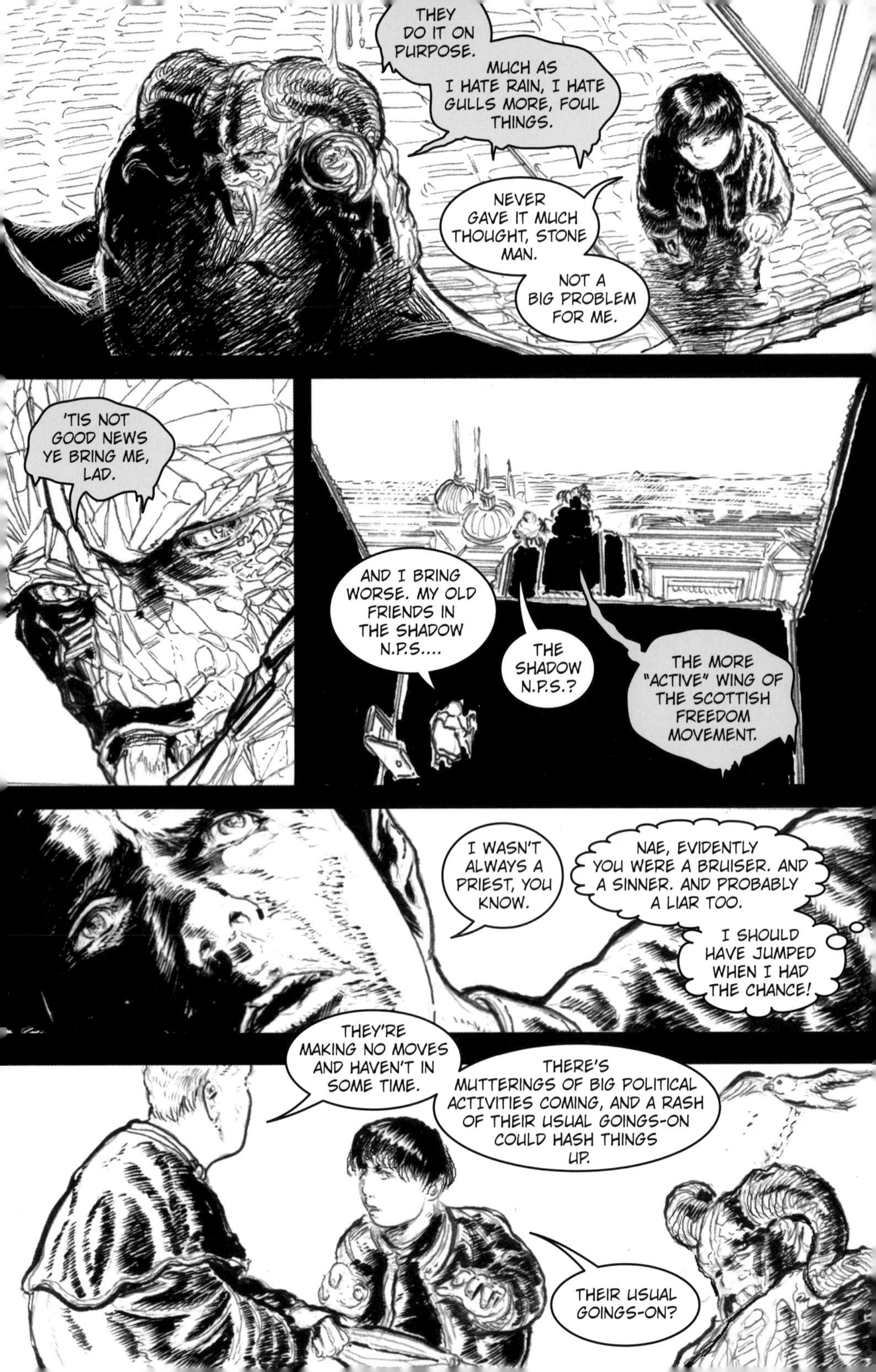
THEY DO IT ON PURPOSE.
MUCH AS I HATE RAIN, I HATE GULLS MORE, FOUL THINGS.
NEVER GAVE IT MUCH THOUGHT, STONE MAN.
NOT A BIG PROBLEM FOR ME.
'TIS NOT GOOD NEWS YE BRING ME, LAD.
AND I BRING WORSE. MY OLD FRIENDS IN THE SHADOW N.P.S....
THE SHADOW N.P.S.?
THE MORE "ACTIVE" WING OF THE SCOTTISH FREEDOM MOVEMENT.
I WASN'T ALWAYS A PRIEST, YOU KNOW.
NAE, EVIDENTLY YOU WERE A BRUISER. AND A SINNER. AND PROBABLY A LIAR TOO.
I SHOULD HAVE JUMPED WHEN I HAD THE CHANCE!
THEY'RE MAKING NO MOVES AND HAVEN'T IN SOME TIME.
THERE'S MUTTERINGS OF BIG POLITICAL ACTIVITIES COMING, AND A RASH OF THEIR USUAL GOINGS-ON COULD HASH THINGS UP.
THEIR USUAL GOINGS-ON?

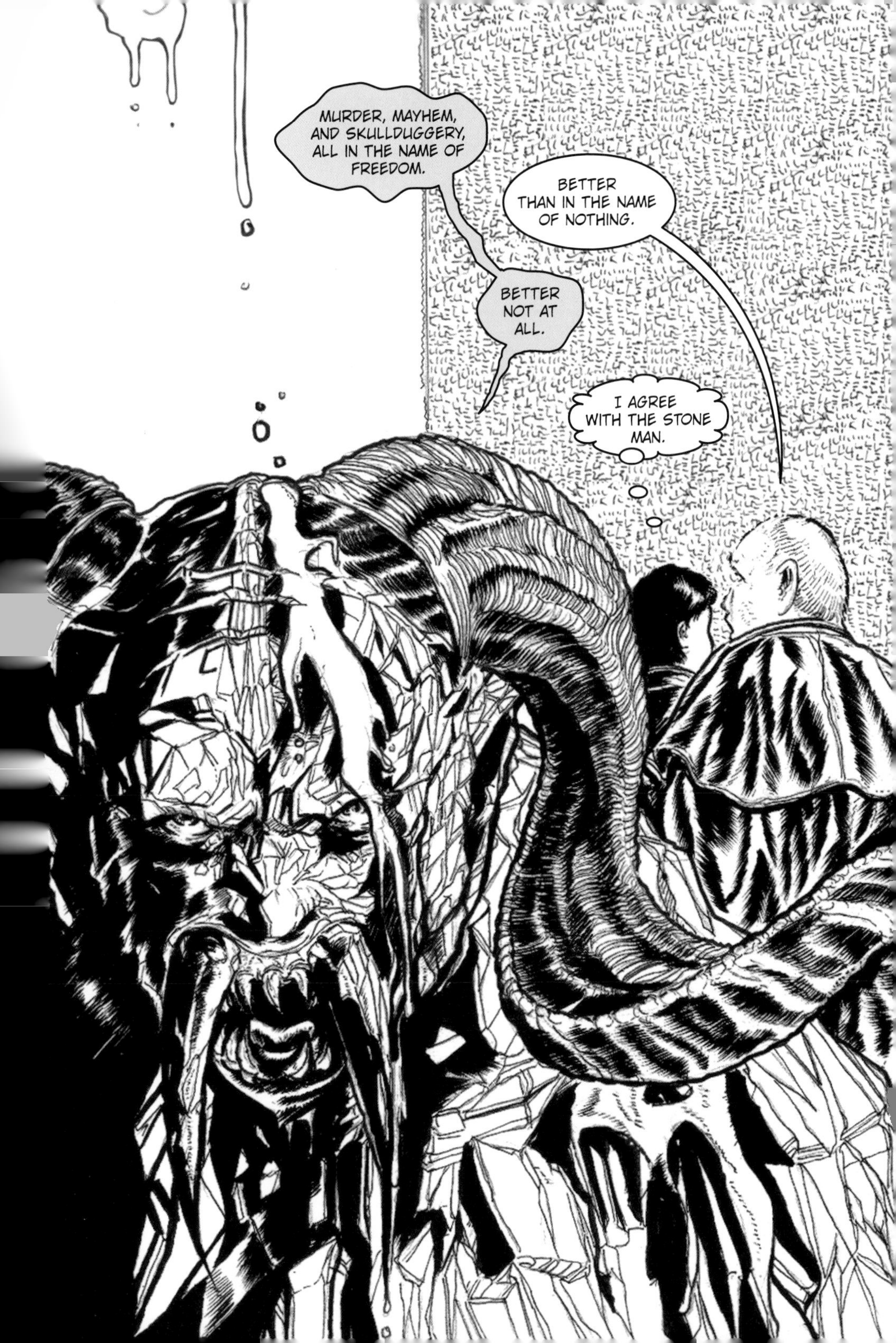
MURDER, MAYHEM, AND SKULLDUGGERY, ALL IN THE NAME OF FREEDOM.
BETTER THAN IN THE NAME OF NOTHING.
BETTER NOT AT ALL.
I AGREE WITH THE STONE MAN.

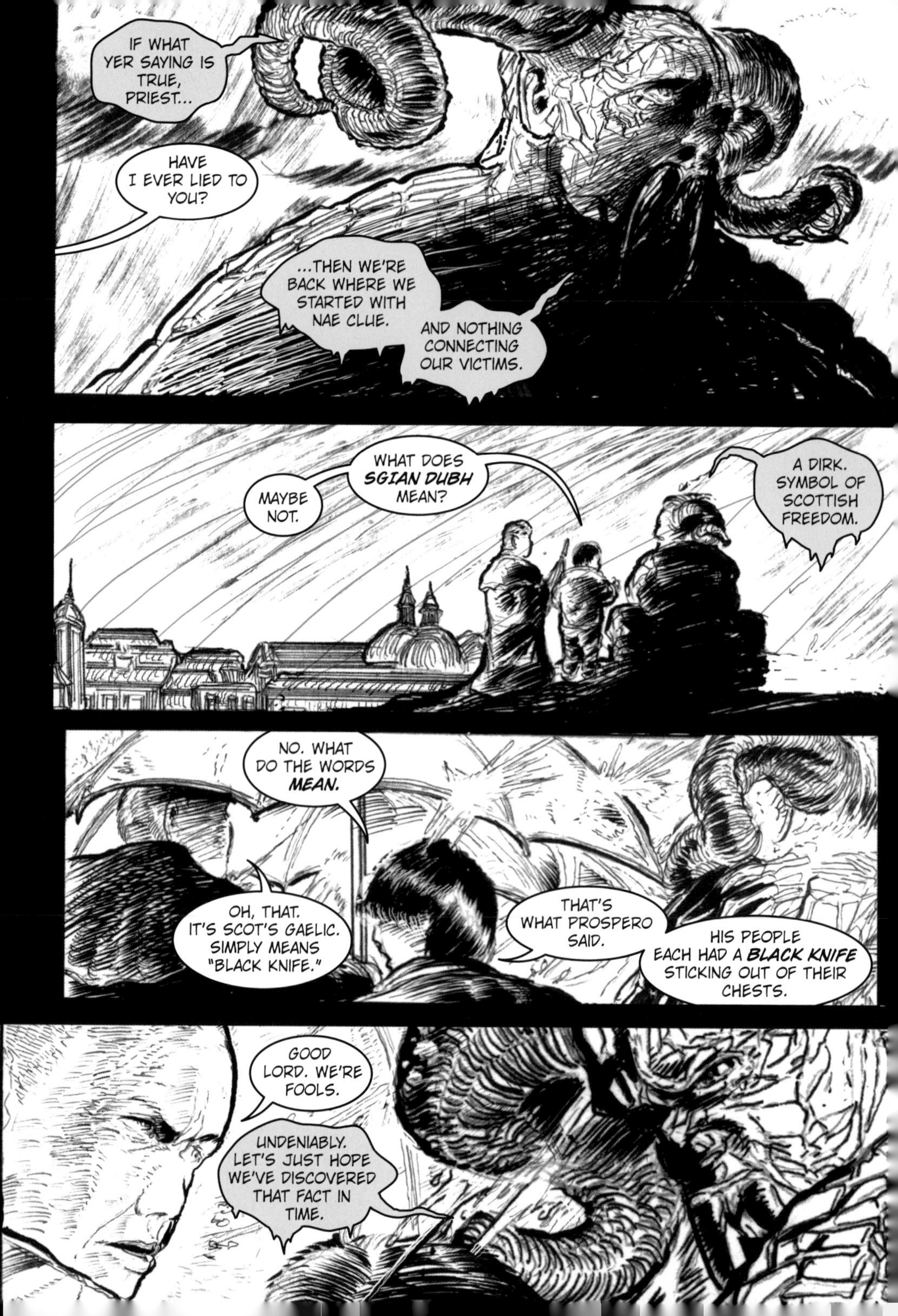
IF WHAT YER SAYING IS TRUE, PRIEST...
HAVE I EVER LIED TO YOU?
...THEN WE'RE BACK WHERE WE STARTED WITH NAE CLUE.
AND NOTHING CONNECTING OUR VICTIMS.
MAYBE NOT.
WHAT DOES SGIAN DUBH MEAN?
A DIRK. SYMBOL OF SCOTTISH FREEDOM.
NO. WHAT DO THE WORDS MEAN.
OH, THAT. IT'S SCOT'S GAELIC. SIMPLY MEANS "BLACK KNIFE."
THAT'S WHAT PROSPERO SAID.
HIS PEOPLE EACH HAD A BLACK KNIFE STICKING OUT OF THEIR CHESTS.
GOOD LORD. WE'RE FOOLS.
UNDENIABLY. LET'S JUST HOPE WE'VE DISCOVERED THAT FACT IN TIME.

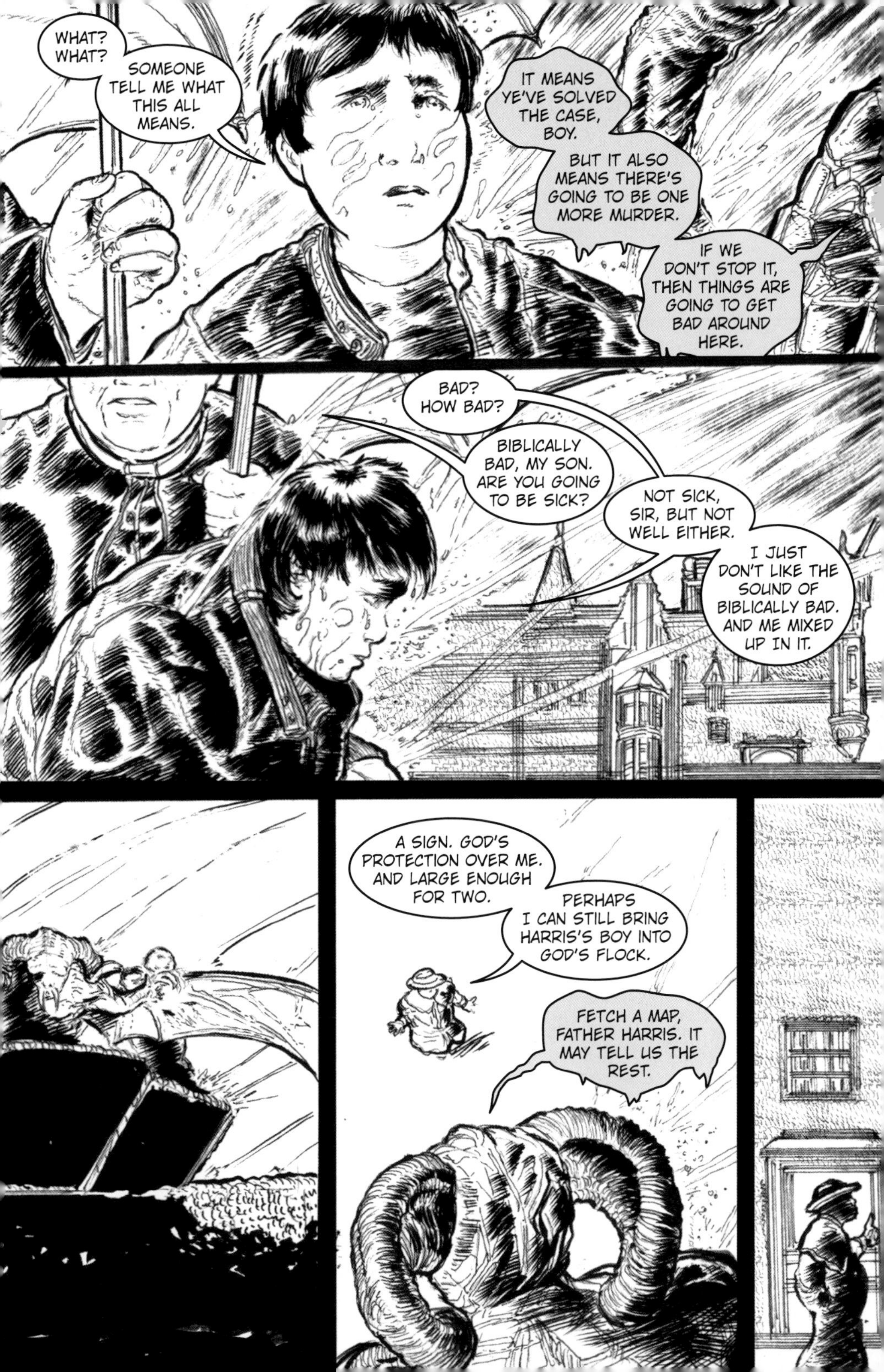

WHAT? WHAT?
SOMEONE TELL ME WHAT THIS ALL MEANS.
IT MEANS YE'VE SOLVED THE CASE, BOY.
BUT IT ALSO MEANS THERE'S GOING TO BE ONE MORE MURDER.
IF WE DON'T STOP IT, THEN THINGS ARE GOING TO GET BAD AROUND HERE.
BAD? HOW BAD?
BIBLICALLY BAD, MY SON. ARE YOU GOING TO BE SICK?
NOT SICK, SIR, BUT NOT WELL EITHER.
I JUST DON'T LIKE THE SOUND OF BIBLICALLY BAD. AND ME MIXED UP IN IT.
A SIGN. GOD'S PROTECTION OVER ME. AND LARGE ENOUGH FOR TWO.
PERHAPS I CAN STILL BRING HARRIS'S BOY INTO GOD'S FLOCK.
FETCH A MAP, FATHER HARRIS. IT MAY TELL US THE REST.

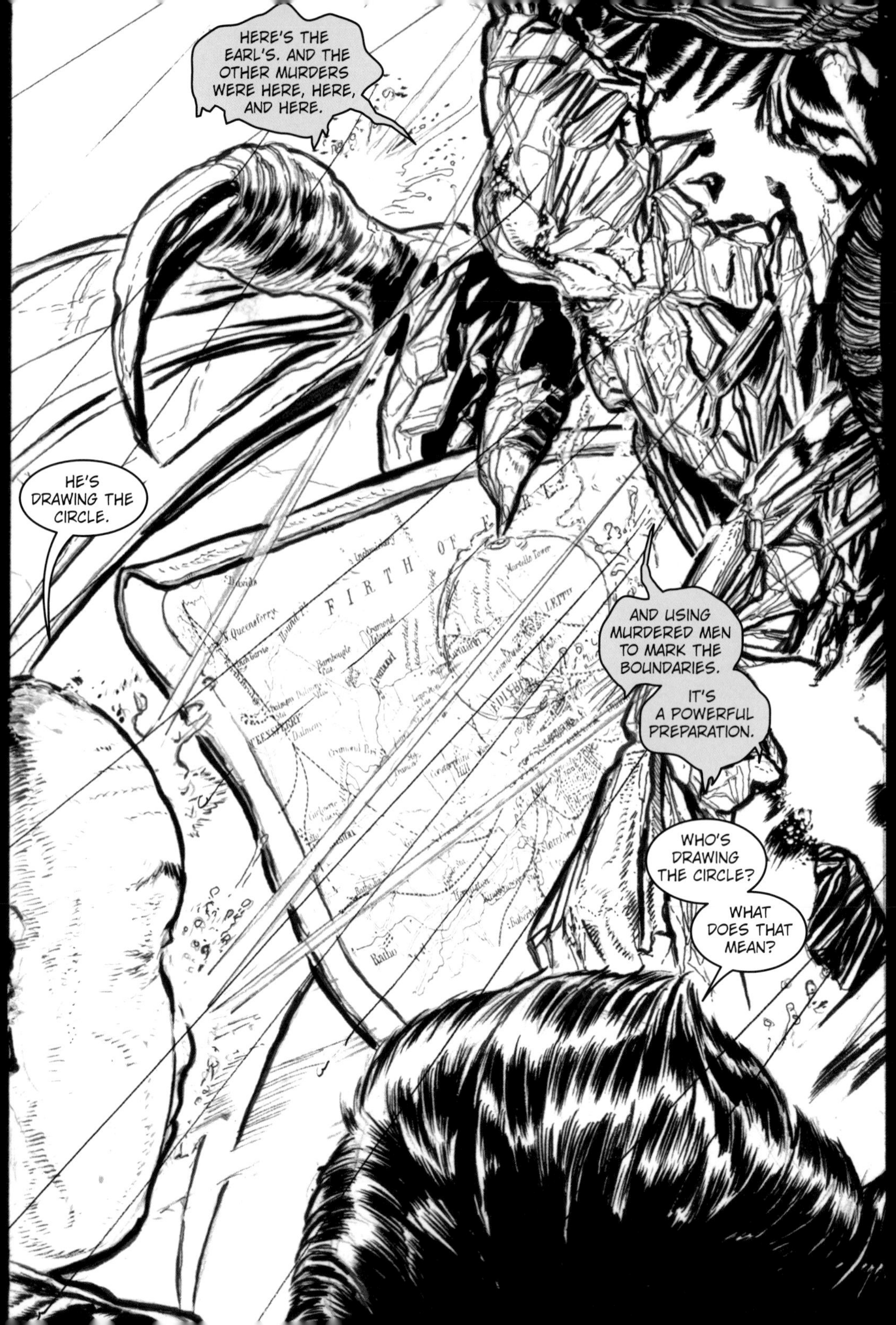
HERE'S THE EARL'S. AND THE OTHER MURDERS WERE HERE, HERE, AND HERE.
HE'S DRAWING THE CIRCLE.
AND USING MURDERED MEN TO MARK THE BOUNDARIES.
IT'S A POWERFUL PREPARATION.
WHO'S DRAWING THE CIRCLE?
WHAT DOES THAT MEAN?
FIRTH OF

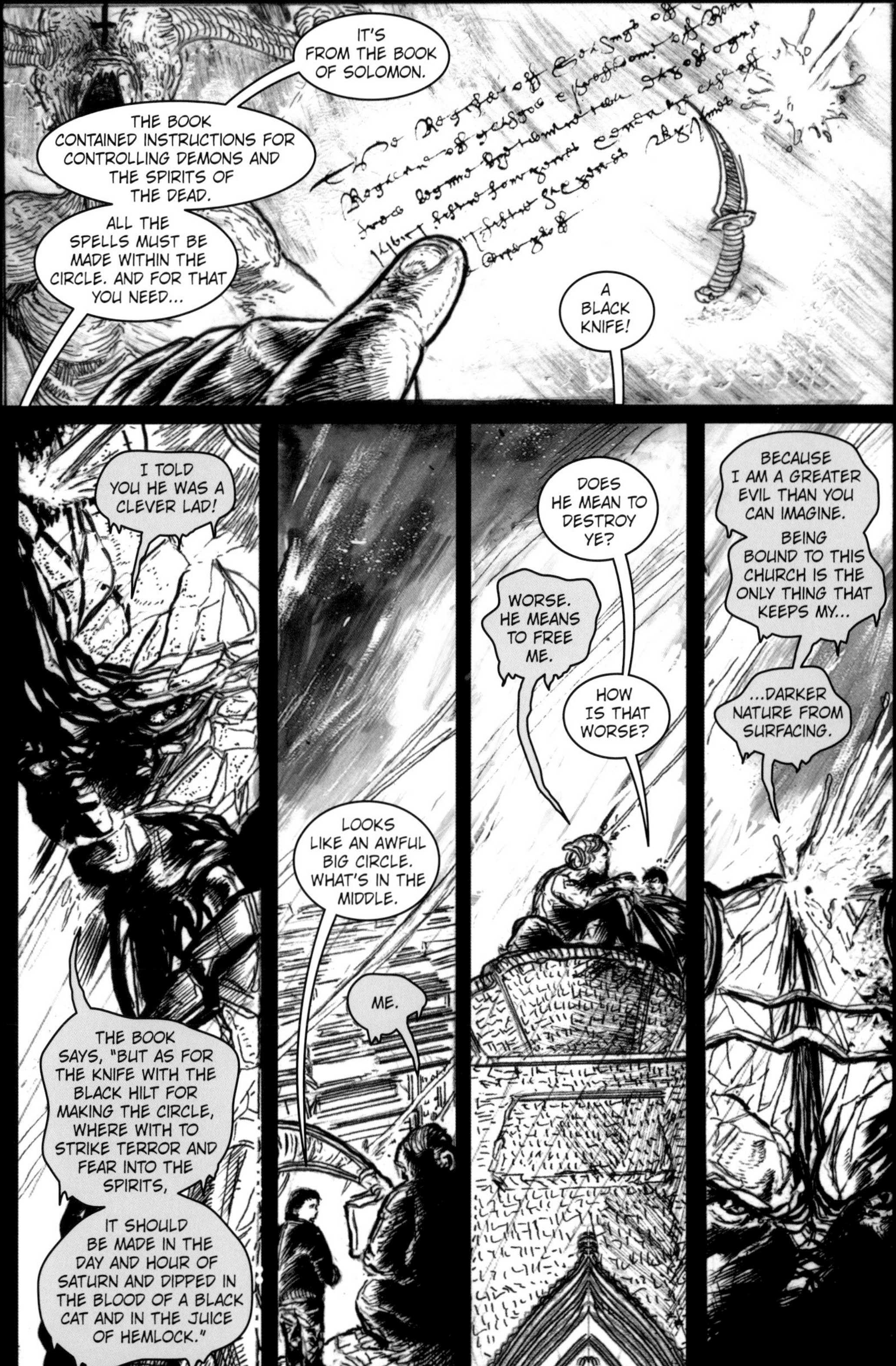

IT'S FROM THE BOOK OF SOLOMON.
THE BOOK CONTAINED INSTRUCTIONS FOR CONTROLLING DEMONS AND THE SPIRITS OF THE DEAD.
ALL THE SPELLS MUST BE MADE WITHIN THE CIRCLE. AND FOR THAT YOU NEED...
A BLACK KNIFE!
I TOLD YOU HE WAS A CLEVER LAD!
THE BOOK SAYS, "BUT AS FOR THE KNIFE WITH THE BLACK HILT FOR MAKING THE CIRCLE, WHERE WITH TO STRIKE TERROR AND FEAR INTO THE SPIRITS,
IT SHOULD BE MADE IN THE DAY AND HOUR OF SATURN AND DIPPED IN THE BLOOD OF A BLACK CAT AND IN THE JUICE OF HEMLOCK."
LOOKS LIKE AN AWFUL BIG CIRCLE. WHAT'S IN THE MIDDLE.
ME.
DOES HE MEAN TO DESTROY YE?
WORSE. HE MEANS TO FREE ME.
HOW IS THAT WORSE?
BECAUSE I AM A GREATER EVIL THAN YOU CAN IMAGINE.
BEING BOUND TO THIS CHURCH IS THE ONLY THING THAT KEEPS MY...
...DARKER NATURE FROM SURFACING.

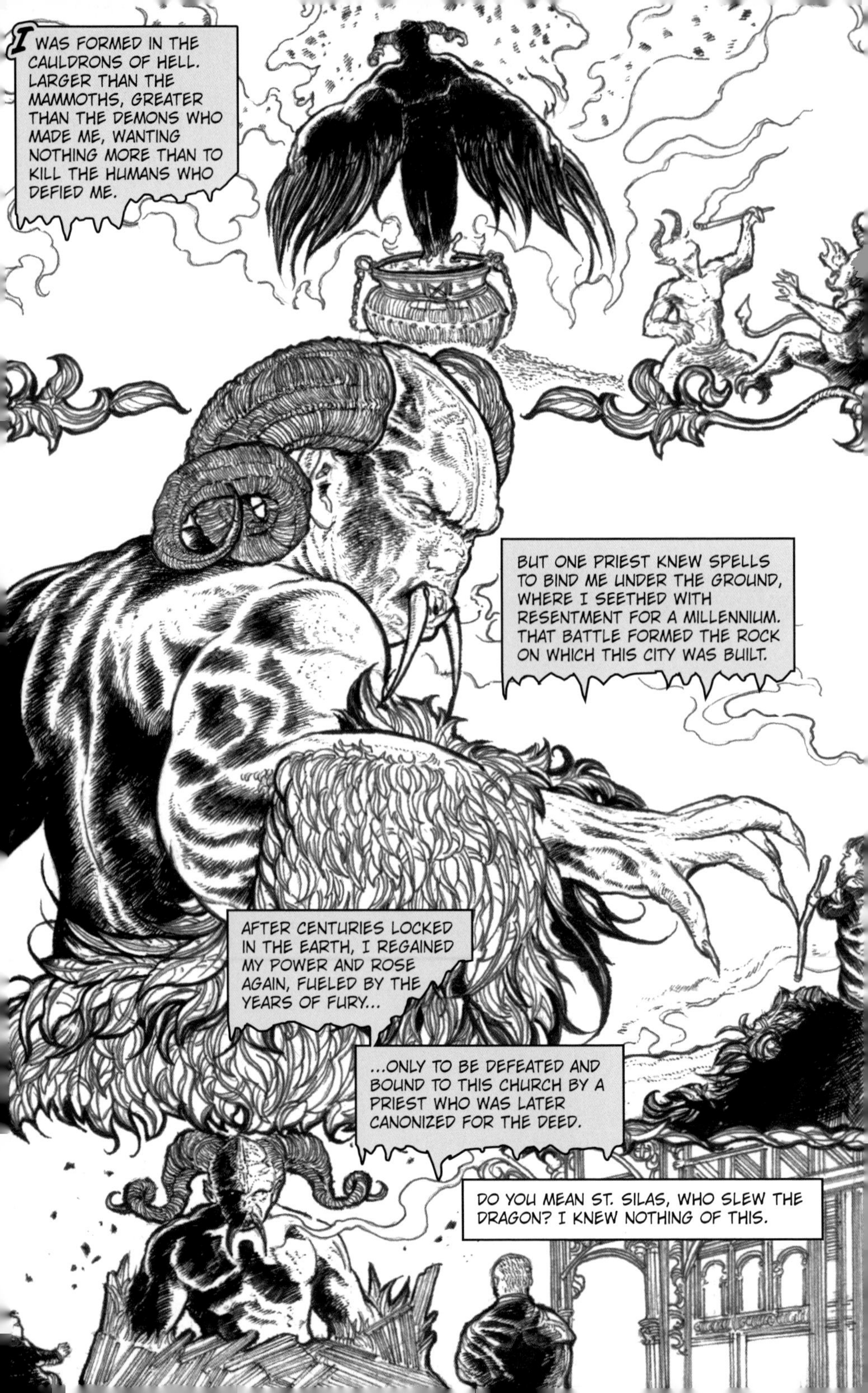
I WAS FORMED IN THE CAULDRONS OF HELL. LARGER THAN THE MAMMOTHS, GREATER THAN THE DEMONS WHO MADE ME, WANTING NOTHING MORE THAN TO KILL THE HUMANS WHO DEFIED ME.
BUT ONE PRIEST KNEW SPELLS TO BIND ME UNDER THE GROUND, WHERE I SEETHED WITH RESENTMENT FOR A MILLENNIUM. THAT BATTLE FORMED THE ROCK ON WHICH THIS CITY WAS BUILT.
AFTER CENTURIES LOCKED IN THE EARTH, I REGAINED MY POWER AND ROSE AGAIN, FUELED BY THE YEARS OF FURY...
...ONLY TO BE DEFEATED AND BOUND TO THIS CHURCH BY A PRIEST WHO WAS LATER CANONIZED FOR THE DEED.
DO YOU MEAN ST. SILAS, WHO SLEW THE DRAGON? I KNEW NOTHING OF THIS.

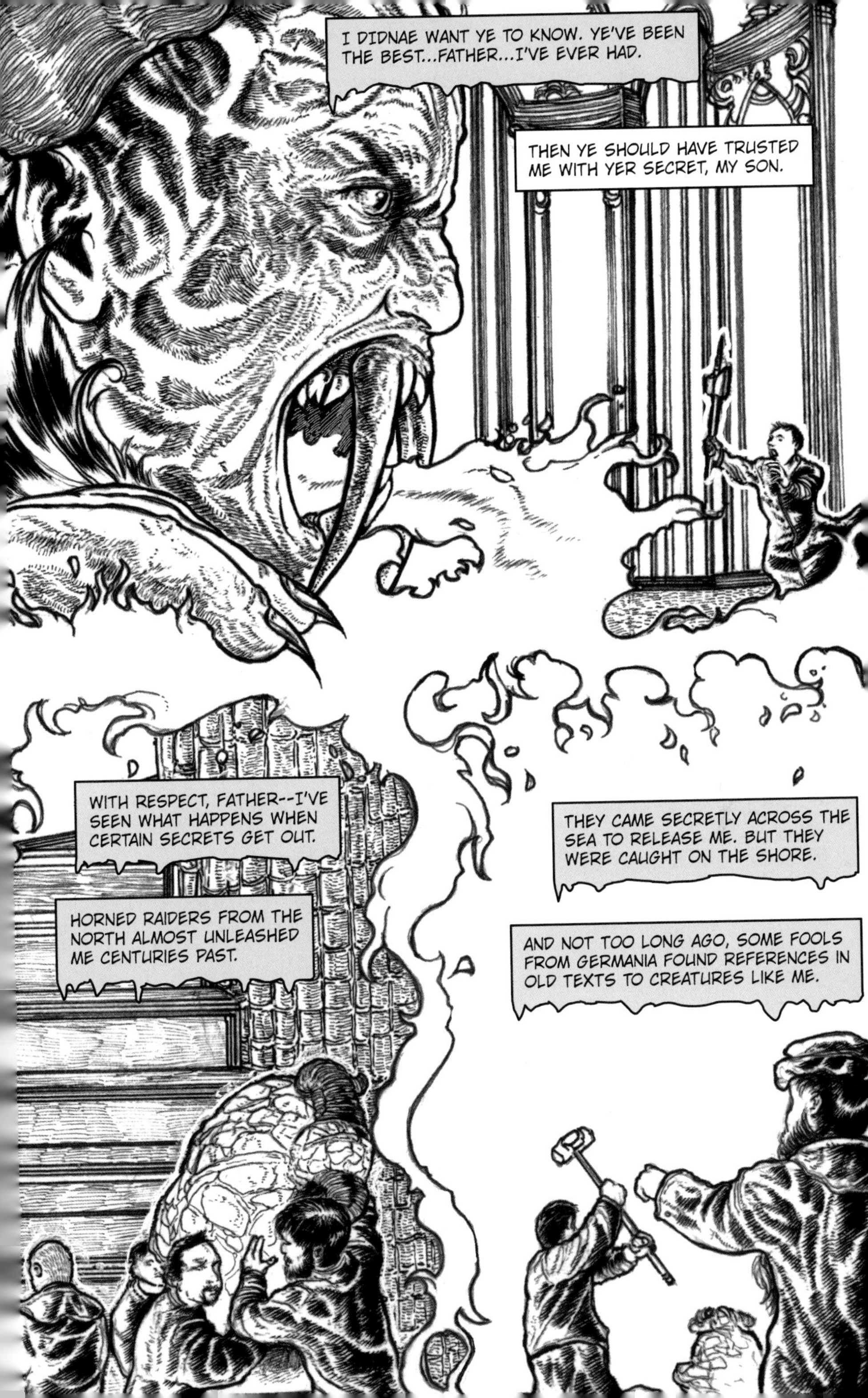
I DIDNAE WANT YE TO KNOW. YE'VE BEEN THE BEST...FATHER...I'VE EVER HAD.
THEN YE SHOULD HAVE TRUSTED ME WITH YER SECRET, MY SON.
WITH RESPECT, FATHER--I'VE SEEN WHAT HAPPENS WHEN CERTAIN SECRETS GET OUT.
HORNED RAIDERS FROM THE NORTH ALMOST UNLEASHED ME CENTURIES PAST.
THEY CAME SECRETLY ACROSS THE SEA TO RELEASE ME. BUT THEY WERE CAUGHT ON THE SHORE.
AND NOT TOO LONG AGO, SOME FOOLS FROM GERMANIA FOUND REFERENCES IN OLD TEXTS TO CREATURES LIKE ME.

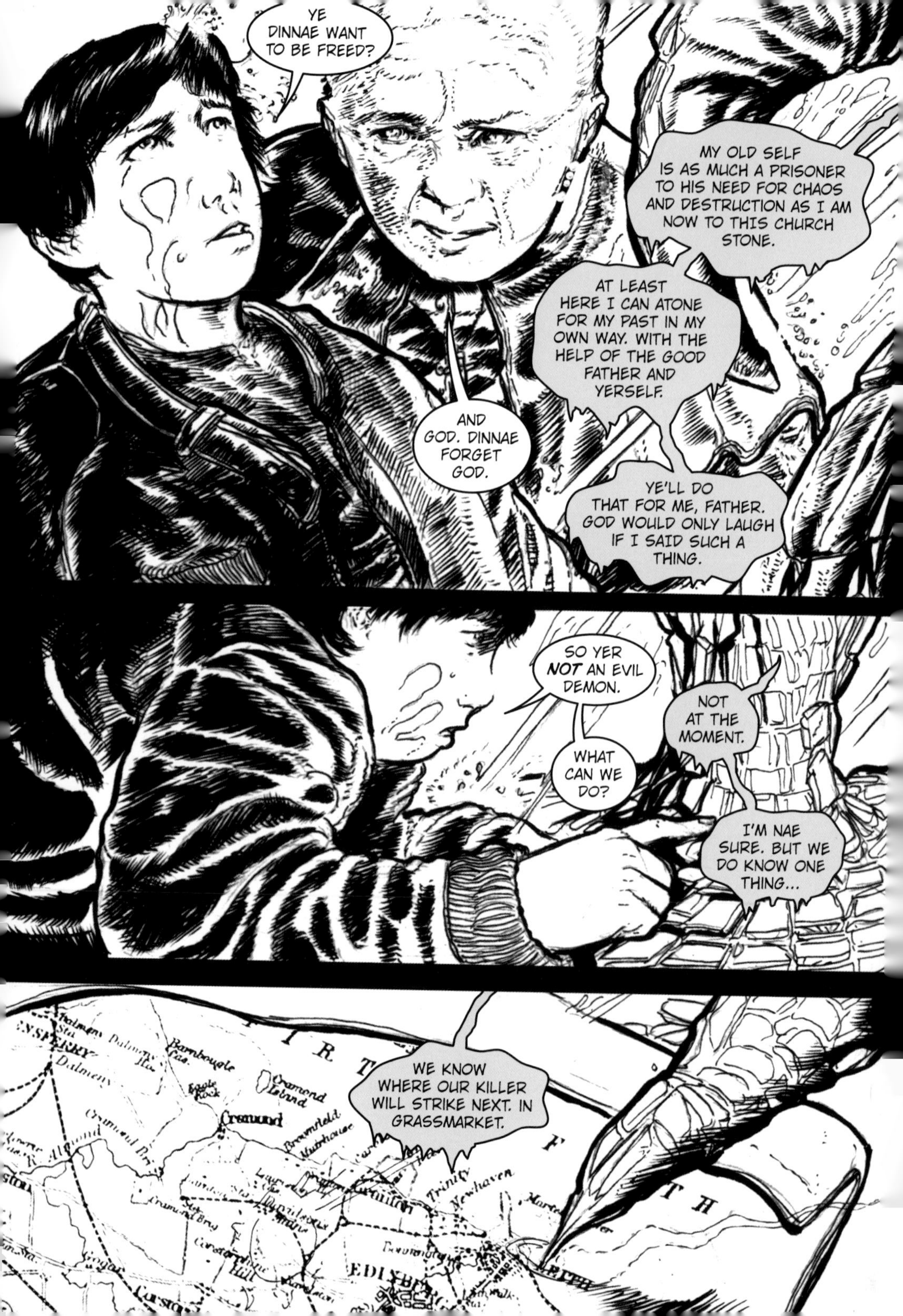
YE DINNAE WANT TO BE FREED?
MY OLD SELF IS AS MUCH A PRISONER TO HIS NEED FOR CHAOS AND DESTRUCTION AS I AM NOW TO THIS CHURCH STONE.
AT LEAST HERE I CAN ATONE FOR MY PAST IN MY OWN WAY. WITH THE HELP OF THE GOOD FATHER AND YERSELF.
AND GOD. DINNAE FORGET GOD.
YE'LL DO THAT FOR ME, FATHER. GOD WOULD ONLY LAUGH IF I SAID SUCH A THING.
SO YER *NOT* AN EVIL DEMON.
NOT AT THE MOMENT.
WHAT CAN WE DO?
I'M NAE SURE. BUT WE DO KNOW ONE THING...
WE KNOW WHERE OUR KILLER WILL STRIKE NEXT. IN GRASSMARKET.

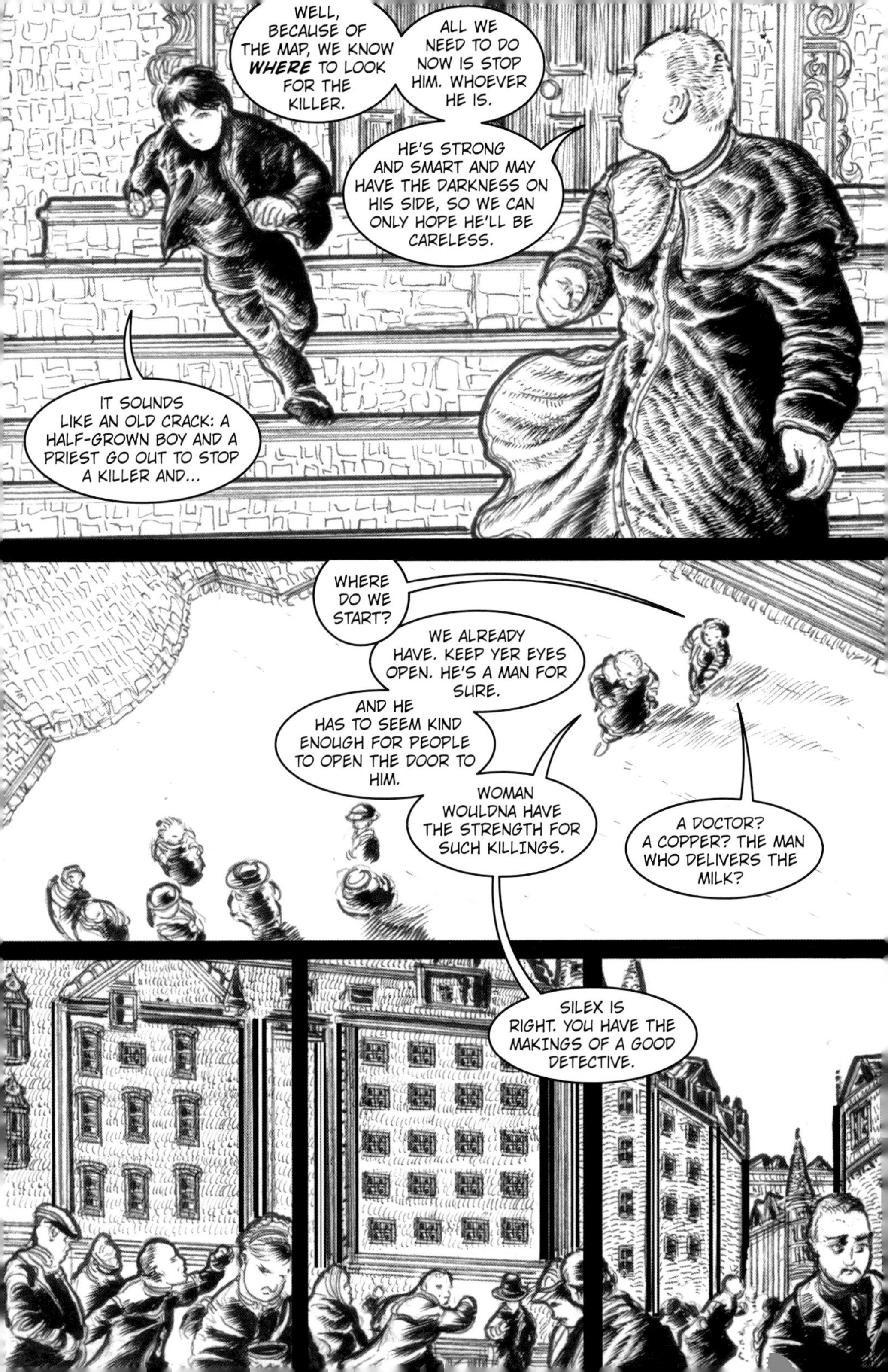
WELL, BECAUSE OF THE MAP, WE KNOW **WHERE** TO LOOK FOR THE KILLER.
ALL WE NEED TO DO NOW IS STOP HIM. WHOEVER HE IS.
HE'S STRONG AND SMART AND MAY HAVE THE DARKNESS ON HIS SIDE, SO WE CAN ONLY HOPE HE'LL BE CARELESS.
IT SOUNDS LIKE AN OLD CRACK: A HALF-GROWN BOY AND A PRIEST GO OUT TO STOP A KILLER AND...
WHERE DO WE START?
WE ALREADY HAVE. KEEP YER EYES OPEN. HE'S A MAN FOR SURE.
AND HE HAS TO SEEM KIND ENOUGH FOR PEOPLE TO OPEN THE DOOR TO HIM.
WOMAN WOULDNA HAVE THE STRENGTH FOR SUCH KILLINGS.
A DOCTOR? A COPPER? THE MAN WHO DELIVERS THE MILK?
SILEX IS RIGHT. YOU HAVE THE MAKINGS OF A GOOD DETECTIVE.

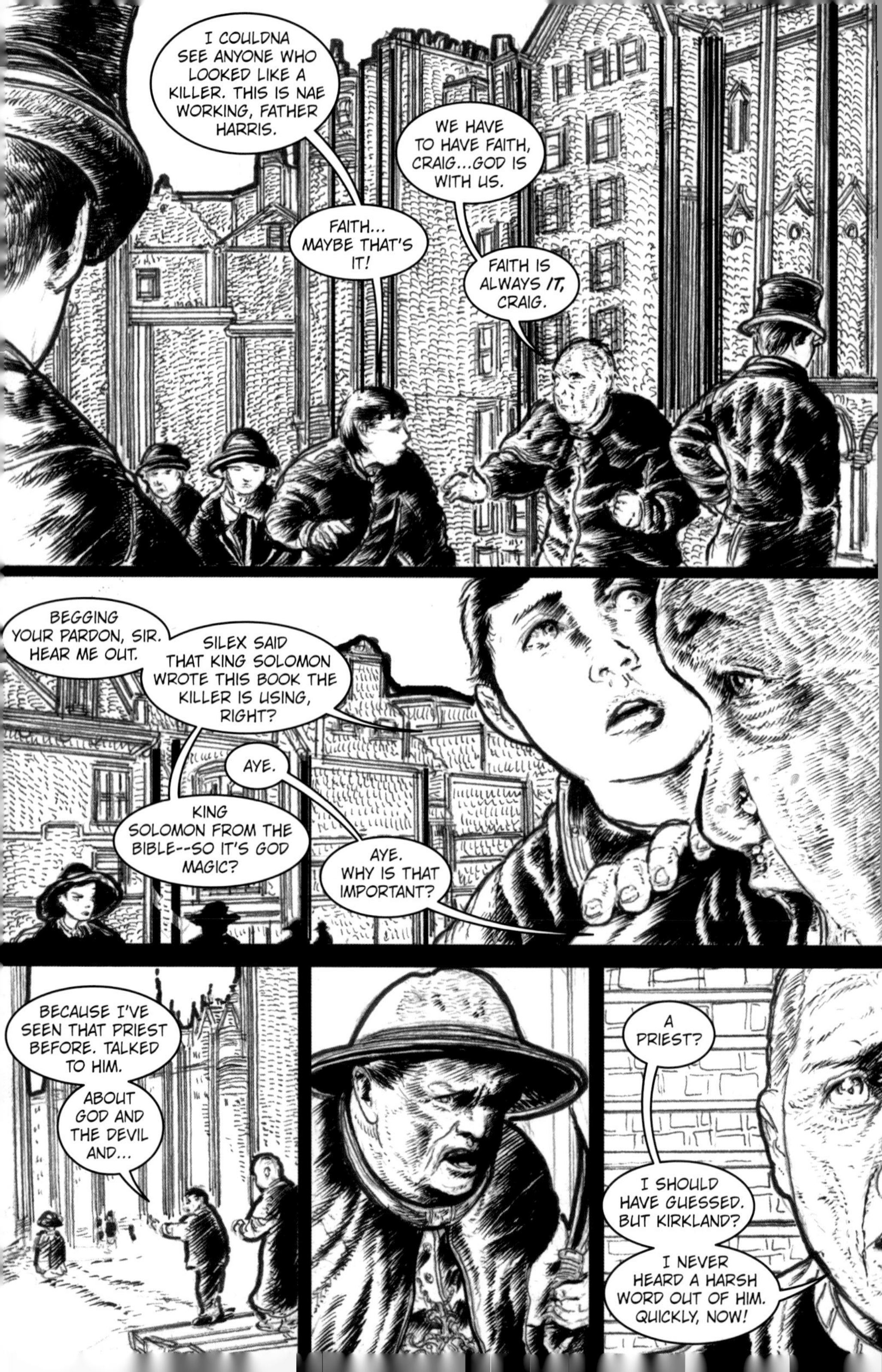
I COULDNA SEE ANYONE WHO LOOKED LIKE A KILLER. THIS IS NAE WORKING, FATHER HARRIS.
WE HAVE TO HAVE FAITH, CRAIG...GOD IS WITH US.
FAITH... MAYBE THAT'S IT!
FAITH IS ALWAYS *IT*, CRAIG.
BEGGING YOUR PARDON, SIR. HEAR ME OUT.
SILEX SAID THAT KING SOLOMON WROTE THIS BOOK THE KILLER IS USING, RIGHT?
AYE.
KING SOLOMON FROM THE BIBLE--SO IT'S GOD MAGIC?
AYE. WHY IS THAT IMPORTANT?
BECAUSE I'VE SEEN THAT PRIEST BEFORE. TALKED TO HIM.
ABOUT GOD AND THE DEVIL AND...
A PRIEST?
I SHOULD HAVE GUESSED. BUT KIRKLAND?
I NEVER HEARD A HARSH WORD OUT OF HIM. QUICKLY, NOW!

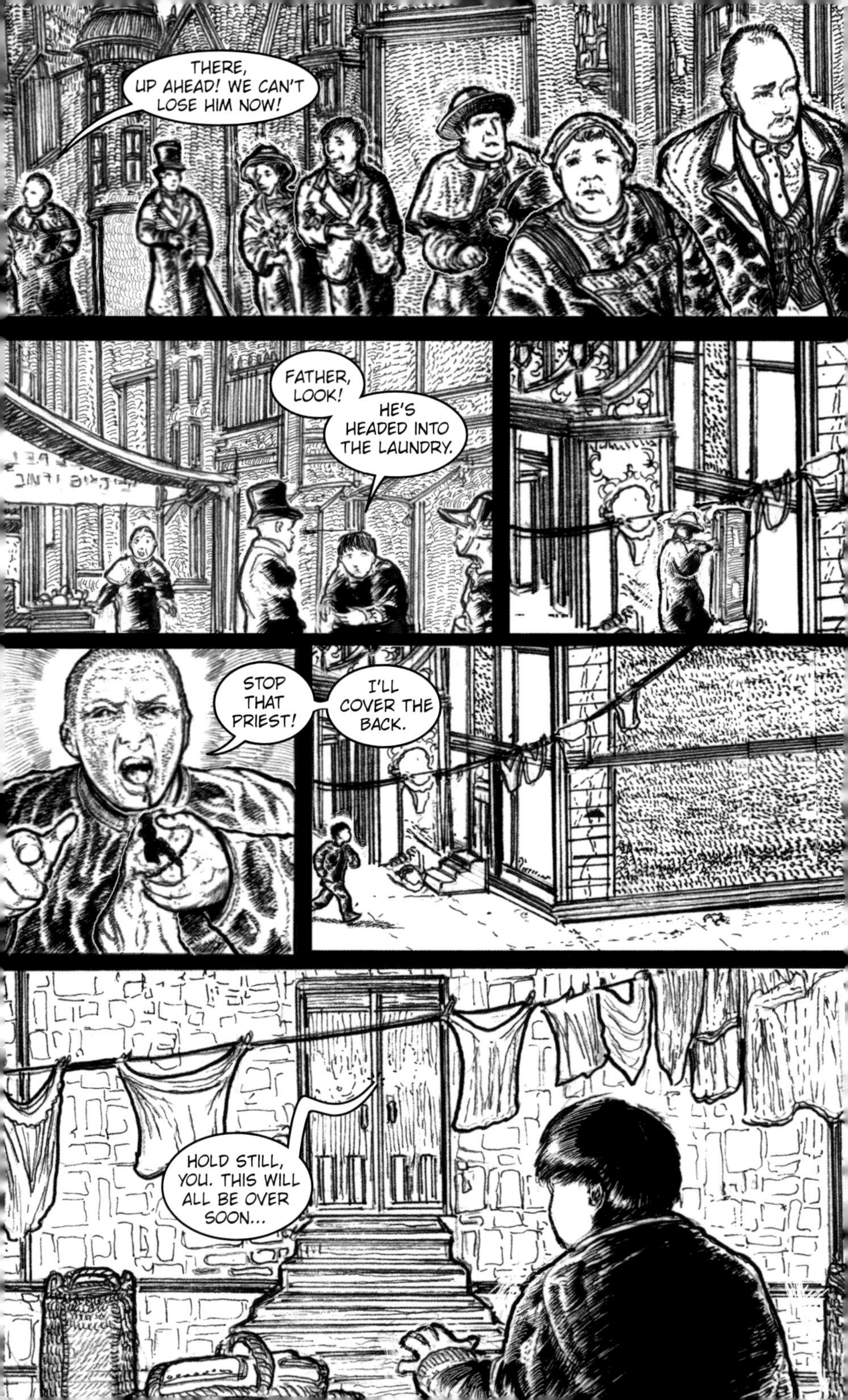
THERE, UP AHEAD! WE CAN'T LOSE HIM NOW!
FATHER, LOOK!
HE'S HEADED INTO THE LAUNDRY.
STOP THAT PRIEST!
I'LL COVER THE BACK.
HOLD STILL, YOU. THIS WILL ALL BE OVER SOON...

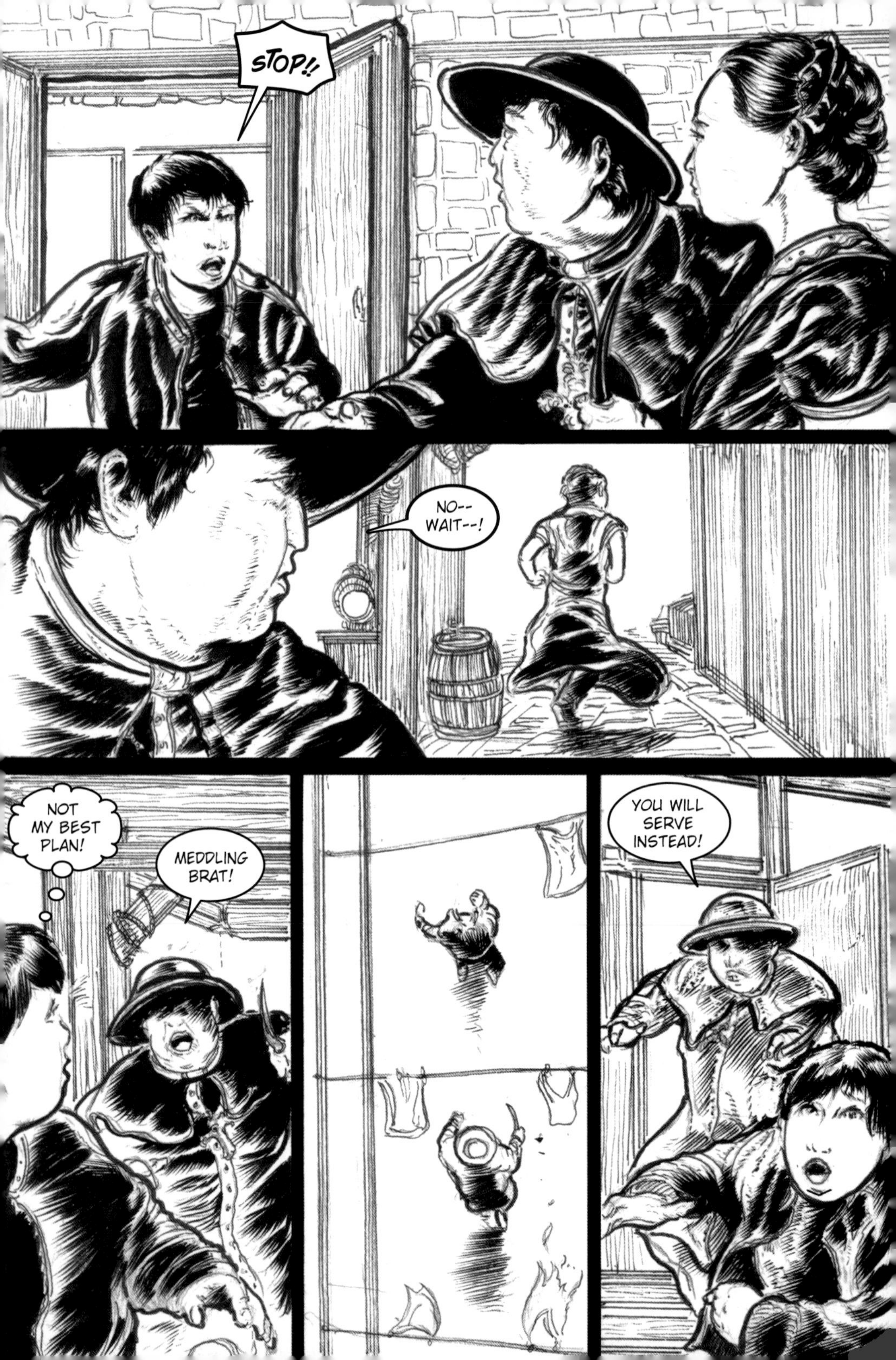
STOP!!
NO-- WAIT--!
NOT MY BEST PLAN!
MEDDLING BRAT!
YOU WILL SERVE INSTEAD!

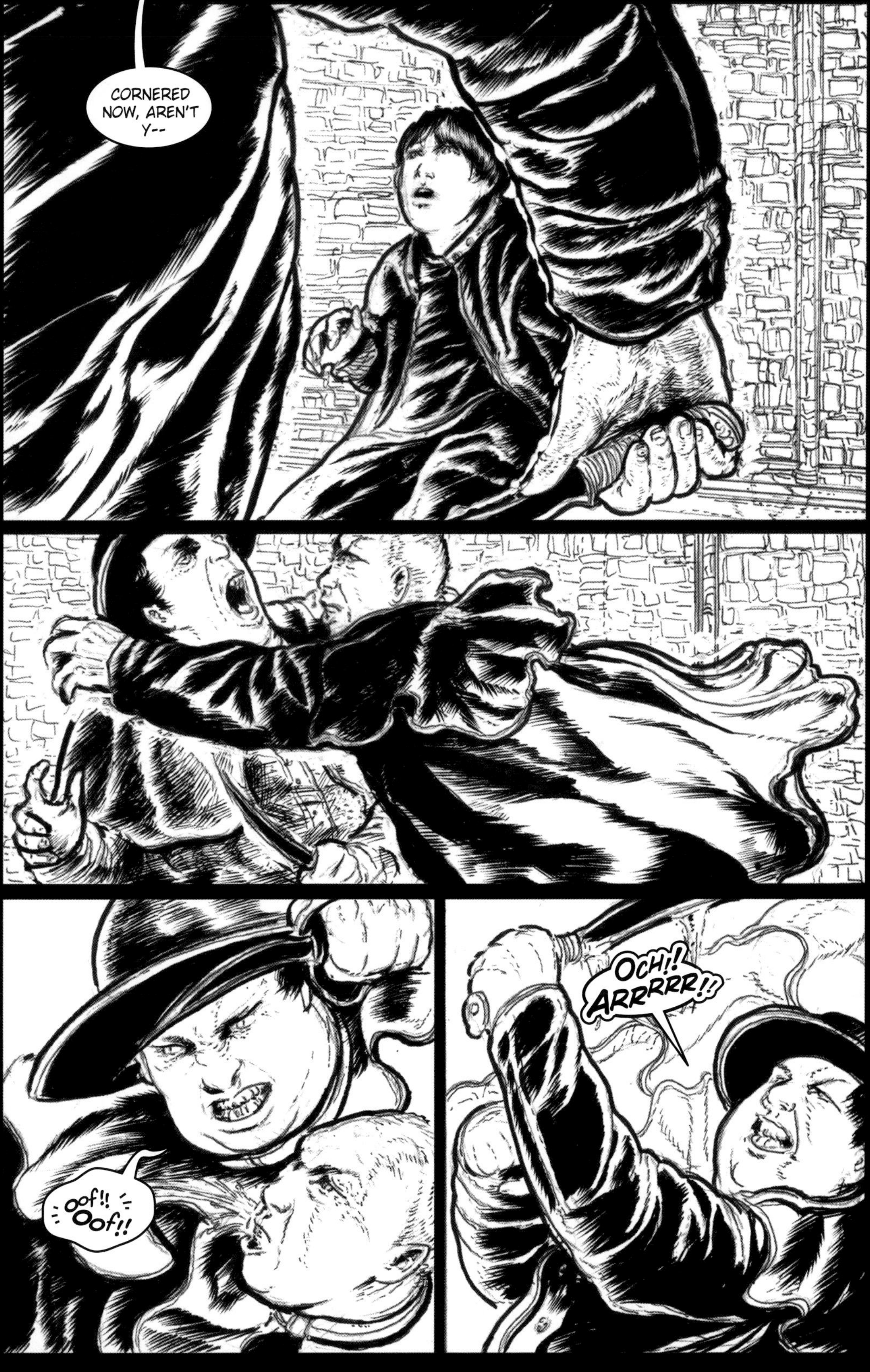
CORNERED NOW, AREN'T Y--
oof!! oof!!
OCH!! ARRRRR!!

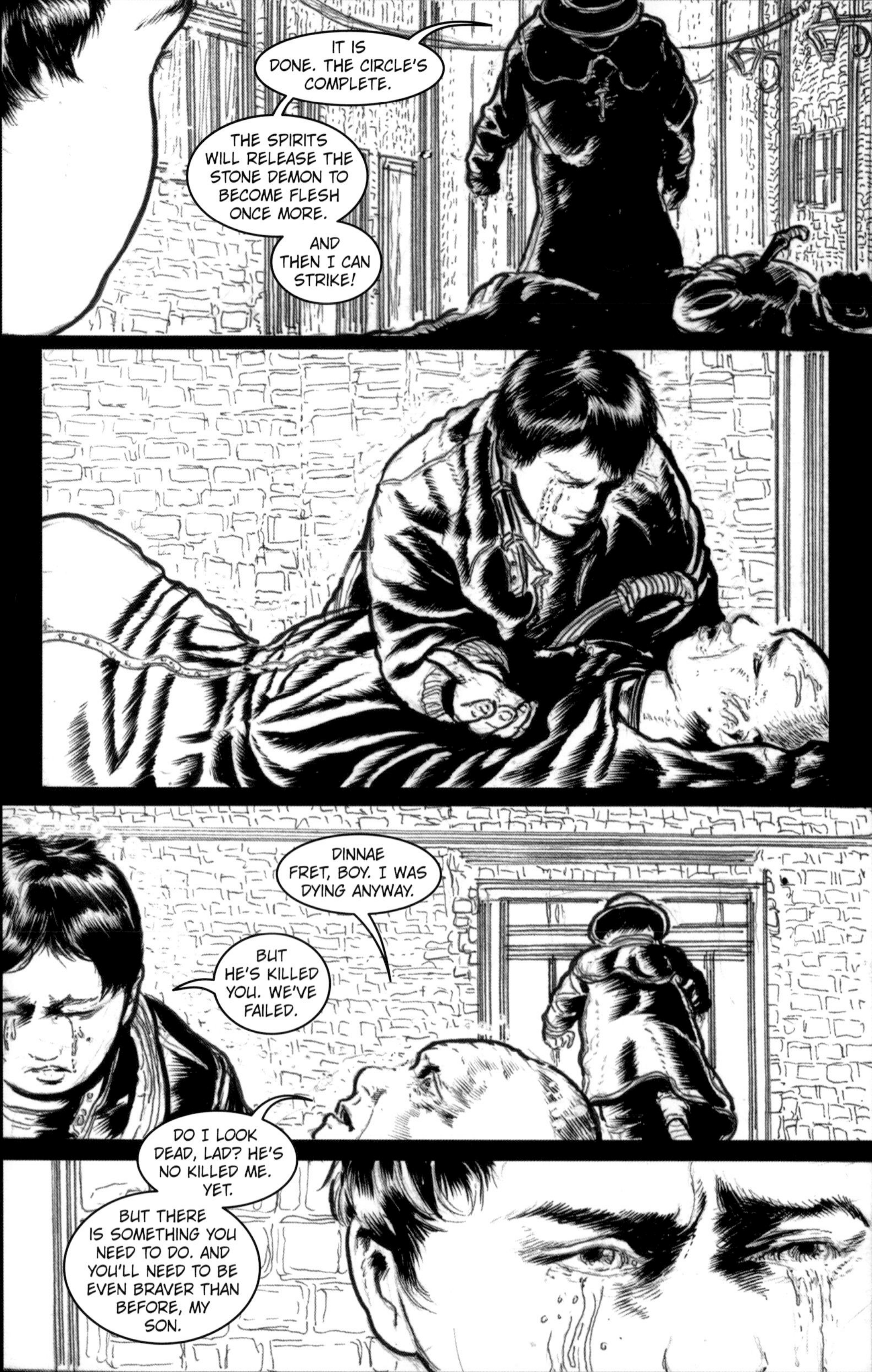
IT IS DONE. THE CIRCLE'S COMPLETE.
THE SPIRITS WILL RELEASE THE STONE DEMON TO BECOME FLESH ONCE MORE.
AND THEN I CAN STRIKE!
DINNAE FRET, BOY. I WAS DYING ANYWAY.
BUT HE'S KILLED YOU. WE'VE FAILED.
DO I LOOK DEAD, LAD? HE'S NO KILLED ME. YET.
BUT THERE IS SOMETHING YOU NEED TO DO. AND YOU'LL NEED TO BE EVEN BRAVER THAN BEFORE, MY SON.

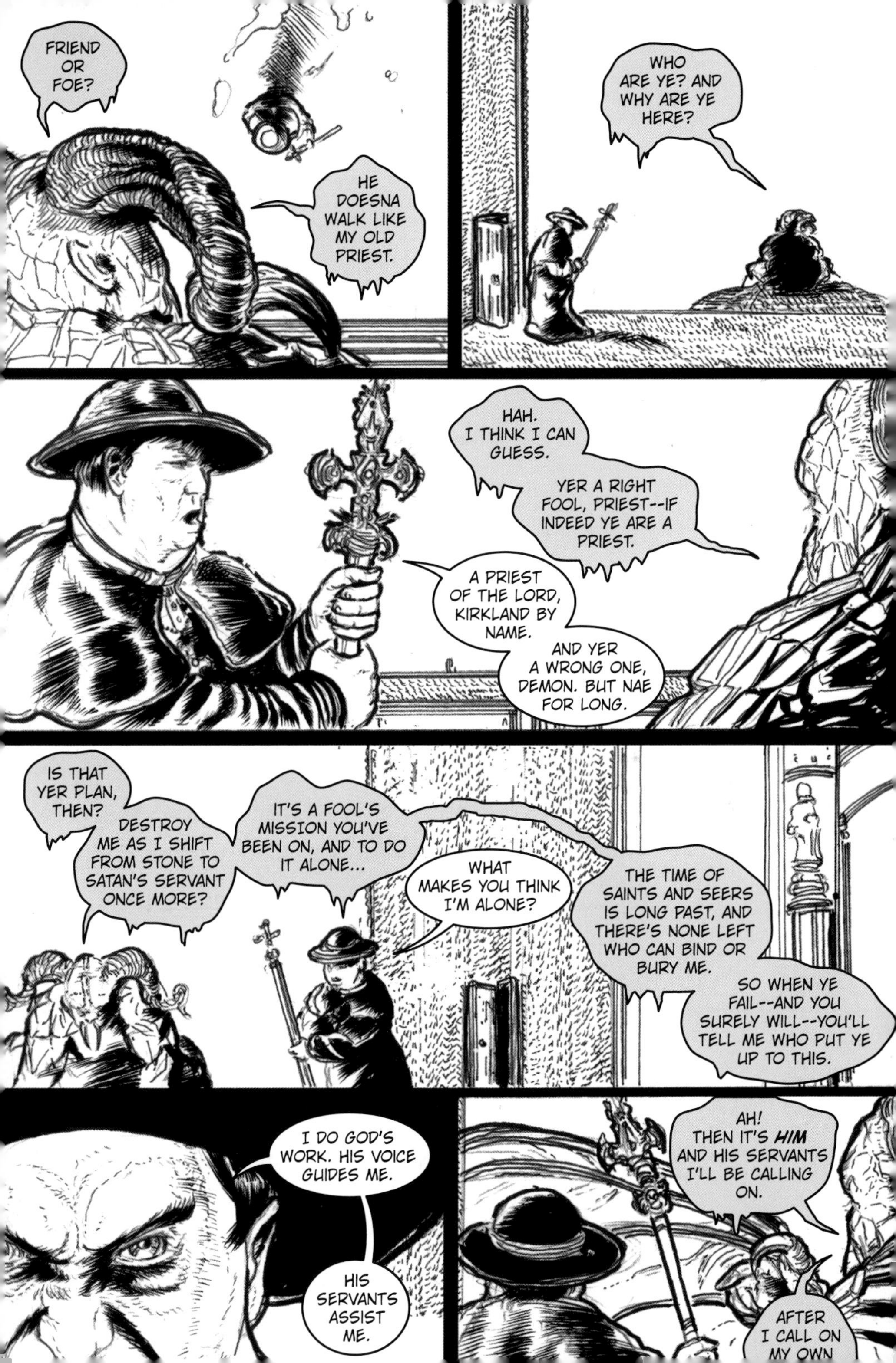

FRIEND OR FOE?
HE DOESNA WALK LIKE MY OLD PRIEST.
WHO ARE YE? AND WHY ARE YE HERE?
HAH. I THINK I CAN GUESS.
YER A RIGHT FOOL, PRIEST--IF INDEED YE ARE A PRIEST.
A PRIEST OF THE LORD, KIRKLAND BY NAME.
AND YER A WRONG ONE, DEMON. BUT NAE FOR LONG.
IS THAT YER PLAN, THEN?
DESTROY ME AS I SHIFT FROM STONE TO SATAN'S SERVANT ONCE MORE?
IT'S A FOOL'S MISSION YOU'VE BEEN ON, AND TO DO IT ALONE...
THE TIME OF SAINTS AND SEERS IS LONG PAST, AND THERE'S NONE LEFT WHO CAN BIND OR BURY ME.
WHAT MAKES YOU THINK I'M ALONE?
SO WHEN YE FAIL--AND YOU SURELY WILL--YOU'LL TELL ME WHO PUT YE UP TO THIS.
I DO GOD'S WORK. HIS VOICE GUIDES ME.
HIS SERVANTS ASSIST ME.
AH! THEN IT'S *HIM* AND HIS SERVANTS I'LL BE CALLING ON.
AFTER I CALL ON MY OWN

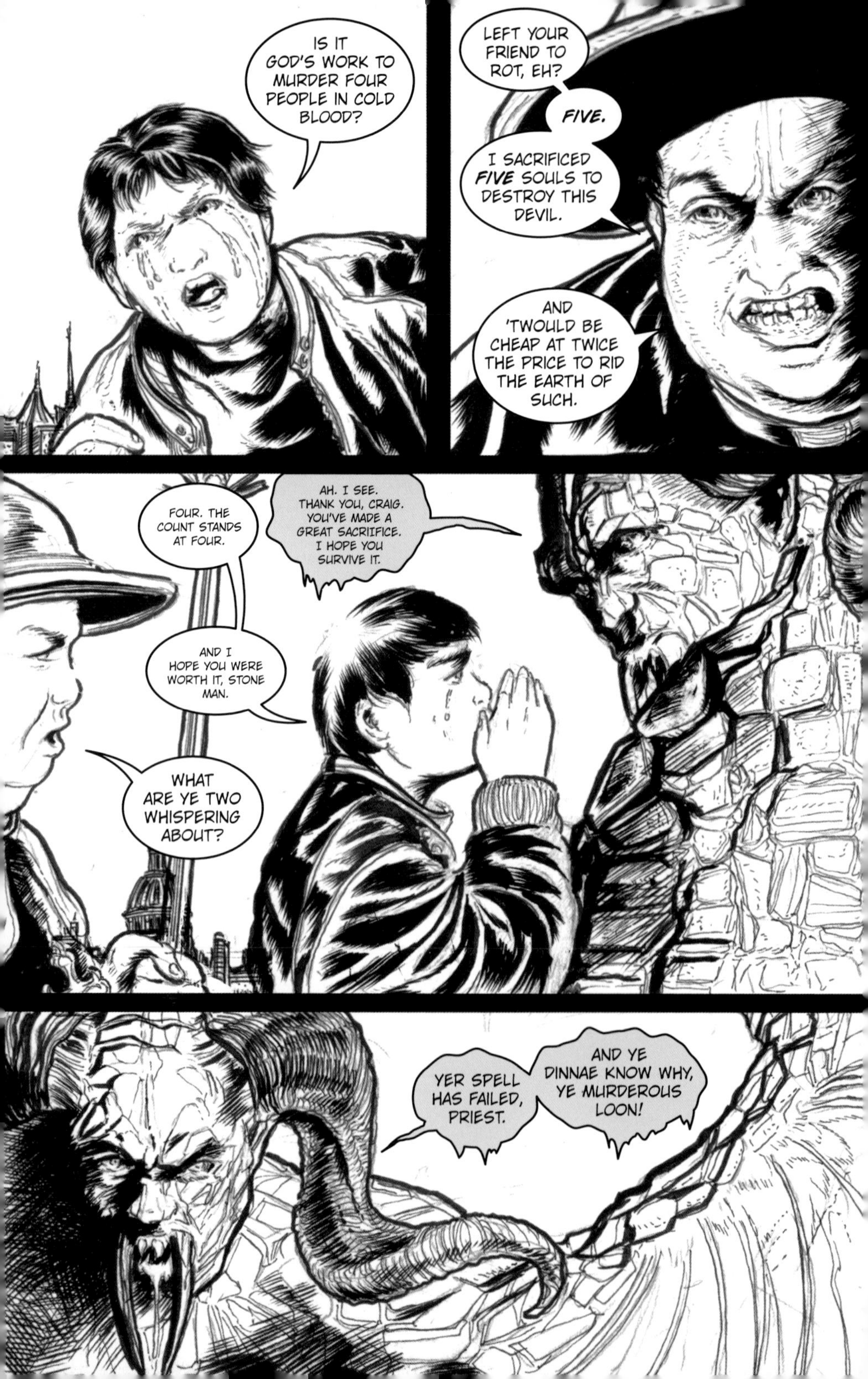
IS IT GOD'S WORK TO MURDER FOUR PEOPLE IN COLD BLOOD?
LEFT YOUR FRIEND TO ROT, EH?
FIVE.
I SACRIFICED FIVE SOULS TO DESTROY THIS DEVIL.
AND 'TWOULD BE CHEAP AT TWICE THE PRICE TO RID THE EARTH OF SUCH.
FOUR. THE COUNT STANDS AT FOUR.
AH. I SEE. THANK YOU, CRAIG. YOU'VE MADE A GREAT SACRIFICE. I HOPE YOU SURVIVE IT.
AND I HOPE YOU WERE WORTH IT, STONE MAN.
WHAT ARE YE TWO WHISPERING ABOUT?
YER SPELL HAS FAILED, PRIEST.
AND YE DINNAE KNOW WHY, YE MURDEROUS LOON!

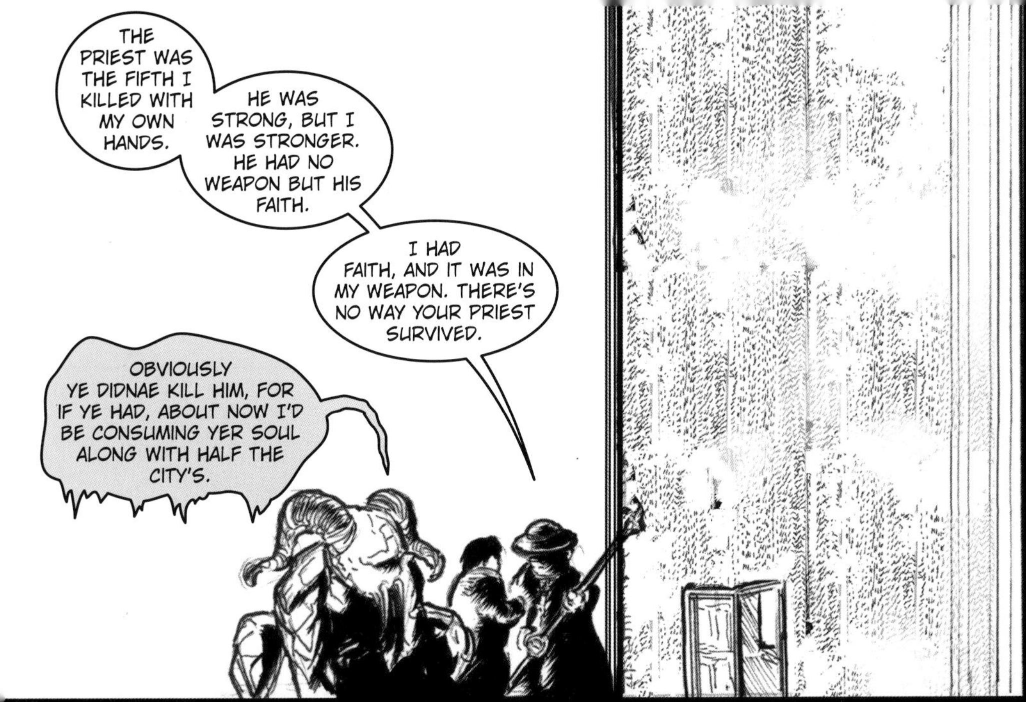
THE PRIEST WAS THE FIFTH I KILLED WITH MY OWN HANDS.
HE WAS STRONG, BUT I WAS STRONGER. HE HAD NO WEAPON BUT HIS FAITH.
I HAD FAITH, AND IT WAS IN MY WEAPON. THERE'S NO WAY YOUR PRIEST SURVIVED.
OBVIOUSLY YE DIDNAE KILL HIM, FOR IF YE HAD, ABOUT NOW I'D BE CONSUMING YER SOUL ALONG WITH HALF THE CITY'S.
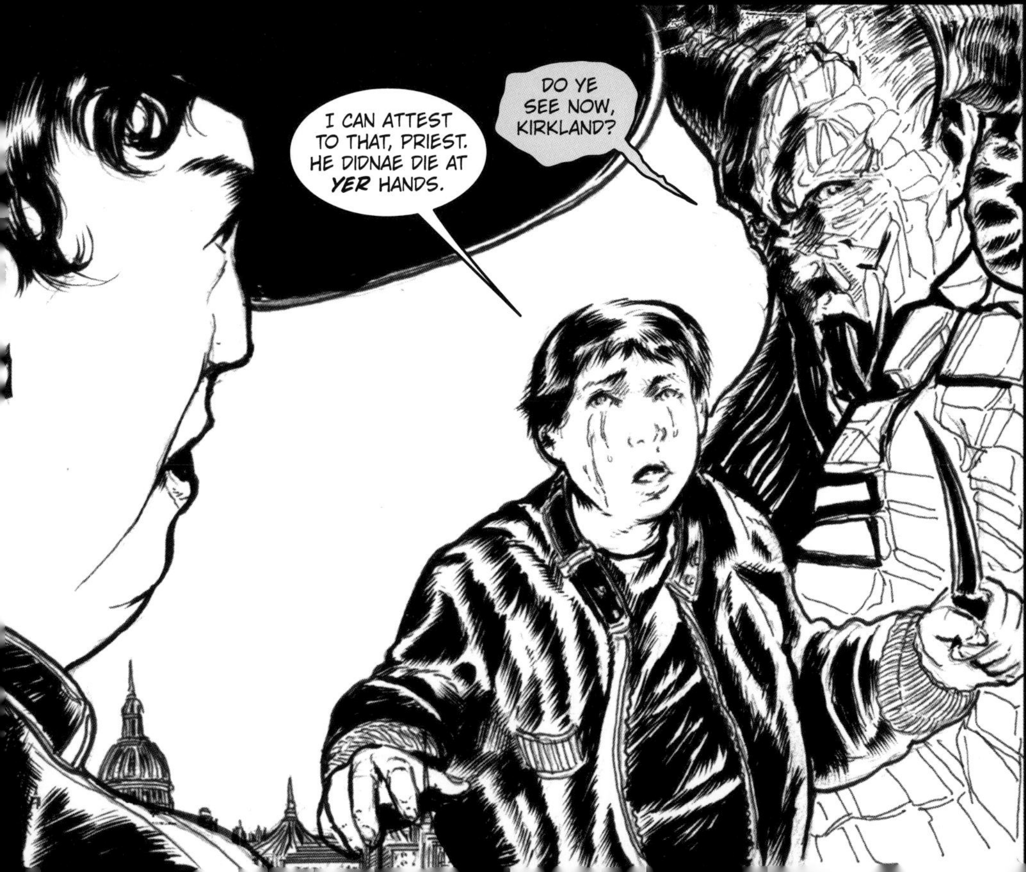
DO YE SEE NOW, KIRKLAND?
I CAN ATTEST TO THAT, PRIEST. HE DIDNAE DIE AT *YER* HANDS.

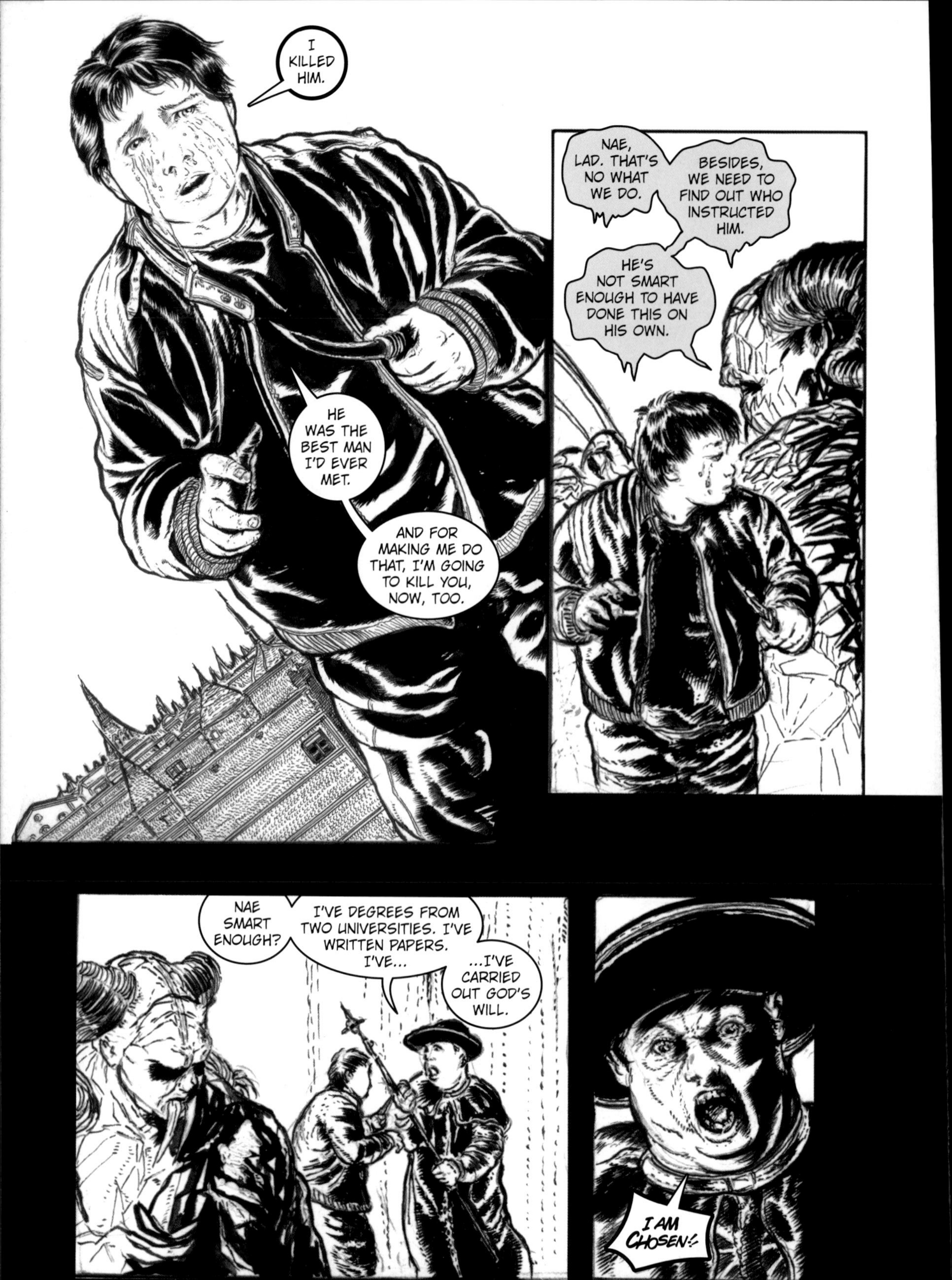
I KILLED HIM.
HE WAS THE BEST MAN I'D EVER MET.
AND FOR MAKING ME DO THAT, I'M GOING TO KILL YOU, NOW, TOO.
NAE, LAD. THAT'S NO WHAT WE DO.
BESIDES, WE NEED TO FIND OUT WHO INSTRUCTED HIM.
HE'S NOT SMART ENOUGH TO HAVE DONE THIS ON HIS OWN.
NAE SMART ENOUGH?
I'VE DEGREES FROM TWO UNIVERSITIES. I'VE WRITTEN PAPERS. I'VE...
...I'VE CARRIED OUT GOD'S WILL.
I AM CHOSEN!

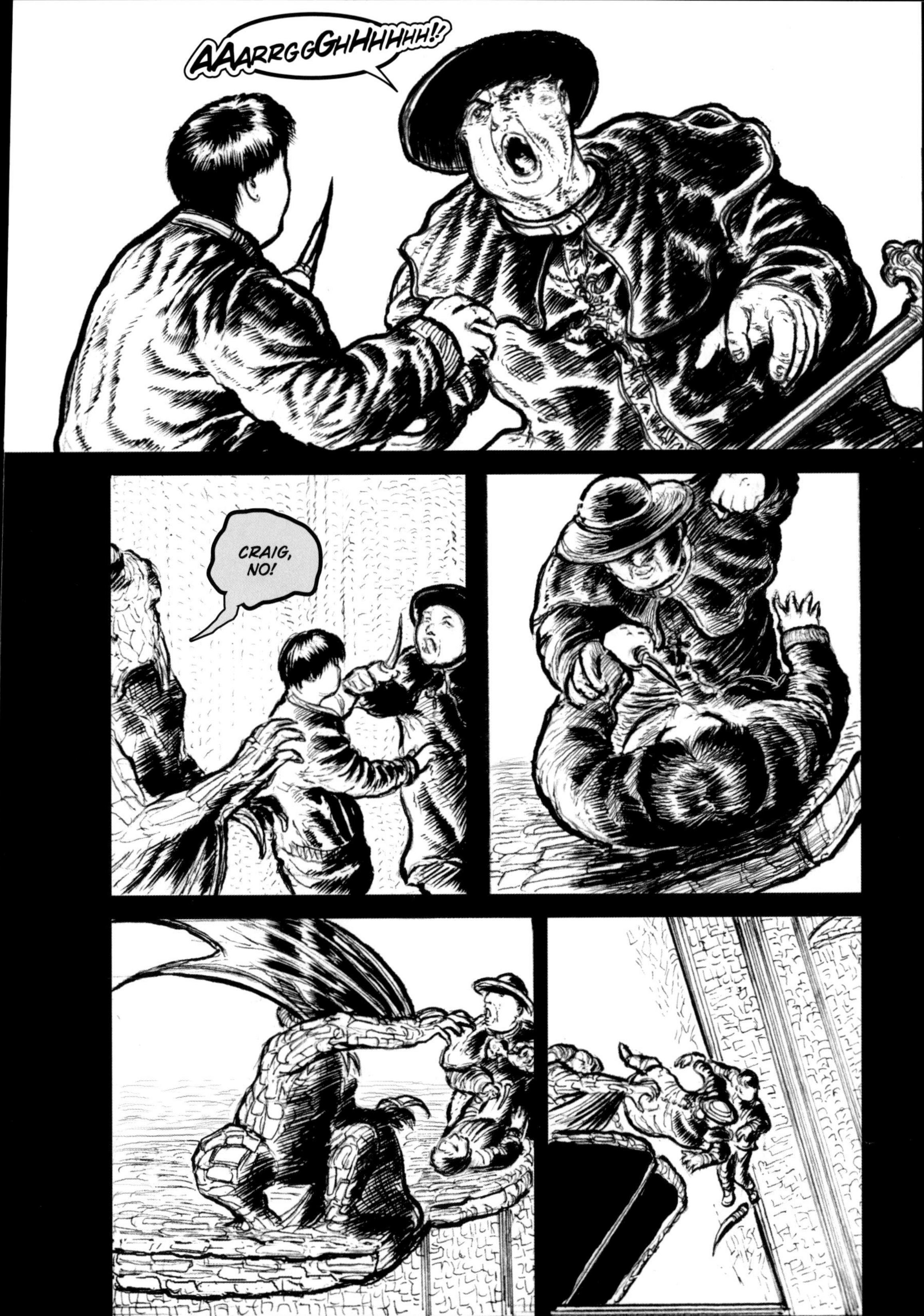
AAARRGGGHHHHHH!!
CRAIG, NO!

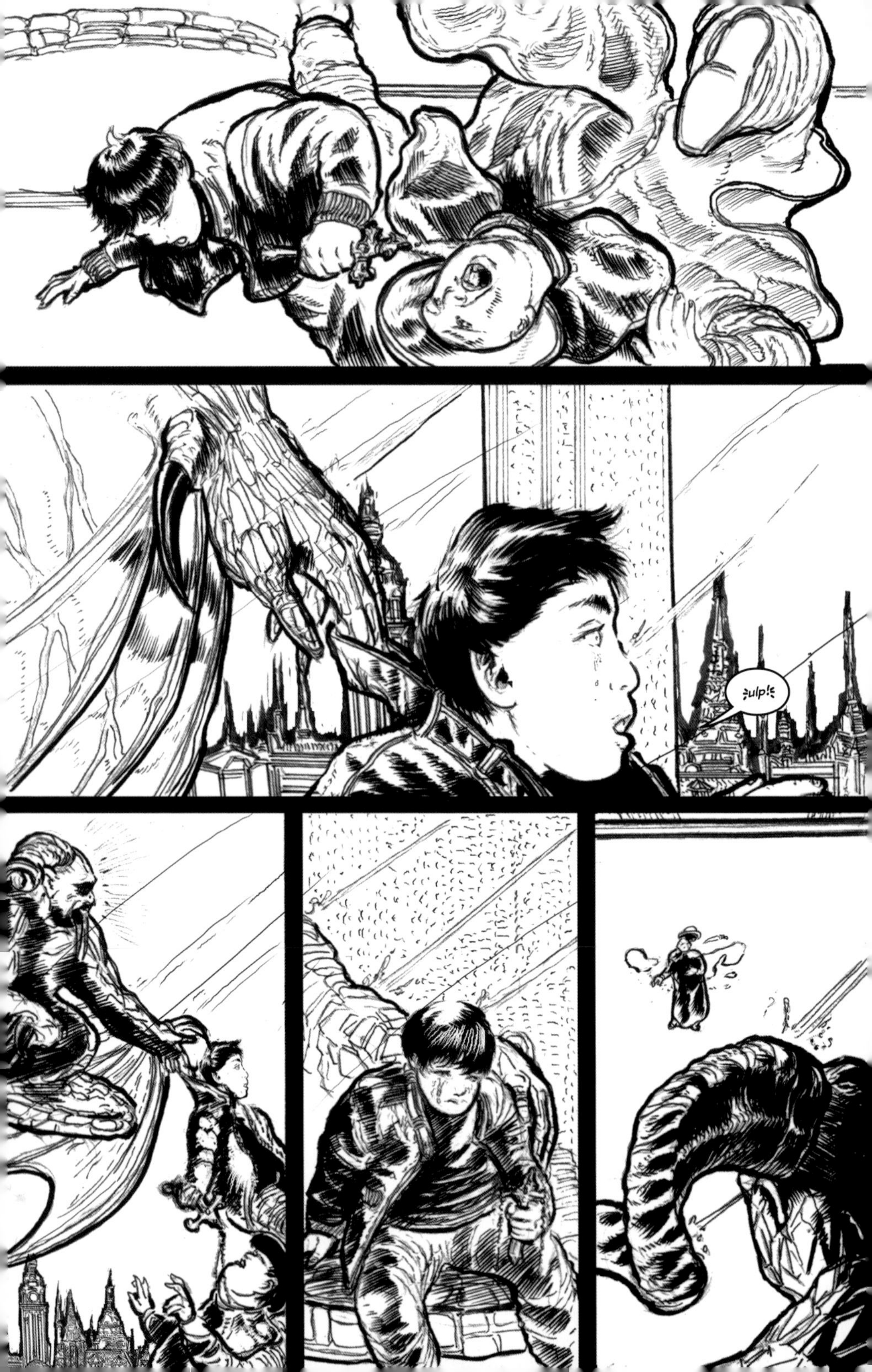

ulp

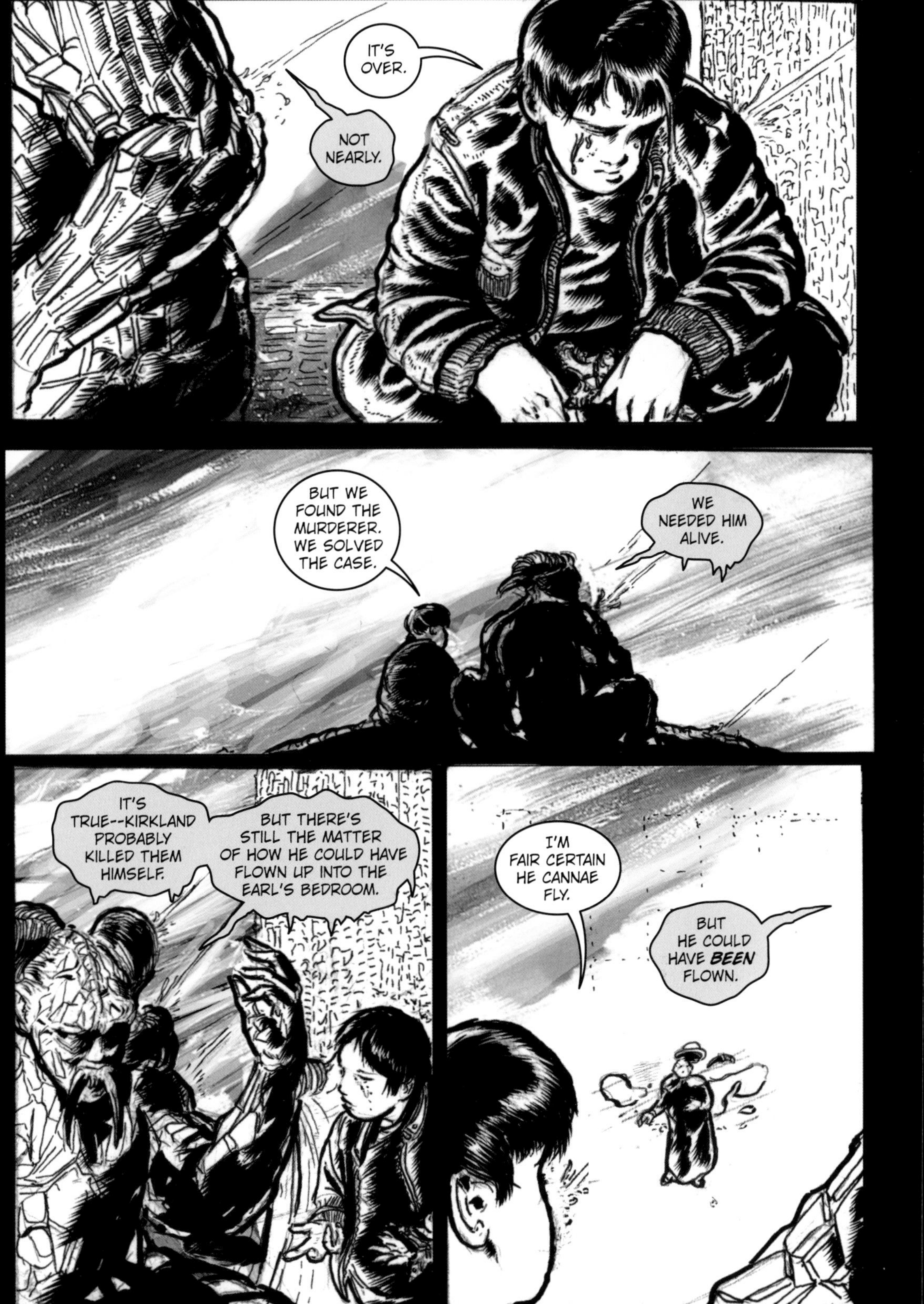
IT'S OVER.
NOT NEARLY.
BUT WE FOUND THE MURDERER. WE SOLVED THE CASE.
WE NEEDED HIM ALIVE.
IT'S TRUE--KIRKLAND PROBABLY KILLED THEM HIMSELF.
BUT THERE'S STILL THE MATTER OF HOW HE COULD HAVE FLOWN UP INTO THE EARL'S BEDROOM.
I'M FAIR CERTAIN HE CANNAE FLY.
BUT HE COULD HAVE *BEEN* FLOWN.

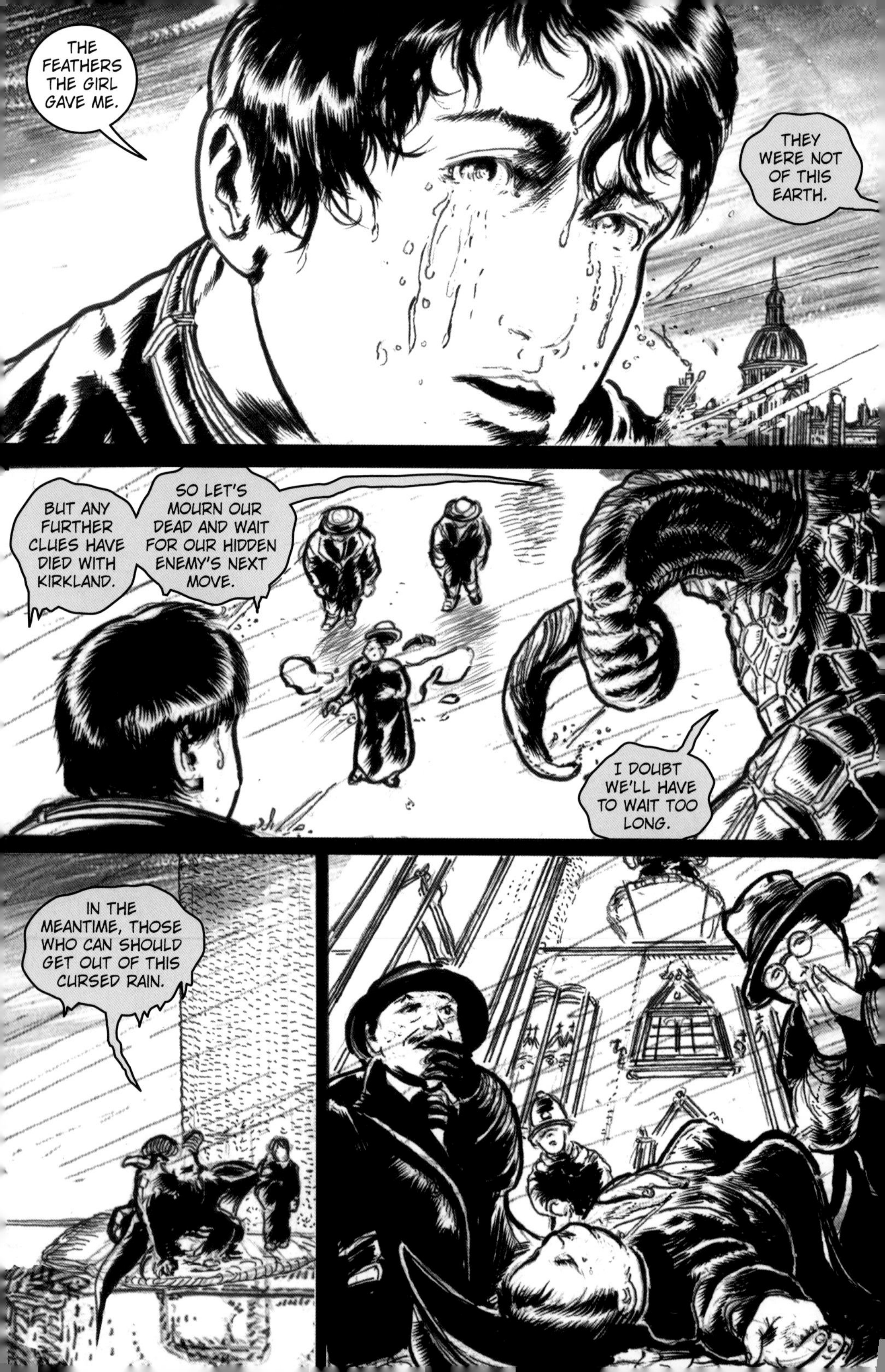
THE FEATHERS THE GIRL GAVE ME.
THEY WERE NOT OF THIS EARTH.
BUT ANY FURTHER CLUES HAVE DIED WITH KIRKLAND.
SO LET'S MOURN OUR DEAD AND WAIT FOR OUR HIDDEN ENEMY'S NEXT MOVE.
I DOUBT WE'LL HAVE TO WAIT TOO LONG.
IN THE MEANTIME, THOSE WHO CAN SHOULD GET OUT OF THIS CURSED RAIN.

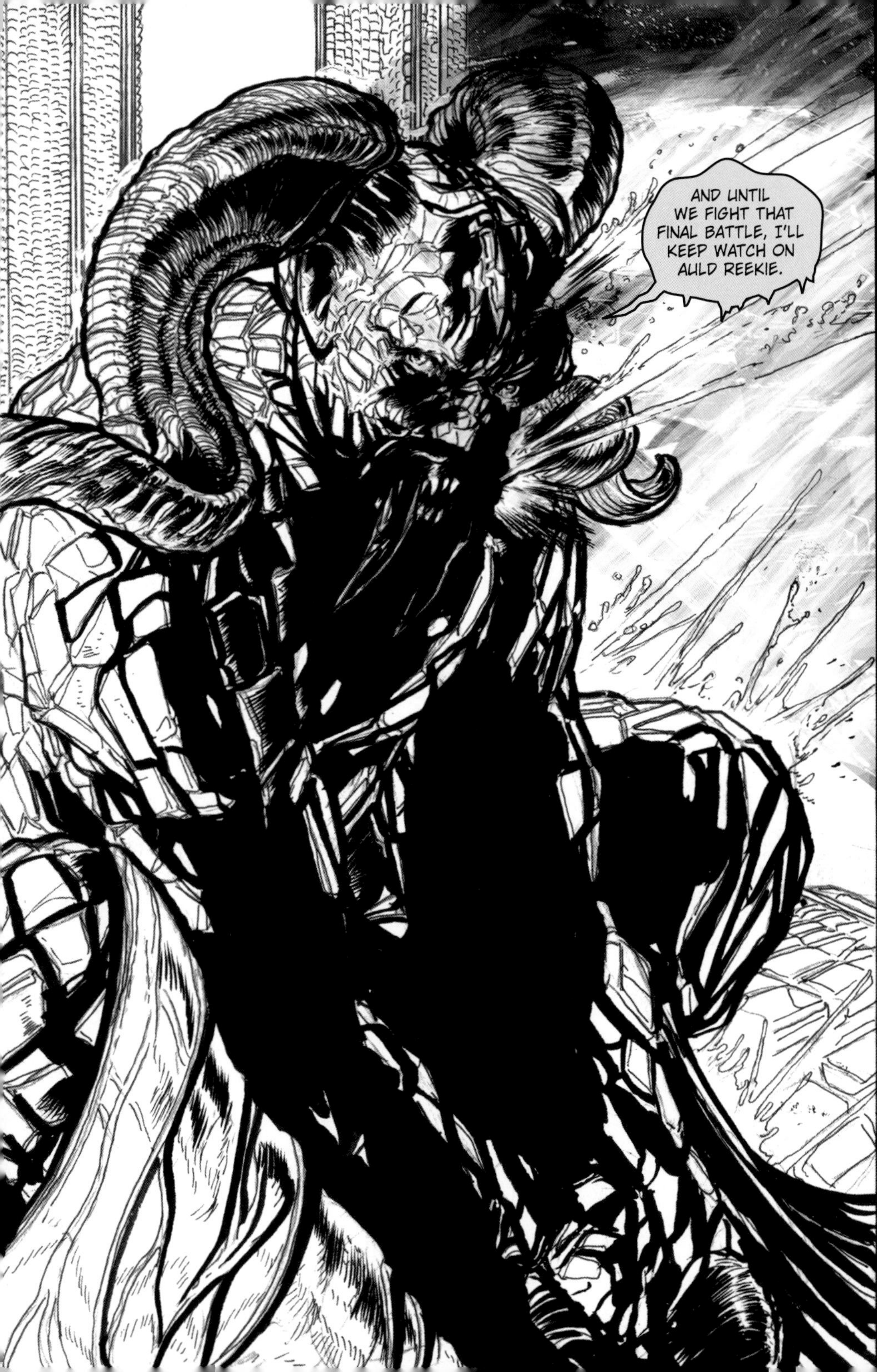
AND UNTIL WE FIGHT THAT FINAL BATTLE, I'LL KEEP WATCH ON AULD REEKIE.

Jane Yolen is the author of more than 350 books, including *Owl Moon*, *The Devil's Arithmetic*, and three graphic novels: *Foiled, Curses! Foiled Again*, and *The Last Dragon*. Her books and stories have won a Caldecott Medal, two Nebulas, and dozens of other awards. Six colleges and universities have given her honorary doctorates for her body of work. Also worthy of note: her Skylark Award—given by NESFA, the New England Science Fiction Association—set her good coat on fire. If you need to know more about her, visit her website at www.janeyolen.com

Adam Stemple is the author of fantasy novels and short stories including *Singer of Souls* and *Steward of Song*. Stemple and Jane Yolen have previously coauthored the Rock 'n' Roll Fairy Tale and Seelie Wars book series. Stemple also performs Celtic-influenced American folk rock. He is based in Minneapolis and online at adamstemple.com.

Orion Zangara is an illustrator and comic book artist who lives in Sterling, Virginia. He is a graduate of The Kubert School, an art trade school with a concentration in sequential art, founded by his grandfather Joe Kubert. Currently he is illustrating a soon-to-be-announced series for Image Comics. And he finds it very strange describing himself in the third person! You may reach him at www.orionzangara.com.